*For Andy, the angel in my life.*

# WHO KILLED LUKE MANDRAKE?

Book I of

**The Goddammerung**

by

**R. L. Migdal**

Volume I:

**Famebeau**

Back in the day, if memory serves me right, life was
one big party where every heart gaped wide, where all
wines gushed forth.

One night, I took Beauty on my knee. —And I found
that I was sick of her. —And I cussed her out.
I armed myself against justice.
I hit the road. O witches, O misery, O hatred, you
can keep the jackpot!

*A Season in Hell*
Arthur Rimbaud

Luke stroked the burlwood stock of the Remington Model 11 twenty gauge shotgun with his fingertips. Freedom from all physical limitations, that was the blessing he imagined his death would confer upon him. Freedom from pain at least, he was guaranteed that, he supposed. Either way, he had understood the deal he was making, when he set out on his drug-fueled sprint to stardom. From the start, his own untimely demise had loomed ahead with inevitable finality.

With its dainty bullets, auto-loading feature and low recoil, the Remington was a sensible choice. A classic, highly collectible and suitable for small game hunting, it was the gun for a sportsman who was also a showman, and a favorite with taxidermists and museum specimen collectors. Not your weapon if you wanted to make a Grand Guignol statement by leaving a messy headless corpse, but certainly the instrument of choice for a suicidal rock star with angelic good looks. Administered by mouth, the gunshot would leave the face perfect and the body easy to identify.

But suicide was not what Luke Mandrake had been thinking about, when he added the Remington to his collection of firearms.

Still, he had arranged for a friend to make the purchase. There was no point in Charity or his Mom catching wind of it. They would only object, even though he had already explained to them repeatedly that his arsenal was essential for the protection of home and family.

Home was the 5000-square-foot chalet overlooking the Willamette River that he and Charity had recently purchased. The nostalgic quaintness of its mullioned windows and solid, half-timbered architecture had charmed Charity, his antique-obsessed wife. The built-in oak gun cabinet with its advanced thumbprint-activated lock was what had sold Luke on the place.

Luke worried about intruders. Paparazzi, thieves, crazed stalkers, presumptuous fans, uninvited salesmen and renegade drug dealers–they clustered around him like flies. It was one of the consequences that ensued upon achieving worldwide fame. Yet Luke could not bring himself to hire handlers. He wanted his real friends to feel comfortable visiting him, wanted privacy for himself and his family. More to the point, he disliked and distrusted police, soldiers–anyone whose philosophy of life veered toward the martial end of the social spectrum. Why would he want bodyguards shadowing him twenty-four hours a day? The last thing he needed was a bevy of hired thugs hanging out in the laundry room, or in the hall by the door, or somewhere around the back of the shed. This was not a way of life, to Luke Mandrake's mind, that was worth the fantastic quantity of money it would have cost him.

Constant vigilance was the price he paid for his stubbornness.

Within days of closing on the house, Luke had begun to feel trapped there, pacing the carpets as if he were locked in a luxurious cage. His fame, like the bars in the leaded windows, separated him from the society of fellow miscreants and weirdos, from the liberty and the anonymity that had once been his own.

*I have to do it. I have to be free.*

Charity believed in reincarnation, and although Luke was skeptical, when she described to him her vision of the place where souls gathered between lives, it was the very picture of a lost paradise. Maybe he really was on his way to that lush and fruitful garden, over which a female deity presided, wrapped in a radiant aurora. If God were a woman, then surely the afterlife would be a haven for lovers, a place for reuniting, a land of peace where wholeness and tender fellowship were bestowed upon all gentle spirits.

Luke raised his head and gazed out over the Willamette, but he didn't see black water dimpled with moonlight. All he saw was a window on oblivion.

He closed his eyes, and prepared himself for the shot.

"I wish I knew what he was fucking up to!" Charity Ball fumed. "He hasn't called back since Wednesday. It's not like him to keep secrets from me."

"Maybe he just doesn't want to piss you off," said the husky voice on the other end of the phone. It was Kaylen, the bass player.

"That's what worries me." Charity thrust her fingers through the pumpkin-colored hair that spiked above her forehead, tugged fiercely at it. Being worried made her angry, so she generally tried not to worry, but right now it was no use. Worry coursed through her veins like amphetamine. "If he's afraid I'm going to be pissed, then whatever he's doing, it can't be a good idea."

The splashing of water sounded on the other end of the line. "Well, what can you do? Did he tell you where he was?"

"No, he did not." Charity bent over and grabbed at a pair of toddler-sized shorts, in a print of pastel stars, which she threw onto the couch. It was followed by a small shoe and a grubby orange slice molded of plastic. "He was furious that I cut off his funds, I can tell you that."

"Luke, furious? I'd pay good money just to hear him yell at you."

"Oh, he didn't yell, he never does. But I could tell." A sloshing noise informed Charity that Kaylen was in the bath. She pretty much lived in her bathtub. The bathroom was basically her office. "When I didn't offer to wire him the money, he made a sarcastic remark. *Send me some cash by homing pigeon, it'll get here faster,* something like that."

"Did he hang up on you?" Kaylen's voice burbled, distorted by a curtain of water sounds.

"No, of course not. He went on kissing my ass. *You know how much I love you. You're my everything, Boo, you and the kids.*"

"Awww. He's so sweet! How can you stay mad at him?"

"That fucking bastard!" Charity burst out. She made a violent motion, hurling a tiny sandal onto the heap. "Why is he being so secretive?"

"He's hiding from you because he's ashamed."

"You're right. He doesn't trust me anymore. I wish I'd never organized that stupid intervention!"

"Well you were just trying to save his goddamn life, Charity. If that annoys him, too bad."

"Yeah well . . ." Charity collapsed onto the couch next to the pile of kid-clutter. She felt like she ought to be sorting through it, but she just couldn't manage to be that organized right now.

"It was a decision we all made together," Kaylen went on, "and it was a long time coming. Maybe giving Luke an ultimatum didn't work, but we had to try *something*." Charity felt liquid pooling in her eyes. Her marriage was on the brink, and this latest stunt of Luke's felt like an act of vengeance. She needed to luxuriate in self pity, even if it was only for a few minutes. Hot tears spilled out, made sooty mascara tracks down to her chin.

"If he really gave a shit about us, he'd be here right now!"

"He adores you, Charity. Anyone can see that. He's just got a problem. It's not about you."

"Maybe not, but it should be!" She managed a self-mocking laugh.

"Totally!" agreed Kaylen. Charity sniffed. She was feeling a bit better. She had to pull herself together. So much to do . . . .

"Luke should be grateful that you're–" Kaylen began again, but she was interrupted by an electronic boop, and then another.

"Hey, I've got another call coming in, I have to take it. Thanks for helping me get through this, Kay. See you at the studio tomorrow?"

"You got it."

Charity pressed a button on the cordless phone twice, *beep beep,* and managed to switch to the other line. "Hello?" she said.

"Mrs. Mandrake? This is Michael from Potamic Bank."

"Hi Michael, what's up?"

"I'm just calling to let you know that there was some activity on your husband's credit card account. Someone tried to cash advance two thousand dollars at an ATM at five-sixteen this morning."

Relief flooded Charity's body like an intravenous dose of opiates. *He's alive.* "Can you tell me where the transaction occurred?"

"The transaction was refused, Mrs. Mandrake, as per your instructions."

"Of course, but what was the location?" *Where is he?*

"We don't track that information, Mrs. Mandrake. Not with credit cards. It's a matter of privacy regulations."

*What the fuck?* "The information has to be in the system somewhere." Her anxiety level was rocketing skyward again. She stood up and paced into the kitchen.

"I'm sorry, Mrs. Mandrake. It's not."

Charity inhaled. Shouting at the man would not accomplish anything. She counted to ten as she shifted her bare foot from the spot where it was stuck in a puddle of dried-up apple juice. She released the air from her lungs. "Thank you for your call, Michael. I'd appreciate it if you'd keep me informed of any future activity on the account. And if there's any way at all you can find out the locations of the recent transaction attempts, please inform me." *That information could literally save Luke's life right now.*

"I do apologize, Mrs. Mandrake. I'll certainly keep you informed if and when we have any additional information. And if you have any questions, just call Corporate and ask for me."

"Thanks, I'll do that." Charity clicked off the phone and stood numbly for several minutes. She was thinking about the bank transaction. Why would Luke try again, knowing that she had put a hold on the account? Maybe somebody else was using the card.

Luke had been on the lam for days now, and she just knew he was using again. The period right after rehab was incredibly dangerous: that's when tolerance was lowest, that's when a fatal overdose was most likely. And he always went too far.

She didn't want to involve the police in this if she could help it, but she had to find Luke as quickly as possible. She needed to hire a professional.

Charity crossed the kitchen, making a tiny suction noise each time she had to un-stick her tacky right foot from the linoleum. *I really need to wipe up that apple juice.*

She grabbed the phone book from the top of the fridge. She opened it and leafed to the listings for private investigators. She picked up the cordless, and dialed.

*April 1, 1994* – Portland, OR

Luke floated near the ceiling of the sun room. He gazed down at his collection of old doll parts, placed in careful rows upon the rough plywood shelving. Cracked bald heads stared blankly from empty sockets. Glass-eyed moppets sporting matted hair, baby torsos arched and hollow, these symbols of broken childhood were the Lares and Penates that guarded Luke's sanctuary.

When he saw himself sprawled below, Luke's melancholy gave way to disgust at the body he'd discarded like a pair of ill-fitting jeans. His mortal sheath both fascinated and repelled him, like an unhealthy turd. It was so small, so frail a remnant, bereft of all meaning, a corncob he'd gnawed at until every particle of flavor was gone.

Then the automatic thought came to him: *better put that gun away before the babies get home.*

But there was nothing he could do about it now.

Luke listened to this thought as to a distant voice. *How can I be thinking at all?* Apparently his mind continued on without the need of tissue, nerves or blood.

Luke watched this new thought blossom into his awareness with only momentary interest. The confirmation that he possessed a conscious self that transcended the physical body would have been momentous to Luke Mandrake, the living man. Now the notion arose and passed into the realm of things known without exciting his curiosity any further.

Someone was moving around down there, messing with the thing on the floor that had once been himself, but Luke was quickly losing interest in the person he had been a short time ago, and the fate of his body troubled him not at all.

He merged irresistibly into a timeless, drifting existence. Once he had associated the sensation with the most pleasurable of heroin trips. The temporary escape from anxiety and pain into a glorious omnipotence had long served to prop up the rickety structure of his disintegrating personality. Now the elation that infused him was stripped of its former purpose. Relief flooded him with its dark and blessed waters, and he sank beneath the gentle wavelets with a mental sigh.

*I never have to go back to that gulag again.*

Comforting darkness engulfed him. But oblivion did not follow.

Gradually he became aware of a subtle effect like that of a moving multiple exposure film. Scenes of activity were layered one upon the other, from which there emerged flashes of familiar movement and sound. Here was a man being handcuffed by police officers, there a child's fingers touched the nose of a dog. There again, a singer writhed to the thud of hypnotic music. Luke felt compelled to follow each thread simultaneously, to trace each sequence to its source, or along its path. He could not tell which direction these stories were headed in time, forward or backward.

It was important to try and enter into all the various viewpoints at once. If he could do so, Luke was sure he would achieve a form of consciousness for which he had always longed: a state of being whole, no longer alienated and alone. But each image slipped from his mind's grasp, to be replaced in an instant by a new manifestation. Overwhelmed by an endless series of signals, each of them on its own trajectory of meaning, he could perceive the stream of information only as one profound mystery after another. Taken as a whole, it seemed, the emanations of human consciousnesses amounted to nothing more than a monolithic cypher which, forever changing and in motion, ineluctably occluded its own significance.

Luke began to feel a sense of gravity tugging at him, although whether it was pulling him up, down or sideways was not clear. Bit by bit the tension increased, and soon he raced along, passing rapidly through layered narratives projected onto phantom scrims. Across these screens flowed the flattened life stories of everyone who had ever lived.

As he traveled more and more swiftly Luke's surroundings began to resemble a tunnel of variegated light and color, rushing by all around him in neon streaks. The stream of light was becoming brighter by the moment, and Luke shut his eyes. But it didn't matter, the light burned through him, waxed till it was a white flood, a hurricane of fire. Then everything went black.

Luke was on his hands and knees in total darkness.

He could hear an animal sound, a gasping, panting noise, which he gradually recognized as his own labored breathing. He opened his eyes in surprise.

Red, everything was red, he was looking down into a pool of clotted blood. He started back from the sight, rising quickly to his knees. His hands were dripping red! Luke barked a frantic yelp, stumbling to his feet, and stared around at a vast chamber filled with mammoth pillars, which extended in every direction. The floor under his shoes was covered with a soft, spongy material. Luke held his hands up and the gore fell away from them, fluttered down . . . coming to rest upon a mass of scarlet flowers. *Poppies.*

He plucked a petal from between his fingers, examined it, let it fall. He was standing on a narrow red carpet of the blooms that stretched on, seemingly infinitely, in either direction between marching columns that stood about ten yards apart. As Luke spun slowly around, taking in the vast and empty expanse which extended in all directions, he began to feel vaguely cheated.

This was no garden paradise. What was he doing in this deserted place?

He had read enough stories of near-death experiences to know what usually happens after the tunnel. This place did not live up to expectations. No city of pearl, no singing host. And wasn't Granddad supposed to be here to greet him? Luke hadn't seen the old lush, who had died last year, for over a decade. Granddad hadn't been a scary drunk exactly, just tottering and spastic, and liable to burn you with his cigarette without noticing. Luke had stopped wanting to visit by the time he was eight.

Still, even Granddad would have been a welcome sight in this echoing mausoleum. Luke stood where he was uncertainly, wondering which way to go.

*You are already on the path,* said a sweet, womanly voice in his ear, crystal clear.

*What the hell?* Luke flicked his head and shivered. So far as he could tell, there was nobody in the hall with him, no footstep, no echo. The voice felt intimately close, and yet Luke was certain that the message had come from a long way off, that its source was somewhere far down the poppy path to his left.

At the sound of that musical voice a powerful urge seized him, and he struggled to suppress it. He wanted to bound down the floral carpet as fast as he could go, like a puppy running to its mistress. He longed to trace the summons to its source, ached for it with a keenness that made his heart contract as though squeezed by a fist.

Luke fought the urge, without even thinking about it, and with all his strength. This was the sort of feeling that signaled danger.

Resolutely he turned his back to the road and walked about ten feet across a floor of polished black marble to where the closest column rose up. The pillar was four feet in diameter or more, of a milk-and-butter striped stone, translucent and faintly luminous. Alabaster, he thought, summoning to mind the bins of polished stones that lined his Aunt Suze's gift shop. *The ancient Egyptians carved Alabaster into containers for mummified hearts.* Canopic jars, they were called.

As a boy Luke had been fascinated by mummies, had devoured any book about them he could find. The mortician-priests removed the brains from the corpses and threw them away. But they preserved the organs, the hearts and livers and kidneys, in lidded jars. They believed that the mind and soul resided in the heart.

Luke looked up. The alabaster cylinder disappeared into a haze of sunlight-shot vapors far above.

*How do you open a canopic jar?* he whispered.

*With a canopener.*

Luke placed a hand on the column, which was strangely warm, and it became clear as glass wherever he touched it. Luke passed his hand slowly over the surface and, as if he were wiping condensation from a window, a distant view into another place was revealed. It was the room from which he had just come.

There was his wee empty husk, arranged like a crime scene in a doll's house.

Luke would have turned away, but the scene shifted then and he saw Charity, sitting at her dressing table in their Los Angeles digs. She seemed close enough that he might have reached out and touched her. He watched her select an earring from a small lacquered tray: one of the fire opals he had given her for her birthday, just a few months ago. She was wearing an ivory silk nightie. Hungrily he took in her lean and shapely silhouette, the curve of her neck, the predatory grace in the way she tilted her head back. His heart thudded as she unclasped the silver barrette that held up her hair, and shook out the thick flame-colored locks so that they brushed her shoulders. She stared at herself in the mirror in that mournful, exasperated way she had, so comical and charming, and then rubbed both hands up and down on her cheeks, finally pushing them together so that her lips puckered out.

"L-u-u-uke," Charity crooned through her puffy fish lips. "L-u-u-u-u-u-ke!" She dropped her hands to the dressing table and frowned. "Where ARE you, you secretive little bastard?"

How many times had Charity saved his life? He hadn't kept count, although he was pretty sure she had. This time he had given her the slip. She had no idea he was dead, nor where his body lay.

Luke leaned on the pillar, pressed his bearded cheek against it, his arms wrapped around its girth, tears stinging his eyes. He wanted to shout her name, wanted her to hear him, to let him beg her forgiveness. He wanted to press his face once more between those thighs, into the gateway of existence itself, to tear at the lace panties with his teeth, taste the nectar that had once given him a reason to live. If he could have gone back in time and changed the future, sparing her the news that she had feared for so long, he might even have done it in that moment.

Luke imagined what he would probably see next inside the monolith: the twins. Playing, sleeping, crying, even pooping on their little his-and-her training potties–it didn't matter. He just knew that if he saw the kids he would totally lose it. He stepped back from the column, letting it slowly regain its opacity, to draw a veil over the past. He wrenched himself around, and stood there for a while, his emaciated shoulders jerking in little spasms. But at the touch of the teardrops coursing down his cheeks and trickling into his beard, he stopped crying.

So surreal, the tactile reality of this place, of himself. What seemed to be the living flesh he wore must surely be some sort of complex mimicry, yet it felt so genuine . . . right down to the burning pain in his gut, the malady from which even death had failed to free him. Luke sobbed a little laugh. It seemed that the joke was on him.

He stumbled back to the path and stood there for a moment blinking, tired and resentful and forsaken. Ahead of him on the track something, or someone, beckoned. He could hear the voice still, murmuring *come to me . . . come!* So close the whisper sounded, that he could almost feel breath against his cheek, a wisp of hair brushing his neck. *Come to me, Luke.*

The distant presence seared him the way the sun bakes hungover beach bums, touching their closed eyelids with fire. The blazing heat of her encompassed all that Luke feared, all that he so desperately needed. There lay madness: not merely the onset of it, but the source of it. At the very thought of proceeding down that path, the panic arose, the same terror that gripped him whenever he wandered near enough to the gorgon to be seized in her inexorable embrace. It was, in a word, *Mom.*

The road lay before him, a raw umbilical cord, a scarlet vein splitting the white stone border of the flower bed. *Come, come here to me.* Luke knew very well that his panic proceeded not simply from the fear of being caught, but from an overwhelming desire for it. His was the terror of the wayward child whose petty crimes cry out for punishment.

With a sudden movement he leaned down and touched the petals of a living poppy, the red poppy he had so loved to paint. He looked at his feet and saw that he was crushing the blooms under his black converse sneakers. He swept up thick handfuls of the blossoms, yanking their stems and uprooting whole plants from the soft loamy soil. He had an urge to throw himself down on the flowerbed and swim away, churning up the path in a shower and splash of torn petals. He almost believed that if he tried it, he could.

*Come to me, Luke. Come.* The voice lured him on, and in a burst of fatalism he lurched toward it.

"What the fuck," he mumbled disconsolately.

*Slip-slap, slip slap.* As he walked down along the border of the poppy bed, a path two feet wide and smooth as glass, his sneakers made gentle sounds against the snowy marble, and the tiny slaps bred a rustling nide of echoes that fluttered up to fill the hall. No other sound could be heard. *Slip-slap, slip slap. Echo-echo-echo.*

In blind resignation he trudged along, a twisted chain of poppies crowning his pale head. He was a gaunt heifer, ungainly and pocked, being led to market. He had decked himself in the garlands of sacrifice, knowing himself to be unworthy of the honor. Now there was a mantra that he muttered, and the words that he comforted himself with were: *She can't want me. She must be mistaken. She can't want me.*

Surely when he finally stood before her, whoever or whatever she was, and she gazed into the depths of his puny, selfish, undeserving soul, she would dash him into oblivion with a contemptuous wave of a finger. And wouldn't that be sweet?

*Slip-slap, slip slap. Echo-echo-echo.* The march went on and on, and the sounds of his footsteps bounced and whispered away into the distance. The mist above was clearing, beams of light cut through the gloom, and peering ahead Luke thought he could see a figure between the alabaster columns.

*Slip-slap, slip slap. Echo-echo-echo. Slip-slap, slip slap. Echo-echo-echo.*

Luke raised his eyes again and now the figure was large enough to make out. It was a woman seated before a shield of polished gold which caught the light so that flames appeared to be playing around her head. She wore a helmet-like, striped headdress and wide jeweled collar, and held a naked sword in her right hand. Even from so far away, her beauty was shocking.

There she sat like a colorful statue, a mannequin. The graceful and womanly curves of the goddess, her childlike, oval face and enormous eyes sent electric signals through his body and he halted, overcome with terror.

What was he doing? If he could see her, she could see him, and was probably already planning how many pieces she was going to slice him into with that sword. Or else she was going to incinerate him with her eye-beams, or whatever it was she did to her visitors after luring them into her trap. What had he been thinking, walking straight toward her, straight into the maw of doom?

Luke looked around for a place to hide. *Dodge behind a pillar—* that appeared to be his only option, and what a pitiful one it was.

Luke tried to appear nonchalant as he strolled away from the path and glanced at one of the columns, casually placing his hand on it. Instantly there arose from it a terrible clamor of shouts, shrieks and whinnies, crashes and crunches, rumbles, skids and bangs. In the transparent space between his fingers he could see a huge cloud of brown dust. In the foreground, a severed arm lay in a puddle of dark blood, a spattered bronze bracelet encircling it between bicep and elbow.

The clang and clash resonated through the hall. Luke snatched his hand away, and the noise faded abruptly.

He glanced up, and though the seated figure off in the distance did not betray any sign of having noticed him, Luke took a hasty step behind the pillar. That was when he slipped. He caught himself as he fell, hands smacking the stone column. A new sound redounded in the open space: boys chanting together in a language Luke had never heard.

An old man's thin treble rose in singsong phrases that the boys repeated word for word, sitting cross-legged on the floor of a stone chamber. Luke forgot the need to quickly mute the sounds. He stood transfixed by the chorus of young voices in unison, the echoes harmonizing as their chant wove its simple pentatonic melody.

The music of the verses was magnified there in that hall, reverberating into eternity. Luke closed his eyes and allowed the chant to enfold him in soft waves. This was what he'd been looking for, this piercing healing chord, these hypnotic cadences. His bones thrilled to it, sending restorative vibrations into every cell.

The lesson ended and Luke watched as the boys bowed to the old man and departed, two and three at a time. Luke pulled his hand away from the stone and looked around at the thousands upon thousands of columns.

What was the deal? Did every one of these pillars represent a person who had died and ended up here? Were these columns living archives, records of individual memories? If so, there must be billions of them.

Or were they doorways, tunnels between this place and the world of the living?

Luke peered around the pillar, examining it. The surface of the stone was perfectly smooth and featureless, the base inlaid with marble in a pattern of alternating white and black blocks.

Glancing warily at the enthroned lady, Luke dashed toward another column, and inspected it. It was identical except for the pattern on the base, which was composed of black leafy swirls. Nearby, another had a base featuring flowers: white on black, then black on white.

What had the base of *his* pillar looked like? Luke realized with alarm that he couldn't recall. Would he ever be able to find it again?

Luke felt panic rise and send a searing spurt of bile through his belly.

He turned and ran back toward the path, in the direction of the pillar that connected him with Charity, and with everyone he had ever loved. Luke had pulled up the poppies there. Surely he would be able to recognize the spot.

Luke ran on and on, scanning the poppy carpet for flaws, watching the white strip alongside it for torn crimson petals. How far had he walked already? The flower causeway rolled past his feet in unrelenting perfection. The soft scuff and tap and squeak of his worn soles, his rapid breathing, all echoed momentously in the enormous empty space with its impossibly long pillars. This chamber, he now divined, had been constructed as a vast resonator, a musical instrument made on a titanic scale.

On Luke ran. It seemed as though he had been running and staring at the ground for hours. He couldn't possibly have walked this far. He stopped, huffing and gasping for breath, hands on his knees. *Charity. Where are you?*

He was *not* going to start crying again. He filled his lungs with air.

"Chariteee! Chaarriteeeeeee! Chaaaaariteeee!"

The echo of Luke's plaintive, gravely cries set the strings in the heart of the vast chamber thrumming. Tuning the moaning chord to the key of his pain, Luke screamed his wife's name again and again. A braying that reverberated through the hall, a harsh trumpet announcing disastrous news, his voice gradually transformed into a croaking noise, and at last subsided into a creaking, whispery sob.

His spent form lay curled up in the poppies. Squeezing his eyes shut, Luke wished himself away, into nothingness.

*April 1, 1994* –Brooklyn, NY

*Had a dream about Luke Mandrake last night. I'm not particularly a Shambala fan, but for some reason the dream really affected me, and left me quite upset.*

*I'm in a bright space where there are flowerpots, and broken dolls on rough shelves. I'm standing there with Phil, Aron's friend from work.*

*"So this is the room where Luke Mandrake died," I say. "Right in this corner is the spot that leads backward in time, to the very moment!"*

*"Then if I go through, I might be able to stop him–change history!" Phil says. His large, rather bulbous eyes are gleaming in his dark face. "I'm going to try and do it!"*

*Before I can stop him, Phil walks over to the corner and instantly disappears, like a light winking out. I realize with alarm that he might not be able to get back from the past. It seems unlikely that Phil will succeed in changing history, and I fear that he has simply sacrificed his own life for nothing, adding tragedy on top of tragedy.*

*I wake up before learning the outcome of Phil's experiment.*

Rosetta Stone put down her pen and rubbed her forehead. She picked up a blister-pack and pushed two tiny red pills out through the aluminum backing. She swallowed the decongestants with a swig of water, and re-read the page in her journal.

*What did the dream mean?* she wondered. *Am I feeling threatened by Phil's friendship with my husband?*

*Mon Dieu, it's not Phil she ought to be worried about!* Jean-Baptiste drifted in the corner near the mantelpiece. Rosetta could not hear his thoughts. Why bother whispering in her ear? She never listened to him anymore.

Rosetta continued her self-examination. The appearance of Luke Mandrake could be an oblique reference to Phil's bisexual leanings. *Was the dream an unconscious expression of hostility toward Phil and Aron?* She searched her heart, but decided it was not. Whatever it meant, the dream had only made her anxious about Phil's safety.

*Actually, chérie, it's a reference to Phil's secret heroin addiction.* Jean-Baptiste closed his eyes and tried to ignore the sour tang of the ashtray on the windowsill. He was sick of sucking butts. Besides, he had used up all the juicy ones, and there was nothing left to smoke but burnt paper and ash.

Rosetta read the dream over once more, She left the journal lying open on the table, and got up to wash out the coffee pot.

Jean-Baptiste's eyes followed her movements. The tall body, ripe with affection and poetry, bent and turned quickly as she worked. With her broad shoulders, long breasts and lean, boyish limbs, she exuded competence and sexual vitality.

She was strangely lovely–her face was striking, with arched, strongly marked brows that lent her features a stern expression. Her green eyes had a thoughtful, penetrating quality that people found unnerving. Combined with the delicate high cheekbones, the pixie nose and bee-stung lips, the effect was both sultry and charismatic.

*Captivating,* Jean-Baptiste thought. He was not the only one who felt this, he well knew. But she was his–his to watch over, his to protect.

As she rinsed the espresso basket, Rosetta scanned the exposed brick wall above the sink. Not one cockroach could be seen. Rosetta had looked on as her roommate Bob gleefully eradicated them in a holocaust, squirting jets of poison from a can while the insects zipped from crack to crack. The bugs had run, dropped and died. *But the poison lingers on,* Jean-Baptiste thought, *saturating the brick, infusing the air with deadly fumes.*

Rosetta set the loaded espresso pot on a burner. She then grabbed the sponge and scrubbed off the black deposits of slime that had accumulated around the base of the faucet. After that she sniffed her hand. It smelled of rancid sponge, so she rubbed her thumb on the pop-up squirt top of the dish soap bottle, dislodging some of the dried-on crud that was crusted around it. She worked this up into a thrifty lemon-scented lather, and washed her hands. The coffee pot began to clear its throat noisily.

*Ah, the infinite horrors of material existence.* It was sometimes difficult for Jean-Baptiste to fend off his distaste for the grotty details. He had been traumatized by grotty details. Memories from his days among the living haunted him. *The rivers of stinking sewage that flowed through the streets, carrying disease to every door, a stew of dead leeches, high colonics, basins of bloody phlegm spat out by consumptives . . .*

Jean-Baptiste shuddered. He reminded himself that Brooklyn in the 1990's was nothing like Paris in the 1660's. Still, he could not permit himself to become complacent. He had a job to do. *Danger still lurks in the most ordinary places.*

Beyond the perils of toxic fumes, lightning, bad mayonnaise and rusty nails, the greatest threats to Rosetta's safety, Jean-Baptiste knew, were psychological. *And here she is once again, careening toward the most common of catastrophes: the betrayal of love, the grief that saps one's soul and leads to rashness, madness, illness and despair.*

And he could not warn her, for Rosetta had long ago ceased to heed his advice. She would have to make her way through that thicket without his guidance. Fortunately she had inner resources, she was both an artist and a seer of sorts. She had access to her subconscious, and she used it fairly well.

That she had dreamed of Luke Mandrake was hardly surprising. The spectacular scandals that had lately battered and nearly wrecked the lives of the reluctant punk messiah and his wife, had made them potent symbols in the collective unconscious. Luke was already treading the final steps on his road to ruin, Jean-Baptiste surmised. The musician had nearly died some months ago in Paris–had gone into a coma–the papers had been full of the news. Overdosed on pills, was it?

*Looming tragedy, there's a fine topic for Rosetta's dreams,* Jean-Baptiste mused bitterly.

Rosetta, deep into her cup of coffee, was now calculating expenditures. Rent and utilities, quarters for the laundromat, groceries, toothpaste and condoms, beer and wine, jelly beans and chocolates–it was an exhaustive list. She added in the cost of a standard ad campaign: wheat paste for posters, printing, and postage for an announcement to the band's mailing list. When the budget lines were totted up, she concluded with relief that there should be enough money left over, even after throwing an Easter party, to pay for linseed oil and film.

She wrote out a check for $1100, and addressed an envelope to the landlord.

"Mom!" came a voice from below. "Mo-o-o-om!!" Rosetta made her way down the stairs, followed by the silent and invisible figure of her guardian spirit. She opened the door to her son's room.

"What is it, Antoine?" she asked softly.

"I can't find my glasses!"

"Uh-oh. Did they fall down the side?"

"I don't know–I thought I put them over here."

"Do you want me to come up and help you look?"

"Just–just gimme my old glasses. I can't see."

"Okay sweetie," Rosetta said as she entered the room, searching on the dresser top with her eyes.

"It's–they're on the desk." The boy's eyes were big and blue, and like his mother he had an elfin look.

Rosetta ducked under the loft bed, into the cubby where the desk resided, raising a finger to touch the red heart she'd painted on the wood directly below where her son slept. Secretly she thought of it as a charm of protection, a fancy which Jean-Baptiste found irritating.

*I'm her protector,* he thought jealously, *she should know that. I'll take care of Antoine.*

"Aha!" she said, and handed the old spectacles, molded of heavy plastic and mended with tape, up to Antoine. "Let me know if you need any more help," she said cheerfully.

"Thanks Mom," the boy replied in a tragically failing tone. It wasn't merely for effect, he was filled with dread. In a fifth grade classroom, wearing tape-mended glasses was social suicide.

"Want a hug?" Rosetta asked.

"Sure."

"A million hugs a day, that's all you get," she smiled. "After that you're cut off."

*You're cut off!*–that was something Antoine's father used to say. Rosetta had been making the same joke to Antoine since before he could talk.

He didn't seem to be tired of it yet. "Mom, I haven't had my million hugs today," he'd say sometimes. Rosetta climbed up the ladder and gave him a quick, heartfelt squeeze.

"There's clean clothes in the laundry basket," she added. "Did you get all your homework done?"

"Yes."

"I love you sweetie." She dropped a kiss on his head. The loft bed creaked as she swung round and climbed down.

Rosetta had designed and constructed the massive piece of furniture on the cheap, creating space for a school desk in Antoine's tiny bedroom by splitting it horizontally. She'd shaped the wood with a handsaw and chisel, spread newspapers on the floor of the living room, and painted it in bright colors.

When it came to inserting the long screws that held the pieces together she'd asked Aron to help her, but after a few minutes with the screwdriver he'd cried, "My hands! My hands! How will I play guitar, if I injure my hands?"

Rosetta had quietly finished the job herself. The bed was still standing. *A miracle,* Jean-Baptiste thought.

Rosetta moved through her morning routine, making sure that Antoine ate breakfast, and got out the door in time for the school bus. She then made her way to the sun porch, and stood staring thoughtfully at her current painting.

This seemed to Jean-Baptiste like a good opportunity to go upstairs and attempt to extract some tobacco from Aron's jacket pocket. But just as he reached for the coat, the phone rang. Seconds later, Bob emerged through the French doors that led to his room, and stared at the answering machine on the windowsill. He waited to find out whether the call was for him.

*"Hi Rosetta . . ."*

"Rosetta!" Bob called down the stairwell as the message went to tape, "are you around? Telephone!"

"Okay, thanks!" she called back. A short while later she emerged from below and pressed the playback button on the blinking machine.

*"Hi Rosetta, this is Virginia. I'm just calling to firm up about tomorrow . . . it's supposed to be a pretty nice day . . . Ah, I'm going to go to the garden center early, to get some supplies, then head over there, maybe around ten? So let me know if that's okay. And hey, thanks for letting me do this . . . I can't wait to get my hands in the dirt, you know? Ha ha. Okay, well, call me back. Love you! Bye!"*

Rosetta punched a series of numbers into the phone, waited for the outgoing message to finish, and spoke.

"Hi Virgie! Tag, you're it! Anyway come whenever you want, I'll be up. Hey, by the way, Jessie's coming over with the girls at some point to decorate Easter eggs, so you can stay for that if you feel like it. It'll be fun. Um, trying to figure out about food, who's going to be around for what. I was thinking we could do a brunch. Let me know. Love you back! Byeee."

Rosetta clicked off and immediately placed another call.

"Hello?"

"Hi, Jessie?"

"Oh, hi Rosetta!" Jessie's voice sounded even more tired and strained than usual.

"How's it going?"

"Oh, not so great. Peter moved out last night."

*"What!?"*

"Yeah. It's been brewing for a while now. He's been sleeping in the basement for weeks."

"Oh my god, I had no idea. What's going on?"

"He told me he was seeing somebody else. And–and he said he wasn't going to stop seeing her. And–I just–couldn't . . ."

"Jessie . . . Oh, you poor thing!!"

". . . I just couldn't have him sleeping in my bed after that, you know?"

"Of course, of course not!"

"Anyway, I don't blame him for finding another place . . . he's been getting eaten alive by fleas down there."

"Wow. I can't believe this is happening!"

"It's happening. He even wrote a song about it. *Fleabag Daddy.* It's pretty funny."

"My god." Rosetta didn't know whether to laugh or cry. "I'm so sorry."

"Oh, Rosetta. I don't know what I'm going to do. He's never made much money with the band, but–but he was at least available to babysit. And I don't know how I'm going to make ends meet now, with just the riding lessons. Sometimes I drive all the way out to Long Island, and then my student just blows the appointment off, you know? And then I don't make anything. If I have to pay for babysitting too, it's going to wipe me out."

"Oh, Jessie. You don't deserve this."

"What really kills me is, I'm so close to a breakthrough at work,"

Jessie sighed. "Do you know who I gave a lesson to the other day?"

"Who?"

"Well, it was this really nice guy named Bob. He needed to learn to ride for a movie he was in. During lunch break we chatted a while. When I stopped by the office the girl at the front desk was going wild.

" 'I can't believe you *talked* to him!' she said.

" 'You mean Bob?' I said.

"And she screamed, 'Bob!? That was *Robert De Niro*!' "

"Ha ha, not again!" Rosetta said. "It's like what happened with Joey Ramone!"

"Ugh, Joey Ramone. It was so creepy, the way he chased me around the club like a horny stork. I was like, *who is this freak*?!"

"Which is why you ended up in the music video. I think your mental block against recognizing famous people is a real gift."

"Apparently that's what they like about me."

"Remember that time you met Phil Lesh at a party, and asked him what band he was in? Ha ha."

"Oh god. At least Peter didn't grab a guitar at that moment and launch into *The Grateful Dead Must Die*."

"Ha ha ha! That would have made for a perfect evening."

"Anyway . . ." Jessie sighed again. "I'll have to look for a full time job, now."

"What were you thinking of?" Rosetta bustled around in the kitchen, dragging the phone with her on its long cord.

"Peter's Mom is helping me buy a computer, and I signed up for a design class . . . "

"Oh, that's a great idea. I'm sure you'll be good at it." Rosetta turned on the faucet, and the espresso pot clattered in the sink.

"Yeah, I think so. It's interesting, and I'm learning a lot about typography . . ."

"I'd like to do that–learn to use a computer. It's so useful for doing paste-up."

"Yeah," Jessie said sadly. "But how am I ever going to have time to paint again?"

"I can't believe Peter is doing this," Rosetta said as she filled the little aluminum basket with fragrant powder. "It's so selfish."

*More coffee already?* Jean-Baptiste thought disapprovingly. He desperately needed a smoke.

"That's Peter," Jessie said. "When we were first living together, he decided he shouldn't have to chip in for rent, because he had so many fans, he could always crash on somebody's couch for free. Even after Alice was born, I had to twist his arm to help out with expenses."

"Gosh. I never knew he was, well . . . such a . . . "

"A deadbeat? Yeah, I used to think the problem was the drugs. But then he got clean, and I found out, the problem is just HIM."

Rosetta barked a laugh. "Oh, god," she moaned. Unseen beyond the breakfast bar, the black sport coat that hung over the arm of the sofa stirred as though lifted by a weird wind.

"Anyway, how are *you* doing?" Jessie asked.

"Great, except for the two broken legs," Rosetta said bitterly, and then held her breath.

"What!!?" cried Jessie.

"–*April Fool!* Heh heh heh."

"AAAAAAAH–HAAA ha ha!" Jessie exploded. It was her signature foghorn laugh.

"Ha ha ha, he he!" Rosetta always laughed at her own jokes, but nobody seemed to mind. Her laugh was infectious.

"Rosetta!! Two broken legs!–AAAAHH! That's too funny." Smacking noises could be heard over the telephone as Jessie slapped her thigh. Meanwhile, the packet of rolling tobacco tucked into the inner pocket of the black sport coat inched its way out, all on its own.

"HEE hee hee hee!" Rosetta giggled on helplessly.

"Oh noooooo! I can't believe it. You got me again! I totally forgot it was April Fool's Day."

"Seriously though," Rosetta wiped her eyes, "I think I might have landed a gallery."

"Really? Rosetta! That's so great!"

"Well, don't congratulate me yet. It's just a little gallery in Connecticut. I'm going to go out there and meet with the lady next week."

"Well, that's still great news! How did–Alice! Would you please not–" Jessie was no longer speaking into the phone, but she could be heard shouting. "We've talked about this! Give Kimberly back her muffin baby! Right now!"

There was a sound of commotion and shrill childish voices rising. On the stove the espresso pot burbled. Not far away, a fluffy blob of tobacco floated in the air above Aron's coat.

"Sorry Rosetta. I'm going to have to go deal with this. So–are we still on for tomorrow?"

"Absolutely. What time do you want to come over?"

"I was thinking maybe twelve or one?"

"Make it twelve, and we'll have brunch."

"Sounds great.–Kimberly, stop that!–Both of you, sit! Sit down, or I swear I'll start singing *Macarthur Park!*" She addressed Rosetta again. "Should I bring anything? Some eggs?"

Jean-Baptiste silently slid the tobacco pouch back into its pocket.

Rosetta was pouring warm milk into a mug from a tiny saucepan. "Nope, I'll get all the supplies. Just–" Rosetta was interrupted by a crescendo of high-pitched howls on the other end of the line.

"Hold on–" Jessie put the phone down. Tiny shrieks erupted in the distance, as Jessie bellowed, "Someone left the caaake out in the raaaain!"

Rosetta sat down at the yellow Formica table with her Americano and a plate of toast. Eventually Jessie returned to the receiver.

"Oh god. I really have to get off the phone. Thank you so much, Rosetta, we'll talk more tomorrow! Love you!"

"Love you too. Bye!"

Rosetta sat for a few minutes in silence, sipping her coffee. She took a bite of toast and chewed thoughtfully. *Poor Jessie, poor Kimberly and Alice. Oh, poor Jessie!* she was thinking.

Rosetta got up to pee. Jean-Baptiste sighed as he followed her into the bathroom. He was becoming feverish with anxiety, with wondering what he ought to do.

He fingered Aron's toothbrush, then slipped it into his pocket. He didn't know exactly what he was going to do with it, but the dead comedian was sure he could think of something appropriate.

Aron was sleeping in the next room. He had stumbled in a few hours ago, in a foul mood. Jean-Baptiste had overheard his thoughts. He couldn't help it. Aron's memories read like a pulp novel. Jean-Baptiste replayed them in his mind.

*Aron lounges on the sofa in Sherry's midtown apartment. Sherry is a coworker at the office where Aron and Phil are both employed.*

*"Would you like a beer?" Sherry asks, slipping sinuously out of her coat. Aron is mesmerized by her petite, curvaceous body and enormous breasts.*

*"Sure," Aron says. While she is in the kitchenette, he gazes about the tiny flat. The place is decorated in chrome and vinyl. There's a poster on the wall of a kitten sitting in a wine glass. A huge television takes up half the room. There's not a book to be seen.*

*"Wanna watch a movie?" Sherry asks. She is carrying a pair of tumblers and a quart of Budweiser. "I got Wayne's World 2 out from the library."*

*"Okay," Aron says.*

*The videotape features a pair of idiots who want to organize a rock festival.*

*"Just like you, huh?" Sherry says.*

*"I'm a musician, not a promoter."*

*Sherry leans over, flashing her cleavage, and pats Aron's knee.*

*"Maybe you'll be famous someday. Then I can tell my friends I knew you back when."*

*Aron's guts start to churn. He has already moved his personal deadline for being famous forward from 20 to 25, then from 25 to 30, and now to 35. He says nothing.*

*He swigs his tasteless beer. Sherry watches the comedy blankly, not laughing at the jokes. Aron stares at her covertly.*

*She is not amply-endowed with brains, but that doesn't matter. He slides his arm onto the back of the couch, then drops it around her shoulders.*

*One thing leads to another.*

*Aron is manipulating the hooks of Sherry's brassiere. Then, just as the plums are about to be plucked, he hears an irritating sound. It is Sherry's voice.*

*"Aren't you married?"*

*Aron doesn't answer. Sherry takes his hand and moves it away from her bust.*

*"I heard you were married," she says. "Is it true?"*

*Aron frowns. "I only married her because she was pregnant!"*

*"So you don't love her? Are you getting a divorce, then?"*

*Oh, for fuck's sake, Aron thinks. He goes to the fridge and retrieves another quart of Bud. He pours some into Sherry's cup, and refills his own. She does not take a sip.*

*He finishes the bottle.*

*After a long time, the movie ends. Aron makes an awkward exit.*

*Servicing a painful stiffie behind the dumpster of a Ninth Avenue pizza joint, he pictures Sherry dressed in vinyl, with tall boots, like a cheap groupie.*

*Waiting in the subway station, he continues to brood over Sherry's rejection. It takes over an hour for the F train to arrive. Aron guzzles a quart of Ballantine's, wrapped in a brown paper bag. It's been a humiliating evening, and it's all Rosetta's fault.*

*Rosetta is standing in his way.*

He had arrived home still vibrating with anger.

That was when Jean-Baptiste started smoking again. Gathering the butts of Aron's hand-rolled cigs, he'd spent the rest of the night huffing grumpily on his pipe in the back garden.

Being a ghost, smoking was not a carnal act for him, so much as a kind of metaphysical extraction process. Still, the flood of nicotine made him shaky, especially when all he had to smoke was nasty brown butts like little cockroaches. And the more anxious he became, the harder it was to stop.

He stepped out into the yard to enjoy a few puffs of the good, fresh shag he'd pilfered. He still had the toothbrush in the pocket of his coat.

The guardian angel giggled as the toothbrush darted here and there, gathering cobwebs, dirt and dead flies into its bristles.

Once he rinsed it out, Aron would never know.

***Eternity, The Hall of Ten Thousand Pillars***

When Luke opened his eyes he saw a pair of brown feet, sandaled in strips of gold. Each graceful appendage emerged from under a thick and ruffled white drapery and was about the size of a St. Bernard. The enormous toes were no more than a dozen paces away from where he lay in the dirt, inhaling the scent of the mashed flowers beneath him.

Luke sat up, trembling. How could this be? Had she somehow appeared while he wept? Had he himself been transported to her? Or had she been there all along, ensconced on her carved throne of red stone, invisible until now?

His head tilted back as he looked up at the goddess's knees, her magnificent bosom, her luscious arms. If she were to stand up, Luke knew, she would tower over him like a redwood tree. Fire licked around her head, reflected in the gold shield behind it. Still, she had not moved a muscle, and her visage, when Luke glanced briefly up into it, appeared changeless and without a flicker of animation, despite the incandescent compassion written there. Luke turned his eyes from the face of the goddess, with its unbearable, almost tormented expression, to the objects in her hands.

The sword in her right hand was of a dark stone, the color of tarnished silver with a metallic sheen. Luke searched his memory for the word. His aunt Suze had owned a lapidary shop that sold tumbled semiprecious gemstones and rocks organized in big Plexiglas bins. As a boy he had loved to let the stones run through his fingers, had taken a keen interest in learning their names. The sword, he was sure, was carved of hematite, also called bloodstone: heavy iron ore, purported to have healing properties that worked by balancing and invigorating the nervous and circulatory systems. The weapon was at least twelve feet long, and must weigh half a ton, he thought, and yet the goddess held it in one hand as lightly as a twig.

The fingers of her left hand curled around a chalice of massive design, solid gold and studded with chunks of lapis lazuli, each encircled in a thick, raised gold bezel. A brilliant light glinted from within the cup.

The goddess remained motionless, tongues of flame playing around her. Was she a living being, or merely a graven image?

Luke stole another glance up at the oval face framed by tresses, black as a raven's wing, that cascaded over her shoulders. He was instantly mesmerized by the sweetness of her expression. Her enormous green-and-gold eyes were bright as sunlit honey.

Silently she sat on her blood-red throne of porphyry, carved and painted with hieroglyphs, and gazed gently into Luke's eyes. The grail between her fingers sparkled.

Luke's throat was parched, he felt a grinding urge to taste what the cup contained, be it the milk of living light, or an elixir of Lethe, bringing an eternal night. He imagined himself climbing into the goddess's lap, lifting the chalice to his lips. To drink his fill . . . Luke could almost feel the trickle running down his chin.

Yes, that. That was what he truly desired . . . the sweet milk, the forgetfulness of her embrace. He licked at the drops, but tasted only salt. Tears were streaming down his face.

He did not move closer. He remained on his knees, staring up at her now with naked longing, his hands gripping the stems of the poppies on either side of him as if their wiry fibers were all that was stopping him from lunging forward.

Then, with slow and silent grace, the left hand of the goddess released the jeweled cup and she lifted her arm. Luke let out a sob, surrendering himself to her will. In thrall to hopeless yearning he gazed at her, and her lambent eyes smote into his heart.

*This is it,* he thought, not knowing what would come.

A yellow blossom appeared, cupped in the palm of the goddess's hand, and grew bigger until it was a ball of flame, sparking and whirling. Then from the bluish white center of this ball there shot out a fiery beam that drove straight down into his guts, where the burning sensation he had carried with him through the years roared up into a consuming agony. Luke cried out as crackling flames exploded around him, thinking momentarily that his anguished journey had reached an end.

But his thoughts did not cease. Instead a stream of smoky red particles appeared to be passing up the beam and into the ball of fire. As the substance was drawn out of him like poison blood, the wrenching pain subsided. Gradually the band of sparks burned itself out, and ceased.

Luke could see a wound like a stigmata on the goddess's palm.

She closed her fingers around the blackened hole, then moved her fist to just above the lip of the grail, palm down, and opened it. A blinding burst of light emerged from the cup and engulfed the hand for a second or two. Now she held up her palm toward Luke like a benediction. The wound was gone, and Luke's pain had gone with it. He touched his stomach with both hands, and looked up at the giantess.

"Thank you," he croaked. She smiled gently.

With a quick motion the goddess tossed her sword upward, and it hung gleaming in the air. She held out both her arms toward Luke in an affectionate gesture.

*Come to me, Luke, and be at peace.* Her words rang in his mind like a carillon.

This time Luke did not hesitate. He shot toward her, clasped her leg and buried his face in her fragrant robes. She stroked him, brushing the tangled locks back from his forehead. After a while he looked up, feeling a stab of joy when he gazed into her adoring face. He held his arms up like a child and she lifted him gently, cradled him against her bosom.

His face was only inches now from a monumental nipple, which stood erect at the center of an aureole the color of papaya flesh, and he seized it with both hands. A stream of milk spurted out onto his cheeks, dribbled down the plump curve of the mighty teat. His mouth found the thick tip and his lips embraced it. His mouth pulled, a gush of sweet liquid washed down his throat, and he swallowed.

As Luke gulped down the life-giving fluid a sensation of ecstatic well-being filled him. The nourishment flooded his astral body, invading every cell, or whatever he was now composed of that approximated cells. Gradually his awareness expanded, became diffuse, and he drifted away in a nearly disembodied state, dreaming vividly of a journey over sienna hillocks under a cool gray sky.

It seemed to him that he stood before the entrance to a cave of red clay, which he had discovered in the foothills of a small mountain. The opening was narrow, but he knew he could squeeze through it. He would need to bend down to look inside properly, so he reached his hand up to hold on to a fold of earth at the top of the arch. That was when he realized that what he had taken to be clay was living flesh. The mat of dark foliage above the tunnel's mouth was lustrous, curly hair.

Luke inhaled a deep and quivering breath. Before him rose the yoni of the goddess. There was a musky, tantalizing odor, one that he now realized had been in his nostrils for some minutes, and the fragrance bathed his face, sent endorphins and mezcal shots of testosterone into his blood. If he could spend the rest of eternity just standing there in front of this humongous vagina, breathing, he thought, it would almost be enough. But the fire in his veins drove him toward the divine crevice, the gateway to . . . somewhere.

It occurred to him that this was what he had come to this place to do, to pass through this soft, velvety door.

But what awaited him then? It was not to be a rebirth, for sure. He was contemplating a return to the womb, not an exit from it. This was a concept, or perhaps a drive, that had always fascinated him. Yet he had tended to scoff at Freudian science, considering it overly mechanistic. Now he scratched his head at the thought, for to force his way through those carmine lips seemed a sacrilege, indeed the very brutality of the act offended him. Besides, how would he breathe in there? The idea appalled him, yet he could not stop thinking about it.

Then he realized that there was a way to open the door: the hooded, glistening pink knob at the top of the crack.

It seemed an obvious thing now, to stroke it and play with it. Still Luke felt rather inspired as he spit on his hands and got to work, palpating with all his might, and feeling at first rather like a cheese-maker squeezing a bag of curds. The clit immediately began to shrink however, and the more he manipulated it, the smaller it got. Or no, he was getting bigger, and not just a certain part of him. He rubbed more gently, and before long he knelt and took the whole delicious nub in his mouth, licked it tenderly but firmly.

Luke was growing steadily larger, or the goddess was shrinking. He could cup the whole vulva in his hand now. Soon he was untying his sneakers and stripping off his jeans and shorts. He felt a tender touch, someone pulling his shirt away over his head.

And now she was lying under him, nude except for a string of beads around her waist, looking up at him with pleasure and love in her fawn-like eyes. She was a big woman, but no longer a giantess.

*Okay! Whatever size she wants to be,* he smiled as he breathed in the tingling scent of her sweat, *I'll make it work.* But this size was nice, very nice. He could dig it.

He took her hands, kissed the pink fingertips. He stroked up along her arms to her neck, brushing her delicate clavicles, and cradled her face between his palms. He found her plump little mouth with his and fell into a kiss, deep and sensuous. As her tongue probed between his lips, desire drove down into him, through him, and emerged below the belt as an erection of purpling girth and fiery urgency.

Luke gulped air like a pearl diver, then began tracing the deep curves of the goddess's glorious bosom with his tongue, and those of her hips with his fingers. She was a carving on a Hindu temple, come to life. And she had chosen him, had taken him to herself.

*Now this is more like it–this is what heaven was supposed to be.* He laughed as he locked his arms around her narrow waist and rolled, pulling her up on top of him.

"Luke. My sweet and beautiful boy," she murmured, brushing the hair from his eyes, and kissed the tip of his nose, then each eyelid before fastening her lips onto his mouth.

Luke lay back with a sigh as she rose into a primal squat, her fingers twisted in his hair. He felt her ankles brushing along his flanks as he watched himself plunge into her, both of them riding the same wave, a pleasure so intense that Luke nearly fainted. Fuck, fuck, fucking him, her touch like electric thrills all over and he couldn't stop fondling her exquisite body, pinching her nipples as he arched up to meet her, then gripping her hips and thrusting with unleashed passion. She absorbed all his force, shuddered into it and pushed back, screaming and grunting and writhing, yanking at his hair and biting his earlobes in tiny erotic nips. Far too soon he reached his perfect agony, and as time froze and his battering-ram heart stood still in his chest he gazed into the goddess's eyes, realizing she cradled a baby to her breast.

Luke knew in a flash that the baby was himself.

He looked up at her through the infant's eyes, reached hungrily for her teat. His mouth filled with sweet milk, and he drifted into slumber, wrapped in a profound contentment. He was gently rocking on a sea of comfort, enfolded in an amniotic kiss.

But his blissful peace was soon disturbed. From deep below, bubbles formed under the surface, and belched forth. These bubbles contained a noxious gas, Luke knew, and he held his breath, afraid to inhale the poisonous fumes. He bucked and bobbed as the toxic balloons burst around and beneath him.

Luke was bouncing in the back seat of his parents' car. They were on their way to church.

"Jim, watch out! You drove right through that stop sign!" Mom yelled.

Luke was singing a song that he was making up. It went like this:

"Eeya! Eeyah! Dunn da dunn. Eeya! Meeyah! Dunn ta da dunn. Meeeeyah! Meeeeeyah! Dunn. Da da Dunn. Eeya! Eeyah! Dunn da dunn . . . "

Dad turned and growled, "Luke. Stop kicking the back of my seat."

Everything was going wrong. When they got into the car, Luke had asked to sit on Mommy's lap. Dad had said no, he was a big boy now and didn't need to sit on Mommy's lap any more. But Jody got to sit on Mommy's lap every time. Luke was starting to think it would never be his turn.

"Jim, slow down!" said Mom. "If we're late we're late."

"Hey," said Dad, "I'm not the one who had to go crazy with a curling iron for forty-five minutes."

"Meeeeyah!" Luke sang. "Meeeeeyah! Dunn. Da da Dunn."

"Luke! Please stop kicking the back of my seat."

It was stupid and boring being the only one in the back seat.

"Just because you know Jake Pomeroy is going to be there, you wanna get all gussied up," said Dad in his I-told-you-so voice.

"It's a tradition, you know, getting dressed up for church." Mom sounded shrill.

Back when Luke got to sit up front, Mom and Dad didn't used to fight all the time.

Luke sang louder. "Eeya! Eeyah! Dunn da dunn. Eeya! Meeyah!

Dunn ta da dunn!"

"And is it traditional to wear a skirt an inch longer than your goddamn panties?"

"Meeeeyah! Meeeeeyaaahh!"

"Luke!" Dad was really mad. "If I have to stop this car I'm going to tan your hide!"

"Luke, settle down! You're driving your father crazy!" Mom was getting screechy, and Jody started to cry.

Luke curled up into a scowling ball.

Mom turned back to Dad. "You have no right to tell me how to dress," she said with all the meanness she could muster. Dad said something back. It was going to be a long trip to church.

Luke scrunched into the corner of the back seat so nobody could watch him pull his secret friend out of his pocket. Her name was Mia. She was a plastic Tinkerbell figure from inside a broken snow globe. He had gotten in trouble for smashing the globe, but it wasn't an accident. He had needed to get the little fairy out, and now he carried her with him everywhere.

He rubbed her body with his thumb, the way he always did for good luck. Looking first to make sure nobody was watching, he kissed the tiny figurine, then held her to his cheek.

"Meeeeyahh . . . eeyah meeeeeyahhhh . . ." he sang quietly. "Meeeeyaahhh . . . !"

Mia was growing bigger in his hand. She was the size of a Barbie doll, but alive. He rubbed her body with his thumb. Soon Mia was bigger than he was.

Mia looked different now, with a mass of dark curls, red lips, sandals and a diaphanous Cretan gown that left her bosom bare.

Luke jumped into Mia's lap. "When I grow up, I'm going to marry you," he said.

Luke had drawn a picture of this with his crayons.

But Luke was already a grownup, he was a grown man. He was

riding a wave of testosterone-fueled rage, headed for a meltdown, but it didn't matter now. Everyone knew. Everyone left him alone.

Luke was an irascible monster with busy fingers, getting nasty with a girl in the back seat of the family car. Would Mom notice?

In the drawing Luke was huge, as huge as a monster, and had gigantic hands. Flying beside him was the tiny buxom fairy, with a bouquet of flowers, and a wedding veil floating in the breeze. The magical little minx was his very own Mia. He would keep her in his pocket, and never be lonely again. Whenever he got into trouble, she would always come out and save him.

He pushed himself up onto his elbow and looked down at Mia. Mia was a goddess, she was generosity incarnate as she gazed at him with infinite love and surrender. Her nipples were fountains streaming with milk.

Milk was getting all over the seat, but Luke didn't care. He would never let her go now, they would stay here, hidden in a sleeping bag in the back of his Dad's Impala. Here she would remain, incessantly and exclusively available to him, as the car drove all by itself, around mountain bends and up and down valleys, forever.

This was what he had always wanted.

He bent to kiss her, relishing the sensation of milk spurting up into his face.

*April 1, 1994* –Brooklyn, NY

Rosetta gulped the last of her coffee and munched the tail end of her toast. It looked like the rain was going to start again. She went downstairs and shoved dirty clothes into a laundry bag. Aron was still asleep as she wrestled a rickety folding cart laden with clothing and soap up the steps of the sunken entrance to their duplex apartment. Wheels squeaking, she pushed the cart down the street to the laundromat on the corner. On the way she sang:

> *Angelica turns up the Walkman*
> *Chews something green, and sticks out a green tongue*
> *Walks to the desk with a swagger*
> *And offers the teacher a piece of her gum.*
> *"Spit that out!" says Miss White,*
> *"And go back to your seat."*
> *Angelica bares her occasional teeth.*
> *"Teacher, is that your real hair?*
> *Teacher, you're my worst nightmare.*
> *There's a run in your hose,*
> *And a zit on your nose.*
> *Is this your purse?*
> *Hey, teacher, I assed you a question."*

It was the first song Rosetta and Aron had written together. Rosetta still carried a picture in her wallet, from the night in January 1990 when they met at the Rodeo Bar–not the black-and-white photo of Aron playing the lute, but a pencil portrait she'd drawn, based on the photo. He wore a black shirt and his red tie, and in the drawing he was bent almost double over the strings, lips pursed in concentration, his ponytail a molten blob of motion. The figure seemed on the verge of escaping off the page, held back only by a tangle of microphone cables and power cords that pinned him in a web of electronics. On the reverse of the image Rosetta had written, *Aron Delgado and his Pick O' Fire.*

She had invited the musician to move in with her a few months later. With her boyfriend sharing expenses, Rosetta decided she could quit reporting to the Board of Ed each day for substitute teacher gigs. She wanted more time to rehearse and play out, to attend open mics and the shows of other young musicians, and generally to promote their blossoming new wave band. Maybe she would even be able to find time to paint again.

Rosetta had proposed dividing up the chores, but as a single mom she'd felt obligated to take on the lion's share of the domestic work. She'd ended up doing all the cooking and cleaning, though Aron would come along with her to help carry the shopping bags and laundry.

She hadn't really minded folding Aron's frayed shirts. He wasn't very good at folding clothes, anyway. He would mush them together into a vaguely flat shape, and call it a job well done. Rosetta had been content just watching her man incline his body against the outside wall of the laundromat, his thermal-clad kneecap poking out through the enormous knee-holes of his washing-day jeans. He was eternally smoking a hand-rolled cigarette, while his mind swirled with chords and melodies.

Now, stacking Aron's work shirts beside her son's briefs and socks, Rosetta fell into a dreamy prayer. These days she often found herself longing wistfully for any sign of affection from her husband. Somewhere in their year and a half of marriage, he had stopped accompanying her on errands, and laundering the man's long-johns had become an act of nostalgia.

What was it that she pined for? Maybe for something that had never existed. Maybe for a future that was never to be.

When Rosetta returned from the laundromat, the phone was ringing, and she ran upstairs as the machine kicked in.

*Hi Rosetta, it's Virgie–* the machine was broadcasting when Rosetta picked up.

"Virgie! Sorry, I just got in," she panted.

"Modeling gig this morning?" Virgie wondered.

"No, just laundry."

They had met when they were both working as figure models. Rosetta had spotted Virginia in the cafeteria at Pratt Institute, sitting alone at a table, crying into her soup. She had recognized the slender, big-eyed waif as one of the models she'd seen posing in a group at the last Draw-a-thon.

Rosetta had pulled up a chair and offered the distressed girl a sympathetic ear. The cause of grief had turned out to be a one-sided love affair. Rosetta had listened kindly, but hadn't tried to advise the younger woman. Virgie, a biology student, had had the misfortune to fall for a handsome ballet dancer in one of her classes. It was one of the hazards of the trade.

For Rosetta, modeling had long been an important source of income. She knew instinctively how to be the naked lady in the room on the first day of Foundation Drawing class, in front of a flirtatious group of freshmen. She always handled the flushed teens with quiet professionalism, striking a balance between the tactful lack of self-consciousness her role required, and a passionate devotion to the artistic process. The students, as inspired by her aura of conviction as they were by her athletic physique, responded by focusing intently on their drawings.

How many couples in the past decade had hooked up during their hours spent straddling the benches in Rosetta's life drawing classes? As her statuesque form gyrated, sweated or lounged before the young artists, it never occurred to Rosetta to wonder. She didn't dwell upon the effect she had. Likewise she had never even considered dating a student or professor–that would have ruined it for her. In her mind she was onstage, untouchable–a living, breathing sculpture made of fire. The flaming White Heart.

If Aron had raised any objections to Rosetta posing in the buff, she would have laughed them away. But he did not. He hadn't seemed disturbed by it, even that time when a young man came up to her at a party and gushed about recognizing her from the nude drawings of her he had seen pinned to the wall of his dorm room. If the notion of thousands of art students seeing his girlfriend naked struck Aron as being a bit awkward to explain to his mother, he never said so.

The "sit still and shut up" business, as Rosetta liked to call it, was an occupation that required few qualifications aside from vigilance to the clock, and an utter lack of bodily shame. Punctuality was paramount, and the sessions proceeded in tightly structured intervals of time. *The model will begin with thirty second poses. Ten one minute and two five minute gestures. Five minutes break, then two tens, please: one contrapposto, one twist. A long pose: twenty-five minutes on, five off, in a reclining position.*

But she enjoyed the work, the familiar odor of the oil paints, the rustle of newsprint as the students rushed to capture each new pose. She particularly liked having the freedom to compose verses in her head, which she jotted down during breaks.

"They can rent my body," she quipped, "but my mind is my own."

Virgie had moved on to a job at the Museum of Natural History, but she and Rosetta had remained fast friends. A few months after Rosetta and Aron's wedding, the couple rented a duplex near Virginia's place. This year, Virgie was enthusiastically planning out their garden.

"I've been drawing up diagrams, and I consulted my Mom–she's a landscape architect, you know–about the plantings. I know it's not a large space, but the sun is great, and I bet you'll be able to grow a lot of veggies. But you probably want flowers too."

"Flowers would be nice. We had so many morning glories last spring, they were climbing everywhere. They're pretty, but–"

"The blue ones right? Yeah, they tend to take over. That's going to be the big challenge, weeding those suckers out. What do you want to put in as far as vegetables?"

"Tomatoes, definitely. Basil, cilantro, peppers."

"You can also grow some tomatoes in pots on the patio, that's where they'll get the best sun," Virgie suggested.

Aron, who had been searching in vain for his toothbrush, clomped upstairs.

"Virgie says hi," Rosetta said.

"Hi, Virgie." Aron rummaged for his tobacco pouch and deftly rolled several cigarettes, muttering "What the fuck? I just bought this pack."

"Rent's due, honey. Drop it in the mail for me?" Rosetta chirped. Aron scowled as he pocketed the envelope. He rapidly wrote out a check to Rosetta for his share, left it on the kitchen table, and departed.

"He was out till all hours again last night," Rosetta said to her friend as the door shut behind him.

"Hey, is something going on?" Virgie wondered. "You don't sound like your usual, ah, chipper self."

"I'm feeling kind of down," she admitted. "My period is late, and the last one was irregular, just spotting. It's been over two months since I've had a normal one."

"Oh god. Have you told Aron?"

"No."

"If you were pregnant, do you think he'd be happy?"

"I don't know. He's been so distant recently." Rosetta felt tears sting her eyes. "He–he did seem sad about the miscarriage, but it's so hard to tell with him. He doesn't talk about his feelings much."

"What was he like before, when you were pregnant?"

"Well, he's a breast man, and his attitude definitely changed when my tits swelled up and got huge. I think it must have pushed a button somewhere in his reptile brain."

"What do you mean?"

"It's kind of hard to explain. Um, I had constant headaches, and since I couldn't take painkillers or Sudafed like I usually do, I spent a lot of time in bed. I was miserable, had no interest in sex at all. But he would wait on me, massage me. It was surprising how devoted he was."

"Hey, that's a good sign."

"Yeah, but he also became insanely jealous. One night after rehearsal, he and some of the band members decided to go out for drinks. I wasn't drinking of course, so I got a lift home from the drummer Jeremy–he's a teetotaler. Later that night I woke up to see Aron standing at the bedroom door, and he was furious.

" 'Whose hair is this?' he yelled.

" 'What hair?' I said.

"And he was like, 'This hair. I found it in the bathtub. It's Jeremy's hair! What the fuck is it doing in the bathtub?' "

"Oh, my, god. He was out of his mind."

"Totally. I said, 'How could it be Jeremy's hair? He didn't even come up here.'

" 'Then how did this hair get there? Explain that!'

" 'I don't know!' I said. 'I have no idea whose hair that is, or where it came from.' It was awful. He had a look on his face I'd never seen before.

"I said, 'Honey, you're scaring me. You're very drunk, and you seem to have some kind of scenario rolling around in your head, but none of it really happened. What did happen was, Jeremy dropped me off, I came upstairs, I had a bad headache, so I went to bed. Nothing more.'

"Eventually he calmed down and accepted the truth of my story. Then he wrote a song about the madness of jealousy."

Virgie laughed. "Oh, really? Which one?"

"It's called *The Hairy Beast.*"

"Ohh. I wondered what that song was about."

Rosetta was doodling in her journal. The lines clumped together to form a cartoon hairball. *Whose hair am I?* she wrote, and circled it with a thought bubble.

"Anyway, a week later I started bleeding. Aron rushed me to the emergency room, he even paid for car service. They took us to a cubicle with one of those high beds covered in plastic sheeting, you know the ones with railings, that are so uncomfortable? Nowhere to sit, of course. And the doctor didn't come for hours. We waited, and waited, and I walked around in a paper gown, while chunks of placenta and uterine lining dropped out onto the floor." *Our baby left the world in a red flood.*

The cartoon hairball she was drawing coughed up a bigger hairball. *Ack! Ack!*

"My god, Rosetta, it must have been heartbreaking."

"It was horrible, I was crying the whole time. But I was also kind of relieved. Aron wasn't ready to settle down to fatherhood, that goes without saying. I was prepared to rise to the occasion, but the future was looking mighty challenging for a while there."

"Well, it sounds like he was willing to step up to the plate, though, right?"

Rosetta doodled a baby's head, with big astonished eyes.

"I guess. I did wonder if Aron would still want to go through with the wedding. But he said, since his mother had already bought her plane ticket from Tokyo, we might as well go ahead with it."

"His Mom is Japanese?"

"Yeah. She runs a dry cleaning place. She's nice. But . . . augh!"

"What?"

"Virgie, he's never told me he loved me. Not in words. And that feels pretty weird."

"Not even when he proposed?"

"He never really proposed to me. It was my idea."

"Oh. I have to admit, I'm not surprised."

"Yeah, he's no mister romantic. We made a deal. I was so scared he was going to leave me, because of the baby. I had made it clear early on that I wasn't willing to get an abortion," Rosetta said. She sketched an owl sitting on a dead tree.

"But why? Haven't you had an abortion already?"

"In high school, yes. But things are different now. I'm a grown woman, a mother. And this is the man I love. How could I destroy our child? I knew I could find a way to take care of it, come what may."

"I get it. So–what was the deal you made?"

"That I would give him control over the band, if he would agree to get married, and–and keep the baby."

"Oh. Wow. And then you had a miscarriage."

The page in Rosetta's journal was becoming crowded with odd creatures. A knight on horseback skewered a shocked-looking hog with his lance. Above the owl, Rosetta doodled a crescent moon, emerging from behind the clouds.

"Yeah. But by then I didn't feel like I could renegotiate."

"God, Rosetta. I had no idea. That's so intense."

"Yeah. I'm still not sure if he regrets it. Marrying me, I mean."

"But the important question to my mind is, do *you* regret it?"

"Virgie, I love him. I want him to be happy. And I'm painting again, that makes all the difference. I just wish . . . " The pen outlined an anxious girl with a deformed torso.

"What?"

"I just wish I knew whether he really loves me. That's all."

"Well, but he has to tell you that. You're his wife. He has to just say the words. God, it's not going to kill him."

Rosetta looked at the page she'd been illuminating. The deformed girl wore a shit-eating grin. She closed the journal with a snap.

"Yeah, I know. Maybe he just needs more time."

"Maybe so, Rosetta." Virgie sighed. "How long have you guys been together now?"

"Four years."

"Well, it seems to me like he's had time enough."

Jean-Baptiste wandered in the back garden, picking his way on his heeled shoes through a half-frozen mess of dead weeds that hid the beer bottles, butts and detritus of last summer's parties. He never made a sound, standing out by the short chain-link fence that divided the yard from those adjoining it, smoking his pipe, heedless of the drops of rain. Idly he poked at the garbage now and then with Aron's toothbrush.

Mon Dieu, but he was bored. There was no-one to talk to, that was the trouble.

*I must remain alert,* he admonished himself. He glanced through the multitude of louvered windows into the enclosed patio that served as Rosetta's studio. She was shrugging on a paint-spattered jacket, gazing at the picture on the easel, which featured a brown-skinned mother and her young daughter, riding through the clouds in the gondola of a hot air balloon.

The odor of turpentine oozed out from the porch via the screen door. It was a shabby room and cold, with its cinder-block walls and wobbly Masonite flooring, but at least it was dry. Rosetta picked up a tube of titanium white paint, squeezed some onto a wooden palette, then added more colors and mixed a mosaic of blues and greens and gold. As she worked she murmured a poem:

Jean-Baptiste watched Rosetta paint. A bird pecked about in the plantain leaves at his feet. Rosetta sketched mountains in the distance, magic castles in the clouds. As her brush flew, butterfly-winged fairies appeared, dancing in the air around the figures in the floating basket.

*She is living in a fantasy,* Jean-Baptiste thought impatiently. *She is squandering her substance on fancies, and on trying to please that ungrateful husband of hers.*

*The man is occluding her luminosity, and she refuses to see it. How like a woman, to underestimate the importance of her own talents. To put a man above herself, and let him feed upon her soul.*

But as Rosetta worked on, lost in concentration, contented, Jean-Baptiste began to doubt himself. What harm was there in it if, when faced with the neglect of a husband, she resorted to taking comfort in the abundant powers of her imagination?

Rosetta paused and seized a pencil to scrawl a to-do list in the border of her sketchbook. *Scrounge large buckets for planters? Photograph paintings. Antoine baseball game, 11:00 am.*

What good would it do, to shake her from the stupor of her denial? So long as she and her child were fed, clothed and safe, perhaps it would be best if she never learned of Aron's philandering. Besides, he wasn't very successful at it.

Jean-Baptiste was beginning to feel rather guilty about dirtying the toothbrush. *What if the fellow contracted a serious disease? Rosetta would be heartbroken.* He tossed the thing into the weeds, and sighed.

*Let her live in her fantasy world, if it makes her happy.*

He would try to be satisfied with that.

I managed to block out of my mind all human hope. I
pounced on every joy like a dumb, ferocious beast and
throttled it.

I summoned executioners so that, while dying, I could
chomp on the butts of their rifles. I ordered up plagues
to stifle me with sand, and with blood. Misfortune became my god. I lounged in the muck, and dried myself
off in the air of crime. And I ran a scam on lunacy.
And Spring served me up the ghastly laugh of the
idiot.

*A Season in Hell*

*Arthur Rimbaud*

*Eternity*–Famebeau

Luke rose from smothering depths into consciousness with a terrible headache. He opened his eyes to a hard blue sky without a cloud, and the dry heat of a desert sun.

*No way.* Luke squeezed his eyes shut. *There must be some mistake.*

Just now–just now he had been in the arms of a tender, gazelle-eyed houri. Where was she? Where was she, the wasp-waisted goddess with a cloud of black ringlets tumbling down her back? Where was the comforting milk of her bosom?

*Gone.*

Just when he finally had it all, had arrived, so it seemed, in heaven, she had simply vanished. *What was going on?*

"Hello?" Luke kept his eyes closed and felt around near him, his fingers scraping on stones and scrabbling at the loose dirt. *What the fuck?*

The goddess couldn't be far. He could hear the clinking of her bracelets.

*"Hey!"* Luke sat up and looked around. All about him was a blank landscape of yellowish-gray sand and yellowish-gray rocks, without a single tree or plant as far as he could see. It was so hot he could feel an oven-blast of air rising from the ground.

What had happened? How had he ended up here in this desert?

Luke lay back on the sand and closed his eyes again, desperately.

*Goddess . . . goddess! Where did you go? Let me back in!* It was still so vivid in his mind: the scent of her skin, its velvety smoothness, her henna-dipped fingertips . . . if he could only recapture that feeling, maybe he would wake up, and find himself back on her lap again. With all his might, Luke willed himself to be there.

*No. Fuck! It wasn't working.* The sun still beat down on him, and now there was a hot breeze blowing sand in his face. Had it all been nothing more than a vivid dream?

As he lay in fetal position, his arms wrapped around his head, something touched him on the elbow.

"Crawk!" a gravelly voice cawed.

Opening his lids, he found he was staring straight into the beady black eyes of a bald-headed vulture, with a raw pink neck and a collar of thin ebony feathers, like a gleaming boa. Luke sat up hastily. The bird hovered above him for a moment, beating its long pinions so that sand flew up in the air and into his eyes. Then the creature landed on top of Luke's head, and he could feel the weight of it, shifting around up there as it folded its wings and settled on its perch.

"The hell!" Luke lurched to his feet, blinded, staggering as he shooed the vulture off. "Get away, stupid bird!"

The vulture gave a strangled squawk. That was when Luke realized that the clinking sound he'd been hearing was the chain.

There were iron links attached to a heavy bracelet around his right wrist. The other end of the fetter, which was no more than a yard long, was attached to a matching collar.

Luke's mouth opened in horrified astonishment. "What the–?"

The collar encircled the wrinkled neck of the enormous vulture. The monster flapped its wings, showing off the blaze of white across its breast and pinions. Then, chain clanking, tugging painfully against Luke's arm, it landed on the ground nearby and smoothed its ruffled wing feathers with its beak.

"A magnificent California Condor," rasped the creature, "that's what I am, so you can stop looking at me like an idiot."

But Luke was looking at his own arm.

*Crap! Shit! shitshitshitshitshitshitshitshit–*

His arm had been thin before, but now it was so gaunt as to be skeletal. And his skin–his skin was a grayish green, and looked strangely tattered.

Luke touched a hand to his face, and felt the jutting bones, the patchy beard and leathery cheeks. "I'm a zombie?" he creaked in a small, pitiful voice.

"I'm a zombie!" he repeated, aghast.

"To me, you are my delicious prey," retorted the condor pompously, and flapping up to the top of Luke's head, it took a bite.

"What the fuck are you doing?" Luke yelled, grabbing the bird by the neck with both hands, squeezing and squeezing with all his zombie strength. Which was, he discovered, quite a lot. He could feel bones cracking. Of course, some of them were probably his own bones. Luke didn't care. He had to kill the creature at any cost.

Anyway the thing did not die, it just kept flapping its wings wildly, raising a gritty sirocco. Worse yet, it knew his name. On it gasped: "Luke, Luke," so piteously that he finally sat down on the ground, and released its throat.

The vulture spent some minutes twisting its hideous head around, and stretching its neck out, then pulling the head back into its ruff, which was looking a bit sparser after the fray. It smoothed the feathers around the bulbous pink crop that protruded from its chest, then stretched the wizened, rosy neck out again in an obscene display. The carrion bird coughed and wheezed, and gasped loudly during this exercise. Luke waited, sitting cross-legged on the sand with his withered arms folded. The creature's antics would have been hilarious, had Luke not been trembling with fury.

Finally the condor spoke. "Luke. You can't kill me. I'm–"

"I don't care if you can talk. I'm going to rip your fucking head off," Luke interrupted.

"–Already dead," it croaked. "Just like you. I'm a zombie, asshole."

Luke glowered at the bird. "Yeah, right, and you've been eating my–"

*Oh crap*. He felt his head. The top of the cranium was missing.

His brain was exposed.

"*Brain!*" he lunged at the bird and grabbed its neck again. At least he still had his reflexes.

But this time the vulture didn't flap its wings. It hung limply in his grip.

"Luke," it croaked in a tired voice. "Luuuuke."

So Luke let it go. What the heck. It probably hadn't asked for this fate, any more than he had.

"Luke," said the vulture, "give it up. You can't kill me. We can suffer, but we can't die."

"Then stay the fuck away from my brain, bird."

The headache had not faded, and Luke was experiencing a dull pain all over his skin, in his rotting flesh, and now in his cracked hand bones. He was in a terrible mood.

"You don't understand," the vulture creaked. "It's my nature–"

"To eat brains, yeah, sure it is pal. And it's in my nature," Luke yanked the thing's chain angrily, "to wring your neck, so if you don't wanna suffer, leave me alone. Capiche?"

"You are going to have to learn to live with me, Luke. You need me."

"You crazy bird," Luke replied vehemently. "I need you like I need another . . ."

Luke's voice trailed off. The condor cackled.

But the bird had a point. He had to get used to the fact that he had woken up like this, as an undead creature, and it probably wasn't the vulture's fault.

Who had condemned him to take this form? Who could it be, but the goddess?

Luke was royally pissed off. The more he thought about it, the more he was convinced that the goddess had meant to inflict this terrible punishment upon him.

He had known this would happen. He had known it!

She had lured him in, made like everything was just wonderful. She had looked at Luke, damn it, exactly as though she loved him best in all the world. And, sucker that he was, he had fallen for it–just like he always did.

Now here he was, a shriveled zombie, trapped in a living hell, with a vulture chained to his arm.

His eyes, already reddened by the particles of sand, overflowed. She had been . . . Christ, so heavenly, so *perfect.* It wasn't only that she was physically flawless. Much more importantly, she had been brimming over with wordless adoration and understanding. He had finally found someone who offered him unconditional love, or so he had imagined as he lay, blessedly content, in her arms.

He had surrendered. He had *believed.*

*And this–this is what I get. It's all so freaking familiar.*

Luke was still crouched on the sand, his head in his hands, steaming about the goddess, obsessing really, when he felt a weird sensation where his cranium should have been.

"You're eating my brains again, aren't you?" he barked.

"No," said the bird, but it sounded like its mouth was full.

*I am definitely going to have to watch that bird,* he told himself. *Damn carrion-eater.*

This purgatory in which he'd awakened was not bringing out Luke's kinder nature. Cruel thoughts began to seep into his mind, creative methods to bend the vulture to his will. If only he were chained to some unruly wench or pouting catamite, there might be some entertainment to be had. Luke pushed that thought away, of course, before it could take root, but it inspired him in the pursuit of a whole new variety of worries.

Romantically speaking, the prospects ahead looked grim. What kind of sex life could a zombie hope for? Considering the precarious state of his flesh, he was afraid to think what would happen, even if he just wanked a bit. *How long before it rots right off?*

This was such a disturbing idea, that panic began to build in Luke's stomach. He had to do *something*: find help, locate the goddess and beg her to reconsider his plight, or if worst came to worst, discover a way to destroy himself . . . to eliminate himself completely. There were things a guy could not go on without.

Luke was surprised by this thought. Was he really that attached to his penis? It had after all been the most problematic of appendages, so much more demanding than, for example, his silent, long-suffering feet. He recalled the profound alienation and despair that had overtaken him during adolescence, when a flood of testosterone had coursed in his veins, bringing with it gusts of fierce longing, spurts of fury. His phallus had stirred to life, a cantankerous gnome, had begun plaguing him with objectionable suggestions and a constant, prurient itch.

Maybe if the damn thing fell off, he'd be less likely to get taken in by beguiling illusions that were designed to rattle and dismay him.

"Come on," he said to the vulture, as he stood up and began walking.

"Apparently I have no say in the matter," the bird remarked, flapping along a short way above his shoulder.

"Nope."

Luke set out with the sun at his back. At least he could see what was ahead that way. Not that there was anything to see, except for more sand and rocks.

As he trudged along he nursed his rage toward the goddess. *The cunt. The cunt.* That was his mantra, and he scowled as he muttered it in time to the scrunch of his feet in the sand.

A song started to form in his mind after a while, a morbid grinding noise punctuated by angry lashings of guitar. Effortlessly Luke pictured the chords to himself, his ragged fingers twitching into the familiar shapes, his wrists working. He wasn't playing air guitar, it was more of an ambulatory spasm. The music seemed almost to rise from the earth at his bidding, growing in volume. In time the song became a juggernaut, carrying him forward across the wasteland at a run:

> *She lied, she lied to me–the cunt*
> *She oozes treachery–the cunt*
> *She made me a zombie–the cunt*
> *Behold my enemy: the cunt*
> *Hello, my enemy! The Cunt!*

Yowling, Luke careened forward, the terrain around him growing rockier. Soon he was leaping from boulder to boulder in a dramatic landscape of giant stones. The vulture flapped awkwardly over his head, threatening to "call the ranger" in a gravelly shriek that was barely audible above the noise.

Luke heard bass pounding from the crevices, guitar squealing from the clouds, and the beat of the condor's wings was the beat of drums that caused the sand to bounce and shiver. The music built toward a crescendo punctuated by the vulture's raucous complaints: "Help! I'm being kidnapped! Condor #17 is being kidnapped!"

"The Cunt!" Luke screamed, airborne, and skidded to a landing in a spatter of stones, along the dry bed of a stream. Pebbles rattled in twigs of desiccated brush that clung along the eroded sides of the gulch, and the condor pumped the air, yanking Luke's arm nearly out of its socket and raising a cloud of grit. Luke uttered a curse and fell into a coughing fit, waving a hand in front of his face.

"Gear song, mite," a friendly voice spoke from a boulder above. Luke looked around but could not see the speaker. "I remember feelin' that way about a bird, once upon a time." There was something very familiar about the voice and its nasal accent.

"Hello?" Luke croaked.

"But if you're tryin' to get the goddess to do you a fiver, well–she can 'ear you, me lad."

"Who's there?" Luke turned about, blinking furiously. "Show yourself!"

"You're a winsome blighter," the voice retorted cheerfully. "Up 'ere!"

Luke's eyes still watered from the dust cloud, but he could just make out the fellow now, perched on top of a rounded boulder.

"And what do *you* know about the goddess?"

"What do *I* know? If I were swellin' about the bounce, lad," the stranger retorted, "I might claim to know 'er at all. And you?"

But Luke had no wish to recount the details of his acquaintance with the voluptuous deity, and replied only with a suspicious scowl. The stranger went on.

"What's more important, really, is what does *she* know about *you*? Is she aware of your sad plight? And if so, can she or will she be of assistance? These must be the questions you're askin' yeself at the moment."

"Where are we? And how did you get here?"

" 'Ere?" the stranger replied in a puzzled tone. "And where are we roit noo, in *your* opinion?–Eh. Your vulture is, ah, eatin' your–"

"Crap! Cut it out, bird!" Luke shoved the creature off his shoulder.

Robbed of its perch, the vulture beat its ten foot pinions. "Christ, you're blowing sand right in my eyes again!" Luke complained, and started reeling in the chain, hand over hand.

"A clue, a clue!" the stranger pursued. "We're in a place with quantities of sand. Gaff me another 'int."

"Awk! This is abuse!" Buzz creaked. "Call the feds!"

"We're in a goddamn lifeless no-man's-land!" Luke snapped, getting a grip on the condor. "Are you blind?"

"Not exactly," the stranger said mildly. "But I don't see this world through your eyes. And if I could, mite, I'd be blinder than I am now. Roit?"

Luke looked down at his feet for a moment, then squinted up at the man and held out his hand in a conciliatory gesture. "Look, I'm sorry–"

"Give me your 'and," the stranger suggested, leaning down off the boulder and reaching for him. Luke handed him the indignant condor, then clambered up after it.

"Thanks, man," he said, and crouched on the rock, finally getting a good look at the stranger. He was a slender man with shoulder-length, mousy brown hair, wearing sunglasses with small round lenses. Luke's eyes widened and the stranger chuckled, peering at Luke over his purple-tinted shades.

"John Lennon!" Luke gasped. "What are you doing here?"

"Ah, but where exactly is 'ere?" he countered mildly. "We 'aven't established that to my satisfaction."

"Hey, look, I'm sorry about being so rude just now. You're the first person I've met since . . ." Luke looked down at his jutting, exposed ribs despairingly, "since I woke up like this."

"Rotten luck. Ghastly. Freakin' people, you know?" He shook his head sadly. "They're always so obsessed with the morbid details."

"Yeah," the condor put in, "they're like vultures."

"And you are?" Lennon asked the condor politely.

"Buzz. I would appreciate it if you would all call me Buzz," the bird rasped.

Luke still burned with resentment. "That fucking bitch–" he interrupted, but stopped short at a click of distaste from the former Beatle. "That *goddess* should never–"

"Think, Luke. She can 'ear you," Lennon said again.

Luke felt dry tears clogging his throat. "What is this, some kind of fucking . . . some kind of police state?" He croaked.

"Only if you want it to be."

Lennon was looking at him so kindly. The kindness was torture, and Luke badly wanted to rub his eyes, but that would only grind the sand further in. "Am I going to have to stay like this," he moaned, tears spilling at last, "forever?"

"Listen kidder," John said, "I can 'elp you get along in this, let's call it a dimension. But you 'ave to trust me, Luke."

"You know who I am?"

"I watch everything, Luke."

Some of the meaning of Lennon's words was starting to penetrate Luke's poor abused brain, and his tears evaporated in the face of revelation. John Lennon had died when he was not much more than a kid. And he knew who *Luke Mandrake* was?

"And so will you," Lennon went on, "if you want to stay reasonably sane in this bedlam, this sparklin' purgatory I like to call Fimeboo."

"Fime . . . boo?" Luke repeated.

"Fimeboo. It's like, a limboo for the fimous." John was nodding encouragingly.

"Ohh. Famebeau. Heh heh. Nice one," Luke said. "So you mean–"

"Roit," John interrupted. "We're all trapped 'ere so long as we're fimous. Ahem," Lennon went on in a BBC-presenter voice: "We are archetypes, heroes in the minds of the living. We exist because the complex of ideas within the collective consciousness, which we ourselves created through our art, combines with the dreams and thoughts and tributes and prayers we continue to inspire in the living, to generate this manifestation."

"Come on. Are you suggesting that we are both just phantasms, being dreamed by our fans? That's–"

"I'm saying that those energies you created, and the thoughts and dreams of millions of human beings in response, combine to create a cosmic force. And that as long as this force is powerful enough to keep you in this dimension, it will determine the nature of the physical form you take. Fame will literally hold your personality prisoner here.”

“But what–”

“So ‘ere you are in Fimeboo,” Lennon resumed his native Liverpudlian cant. “And ‘ere you’ll stay. Maybe forever.”

“Okay,” Luke said, digesting this. “But eventually–”

“Eventually, so I’ve ‘eard, some of the lads–and lasses too–move on, fade away from the memories of the livin’. Others do everything in their power to ‘old on to their fame, and to their lives ‘ere. And some are going to be trapped ‘ere indefinitely, like it or not–Socrates, Caesar, Hitler, them lot. Mad, most of ‘em, quite mad.” Lennon took a deep breath. “But a few of us ‘ave a proper agenda. We try and give somethin’ back to the world.”

Here Lennon stopped and looked at Luke, clearly expecting some sort of reaction. Luke merely looked down, his jaw set. It wasn’t hard to interpret his silence.

“It’s not the goddess’s doin’, Luke. The vulture, and bein’ a zombie and all. It’s a manifestation, a synthesis of your appearance in public and private thoughts, includin’ I might add, your own. That persona can be changed.”

“So now I’ve got a homework assignment? Wham bam, you’re a zombie, now go figure out how to change yourself back to your real self?” Luke was furious. “She should never–”

“Luke. Believe me, this obsession with the goddess won’t ‘elp you to get on with this part of it. You’ve got to let ‘er go.”

Luke bit back a sullen retort. There was no point in fighting with Lennon over the goddess, when she had already given him the boot. But Luke was not ready to forgive. “She lied to me with her eyes. That’s my point.”

Lennon shook his head. “She wouldn’t do that, Luke. She’s not like that. You’ll understand one day.”

There was a silence, Luke holding Buzz in his arms and stroking the bird absently, frowning down at his knees. Lennon was holding back on him, he could tell. There were certain things he refused to discuss.

"You love 'er too," Luke muttered.

Lennon looked away. "Storm clouds brewin' over Peak Forest, looks like," he remarked.

More silence. Luke was thinking of Charity, of the brusque way she had of handling him during his deep funks. She used to go through the bedroom gathering up all his dirty socks and tee-shirts, and throwing the laundry in a smelly pile on top of him where he lay, on the bed or the couch. He would watch her, oddly comforted by the routine, her grumpy harangue, the feeling of the soft fabric landing gently on his body. Waiting for her to pounce on him like a leopard kitten, smack him back to life.

And then he thought of the goddess, how she had drawn out the pain from him like poison from a snakebite. How she had lured him into her web of ecstasy, offered him the kind of solace that he had once found in Charity's embrace, before . . .

"I love 'er too," rasped the vulture.

Lennon giggled. Luke snorted like a pig. At that, both Luke and Lennon laughed out loud.

Luke laughed so hard his cheeks nearly split open. His eyes streamed, and he guffawed for a while, then fell to snickering. Lennon tittered along, "hee hee hee," bent over, one hand clasped over his nose.

Eventually the bird remarked in an injured hiss, "It's not that funny!"

The two men lost it again, more hilariously than before, batting the air and wiping their eyes with mirth, while Buzz let out a contemptuous croak.

"Ah ha ha! I think one of my eyes is coming out," Luke finally gasped.

"Eee, hee hee," Lennon quivered. "You're literally laughin' your own 'ead off! HOO hoo hoo hoo!"

"Oh god. Oh god," Luke wheezed. "I'm so pathetic. I'm such a pathetic little zombie." He sat quietly for a while, giggling in a sobby sort of way, his head in his hands, then finally turned a serious gaze to John.

Lennon smiled back sympathetically. "What're you goin' to do, lad?"

Luke just shook his head, trying not to start crying real tears again.

Lennon was bracing. "Listen, mite, it's all up to you, you and your talking vulture 'ere. You two can stay in your self-made 'ell, or you can let me show you around paradise. And by paradise I mean, a sort of metaphysical Las Vegas," he chuckled. "Come on, Mandrake," he put an arm around Luke's skeletal shoulders, "It's not all bad."

"Nobody ever asks me what I want," Buzz complained.

"Well then, what do you want?" Lennon nodded to the bird.

"What do I want?" Buzz began in a rattling rasp. "To cut clouds with my wings. To sink my beak into the neck of a ripe bear. To swoop down and alight on deadwood at the timberline. To sup on a gamy goat, eyes still in; feel the pop in my beak and taste the juice trickling down my throat."

"Poetic," Lennon remarked.

"But–I'll settle for brains, served on a doily," the bird croaked, fixing its little black peepers on Luke.

Luke looked at Lennon and their eyes met. Luke gave a shrug, and Lennon shrugged back. "What've you got to lose?"

Luke let out a bitter laugh. "Memmm-reeez," he crooned, "in the corners of my braaaiiinnn . . ."

"Look guys," the vulture croaked, "I'm one of the most endangered birds around. We California condors are gonna be extinct any minute now, all because of lead bullets and toxic trash that ends up in our food."

"And bein' your mates at the apex of the food chain, we apes 'ave nothin' to worry aboot," Lennon proclaimed.

The irony was lost on Buzz.

"Sure, bucko, sure. Then why do your scientists tag us and study us?" the bird lifted its wings and showed them its bright red tags, "Condors die, year after year. Me? A farm kid shot me. How I ended up a zombie bird, attached by the neck to this Bozo, I'll never know. All I know is, my chick is still in the nest, and my mate tends her alone."

"You're a parent, then."

"I'm a mother!" Buzz snapped.

"This bird's a bird," Lennon remarked.

Luke was gazing at a tiny plastic box clipped to the vulture's wing. "Buzz, is that a radio transmitter?"

"You tell me, Bozo. I'm just a stupid bird, remember?" Buzz hopped into Luke's arms and laid her hideous head on his chest. Luke glanced at her beak warily but she only lifted a pinion and held the device up for his inspection.

"Testing, testing," said Luke into the tiny microphone. "Hello, world, this is Luke Mandrake . . . speaking to you from beyond the grave, on WZMB, zombie radio."

"Nobody's answerin'," Lennon pointed out.

"It's being recorded, dumb-ass," Buzz cackled.

"Sshh!" said Luke. "I hear something." The transmitter crackled and emitted a low hum, and a voice said, *"Jake!"* Then there was a high-pitched buzz, a soft pop, and it was silent again.

"That's–that's impossible," sputtered the vulture. "These things never make any noise. They're one-way transmitters."

"And just 'ow *do* you know that?" Lennon resumed. "Bein' a bird?"

"Oh me," Buzz sneered. "I don't know anything. Me, the condor, who can spot a fly crawling on the hide of a mountain goat from a hundred yards up; me, the condor, who can hear the difference between the footstep of a mouse and the sound of maggots chewing–*I could never know anything important*, like the fact that this god-damn radio *never makes a sound.*"

"All right, but it's a supernatural radio now, innit?" Lennon pointed out. "That noise it made, it's a signal of somethin'. That's 'ow things work 'ere. Listen, kidder," he said turning to Luke, "come up to the top of the tallest rock with me, and I'll show you *my* world."

Luke and Buzz looked at each other, then at Lennon. "Lead on," said Luke. Before long the two men and the vulture stood up on top of a flat stone overlooking the valley.

"So tell me, Lad, what is your vista from 'ere? Just describe it to me," Lennon urged.

"Ahrrm. Well, there are a lot of rocks and boulders . . . some dead bushes. It looks like a stream went through here once, but it's all dried up now. And off in the distance . . . I see a . . . well, it looks like a ruin or something. Some broken pillars, I think."

"Turn around," John commanded, and they faced the other direction. "What d'ye see?"

Luke was expecting to see the empty desert he had just crossed, stretched out endlessly before them. But the wasteland appeared to be more like a strip of gold, folding up a few miles off into sienna hills, graceful and rounded. The pinkish-brown terrain seemed everywhere to mimic the female form: delicate faces, sensuous hips and knees, plump bosoms and pert calves marched away into the distance.

"The hills . . . it's Her. This whole world is Her!"

"So at least you can see *that*," Lennon pounced.

"I see the Badlands," croaked Buzz. "There's carrion . . . a dead guy, looks like. Maybe two, and one's about a mile off."

"It looks like a Georgia O'Keeffe painting," Luke remarked. Who or what might be out there, wandering in those fractal, feminine folds? Lost miners, bandits, rogues, madmen? Zombies?

Lennon went on. "Now, close your eyes, and I'll describe to you what *I* see."

Luke squeezed his eyes, shutting out the terrible beauty of the desert hills. "Okay."

"We're sittin' on a tumbled rim of boulders, and a few old mill-stones–a glacial moraine called Froggatt Edge," Lennon said, "a place I like to come and take in the view."

"Froggatt Edge," Buzz croaked, "now that's funny."

"Below we see Hope Valley, with its knobby hills, terraced fields in a patchwork of green and yellow, and the steep streets of the villages of Froggatt and Stoney Middleton. One of the most painted views in England, it is. Me Mum and Dad and me traveled 'ere on holiday, after me Dad came back from the war."

"So . . . we're both sitting on the same rock, but you're in Heaven, and I'm in Hell, is that what you're saying?" Luke's voice had a bitter edge to it.

"Further on past the mountains is Liverpool, with a perfect replica of Penny Lane, and to the North along the coast, Blackpool . . ." Lennon stopped short in his narration here, and Luke waited.

Luke still had his eyes closed, and was trying to picture the place. "Blackpool?" he prompted.

"Beaches, amusement park, you know. Sort of the Coney Island of Northern England." Lennon fell silent again momentarily, rubbing his chin. "These are places that mean somethin' to me, where good things happened and bad, and places where I'm remembered most vividly. So they appear in this dimension, too."

"What are you talking about?" Luke said. "Is it real?"

" 'What is real?' asked the Velveteen Rabbit," Lennon murmured.

"Dear god, no," Luke moaned under his breath.

"I 'eard that," Lennon said.

"Sorry. It's just–my Mom used to love that book. Reminds me of frilly crocheted toilet paper covers with bunny ears, that kind of crap," Luke shuddered. "I used to have nightmares about being stuck in the attic with all the old toys."

"You do look like you've 'ad a few bits loved off," Lennon observed. "Now keep your eyes closed, and stop interrooptin'. "

"Okay."

"Froggatt Edge is where I come to get away and think about the past. Because the past is the only time I 'ave that's really happened, you see? That's where all me juice is. The more I go back in me mind, the more I examine the things I did and said, the more I can affect the outcomes. Roit? By thinkin' about 'em now, I can make certain things that happened more real, and make 'em realer in particular ways."

"You've lost me," Luke said, feeling exhausted. He opened his eyes.

Nothing had changed. He couldn't see Hope Valley, or Penny Lane, or the Ferris wheel at Blackpool. He could only see the barren, seductive hills far away in the setting sun, and it seemed to him now that train tracks scarred the foothills, and tunnels pocked the buttes here and there, and that he saw miners pulling out carloads of ore.

The condor was yanking on her chain, trying to get him to go down into the badlands, no doubt to investigate the corpses.

"What exactly do you do here?"

"Greet fans, make music, media management. Same as before I died, really."

"You're serious? You still have a career?"

"I muck about in the studio, do shows, naturally–but me wife, she's not 'ere. It's not easy without 'er. And I miss me kids, that's the worst of it. Still, I 'ave me work, and just knowin' they're all roit…"

It all sounded like a vast self-deception to Luke. Besides, Lennon's talk of the family he'd left behind was dragging Luke to the edge of his own sanity, and he felt nauseous with fear standing on that precipice.

"Come to Penny Lane with me, Luke. I'll introduce you to the gang."

Luke shook his head. "I wish I could see your world, whether it's real or not," he said. "But even if I could, I'm not ready to meet anybody right now. Not like this."

"At least let me give you some pointers," John insisted, holding up a finger. "First, start with what you 'ave, and build on it. Second, never let your fans go away unsatisfied."

Luke let out a bitter bark of laughter. "That should be easy, so long as they're all wearing blindfolds."

"Third, watch carefully what's 'appenin' in the solid world, but–"

"And how am I supposed to do that? Get a TV?"

"Maybe. Whatever works. Don't worry, we all find a way soon enough."

*Could I stand it?* Luke wondered. *To watch, to love, longing for a look or a touch, and never to be close to them again?*

"But for the love of Mike, don't interfere," Lennon warned. "It only leads to heartbreak, lad."

*To look on as Charity lives out her life, to watch our two little beans grow up . . . to be nothing more than the eyes of a distant ghost?*

Luke heaved a profound and piteous sigh, and held out his hand to Lennon.

"Thanks for the advice. I just wanted to say, you were always my favorite Beatle, and you and Yoko were the coolest couple of all time."

"Thanks lad," said Lennon, coughing a little with emotion. "You and Charity 'ad a good run yourselves. You were, if I may reclaim a phrase from the dustbin of advertisin', the real thing."

"Well, maybe someday I'll be a real boy again," Luke drawled with a bravado that he did not feel. Lennon chuckled, but Luke was still teetering on the edge of hysteria. He suffered from a chronic malabsorbtion of praise, but the compliment he had just dodged had nonetheless elicited recollections that were unbearably poignant.

"I . . . have a few things to figure out first, I guess."

"I'll be 'ere, when your ready." Lennon said. He embraced Luke then, carefully so as not to damage the zombie's fragile physique.

"In a bit," John nodded to Buzz and turned to clamber down the rock.

"Bye," croaked Buzz.

Luke stared out over the desert. Everything was aglow in a glorious light.

"Let's go, Bozo," Buzz hissed.

Luke watched Lennon picking his way over the boulders, somehow walking along the desert ridge and at the same time, his mythical Froggatt Edge.

Luke tucked his chin down against his breastbone, and let his mind go blank. The vulture tugged at the chain, and Luke walked. He wasn't paying much attention to where he was going, and with Buzz flying just above and urging him along, finding the way with her keen senses, his eyes didn't have to stray from the ground unless he needed to climb up or down rocks. He stumbled along through the lovely landscape, and though all the world was bathed in the lavender and gold of a spaghetti-western sunset, he was blind to the iridescent sky and the fiery clouds.

When he emerged from his stupor, it was only because Buzz had found something.

Luke stopped short. There was definitely a body lying among the juniper bushes at the bottom of a gulch.

"Come on!" Buzz screeched. "We're almost there!"

It was a dude, wearing jeans and a denim jacket, dark hair streaked with green. He was on his side, and Luke could see that under the jacket the fellow's bony torso appeared shrunken, collapsed in on itself. The back of the jacket had *Shambala* silk-screened on it in white, with blue water ripples around it, and below that in red, the iconic cover image Luke had drawn for their first and least commercially successful album, *Meat Taco*. Luke had designed that jacket himself, and had sold them at his early shows. Christ, maybe he even knew this guy.

"Buzz, I gotta see who this is."

"Sure, Bozo. Me too."

"What I mean is, no bitey, no eaty–no eating people. Okay?"

"What are you, a moron? Why did we come here, then?"

"Buzz. I'm serious. No eating people, nor any part of a person, ever: living, dead or zombie. Especially not my fans."

"But I'll starve!"

"No you won't. You're dead. You don't need food."

"I'll starve psychologically though. And that's just as worse."

"Buzz–what do you think would happen if I ripped your head off and ground it to bits between two rocks?" Luke wondered grimly.

"Crap." The vulture jumped from one foot to the other. "Not even Hitler?"

"Hitler you can have your way with," Luke agreed.

"All right. I promise."

"Promise what?"

"I won't eat that guy! I won't take even the tiniest nibble. Okay?"

Satisfied, Luke stepped toward the body, and the vulture did likewise, waddling along the ground on her stork-like feet, and hopping up onto the corpse's thigh.

The flesh was dried out and wrinkled, but the person's facial features were intact. He looked familiar, but at first Luke couldn't place him.

Then Luke noticed that the dead man was holding a pistol in his hands. And that part of his head was blown off.

"Oh no. No." Luke backed away. "Not that."

The corpse opened his eyes.

"Luke! Luke, it's you!" he said in great wonder and joy. "I knew I would find you here."

"Billy! What have you done?" cried Luke.

"I love you, Luke," the young man said, choked with tears. He sat up.

"How could you do this? You don't even know me!" Luke said in a cold and angry tone.

The young man's eyes began to fill with horror. "What–what's the matter with you?" he asked.

"I'm a zombie," Luke said. "And so are you, guy. I guess it's our punishment for being such assholes."

The youth was looking at his hands, then at the vulture cocking its head from side to side while watching his every move, then at Luke with his rotting flesh and hollow eyes. "No!" he cried. "This . . . this wasn't supposed to happen!"

"Ugh. Shut up." Luke looked away.

The young zombie leaped to his feet with a wail, and took off at a run into the hilly landscape.

"That went well," Buzz remarked.

"Great," said Luke. "I can already see how much fun this is going to be."

"You should've let me eat him," Buzz remarked. "Put him outta his misery, at least."

"Huh," Luke said, looking at the bird with sudden interest. "You can do that? Just make somebody disappear completely?"

"This beak is the most powerful cutting tool in Nature," the bird creaked, puffing out the pink crop on her chest. "Of course I don't usually eat the bones."

"But you *could* eat the bones, if you wanted to?"

"Ha! That would be a thankless chore," she remarked, preening her ruff.

"I don't want to end up as an animated skeleton," Luke went on, agitated. "Could that happen? Or does it even matter what you do to me, I mean, if I'm some sort of projection of the collective unconscious, isn't my appearance determined by that?"

"Don't ask me, I don't make the rules around here," Buzz pointed out.

"Maybe . . . maybe the bones could be ground up into a powder. A calcium supplement or something," Luke suggested.

"This is getting too macabre even for me!" Buzz squawked. "If you wanna dispose of yourself, don't make me responsible for the job. I'm a scavenger, not a magician."

"Well it was your idea. You said–"

"I was making a joke, all right?"

"Well Christ, I've got to do *something!*"

"*We're live. We've got audio,*" said Buzz's left wing.

There was a voice coming out of the radio transmitter.

"*And record,*" said the voice. "*Rolling.*" It sounded like woman's voice, and it had a gruff, park ranger feel.

There was a crackle and hush of papers moving. "*. . . April First, 1994, Condor number 17,*" another voice spoke, distantly, in a scientific tone. "*Location of body: unknown. Cause of death: unknown.*"

"*Let's track this condor-killer down,*" said the first voice.

Luke laughed out loud.

"I hear somebody," the voice on the condor tracking device said "What's the location?"

"It looks like–no wait. What? The locater is going crazy," the scientist voice grumbled.

"They think I killed you! What should I say?" Luke hissed.

"Grawk!" said Buzz, and pecked at the microphone. She was, it seemed, still annoyed, and had no intention of cooperating now. As her beak struck the device, it issued loud thumps and crackles of feedback.

"Christ. Was that AF17?" the device wondered.

"Ahrrm, greetings, earthlings," Luke began. Buzz gave him a

disgusted stare, and shook her ghastly head.

"Jake, listen to this," the ranger barked.

"Buzz is safe and sound," Luke went on, "I mean condor 17 is . . . well, not alive–" Buzz was making motions with her head as if to say she was laughing silently. "Anyway, she's here . . . we're speaking to you from the afterlife, and we can hear you."

The device was silent, but Luke got the impression that it was breathlessly waiting for him to go on.

"Hello?"

"Jesus, that's not possible," Jake uttered.

"Hello, can you hear me?" Luke asked.

"Roger," the ranger voice said brusquely. "To whom am I speaking?"

"This is Luke Mandrake," he replied.

Jake burst out laughing, then stopped abruptly.

"Look, whoever you are," said the ranger, "it's a federal offense to possess or to alter this device in any way. We will track you down, so I advise you to immediately surrender the transmitter, and the remains of condor 17."

"Buzz, tell them you're all right," said Luke. Buzz opened her beak wide in a hideous grin, but remained silent.

"Can you give me a location?" the ranger lady asked.

"I have . . . Portland? No. Eureka . . . ? Now it's . . . wait–no," the scientist replied, "I don't know what's wrong with this thing!"

"We're in Famebeau," Luke offered.

"Can you spell that please?" the Ranger asked.

"No, I can't spell that, and it's not on the map," Luke snapped. "We're dead!"

"Listen, whoever you are–" The voice of the ranger was oddly familiar to Luke.

"Luke Mandrake. You've heard the name, I presume?"

"You may think it's funny to adopt the name of Luke Man-drake," the ranger snarled, "but his sister is a good friend of mine, and I don't appreciate–"

"Wait, Janice? Is that you?"

"How–how do you know–?"

"Janice, it's me, Luke!"

"Is that you? It can't be . . . Luke?"

"Janice," the scientist said, "what's going on?"

"You dated my sister Jody. We met at Thanksgiving in . . . 1991, I think," Luke went on. "After graduation you moved to California for a job in the National Parks Department, and . . . maybe that's when you and Jody broke up. I'm not sure."

"Just how do you know these things?" Janice demanded. She sounded extremely angry.

"Janice–" Jake put in anxiously.

"You freaking paparazzi jerk," Janice shouted, "It's people like you who ruined Luke and Charity's lives!"

Luke felt a burst of warmth in the region of his zombie heart,

and even if he had been able to make himself heard as Janice continued to curse him out, he was temporarily unable to speak.

". . . And we *will* find you, you condor-killing, lying bastard!"
she finally concluded.

"Thank you for that, Janice," he said quietly. "It means a lot."

There was silence for three seconds. "Luke?"

"Yeah, Janice, it's me."

"No way. It . . . it sounds just like Luke! If you're Luke, where the
hell are you?"

"Janice, I'm so sorry that you're gonna be the first to hear it, but
. . . I died last night."

"It sounds just like him . . . But it can't be." Janice's voice was
strained.

"I can prove it, if that would help," he offered. "Just ask Jody if
she still has Fred the Bacon King's picture."

"What are you talking about?"

"Fred the Bacon King. Just ask her that," Luke repeated.

"Okay, I'm going to go make a phone call," Janice announced.
Luke heard the sound of a chair scooting back.

"Janice, you can't seriously believe–" Jake the scientist began.

"I don't know Jake. But I've got to get to the bottom of this."

"He's lying!" Buzz squawked.

"Uh, was that the condor?"

"Yep," Luke said.

"I don't get it," Jake said. "What is going on?"

"You've tuned in to the other side, Jake," Luke cackled. He was
starting to enjoy this.

Before long Janice came back to the microphone. "Okay, I left a
message for Jody," she said. "But this is just too weird. You probably
got your information from some inside source."

"About as inside as it gets," Luke agreed.

"Janice, I don't see what this has to do with–" Jake began.

"Why don't you find me some coordinates, then?" she replied.

"There's something wrong with the system, obviously," Jake protested.

"There's only one way to find us," Luke remarked, "and I don't recommend it."

"Well, I'm going to wait for a confirmation from Jody," Janice said, "and work on this report." Then she stopped talking, and Luke heard the sounds of tapping on a computer keyboard.

Luke had been climbing the bluffs during the conversation, with Buzz on his shoulder, and was now perched on a huge pink rock above the mouth of one of the tunnels that they had seen from Frog-gatt Edge. He sat staring into the distance, as the last afterglow of the setting sun faded over the indigo hills.

The conversation with Janice had summoned up a storm of conflicting emotions in him. The thought of communicating with his sister excited him, dismayed him and filled him with dread. The possibilities were enticing, but he knew that one conversation would never be enough. And when he imagined any sort of reunion with Charity and the kids, he couldn't help picturing their distress at seeing his gruesome new form. If he meant to try and contact them directly, he had to do it carefully.

But what he dreaded most was finding out that this was all just some delirious hallucination.

Meanwhile, Buzz had begun to gaze with longing at the pulsing gray matter that threatened to spill from Luke's shattered skull. She sidled closer, and Luke looked up at her warily.

"What do you think you're doing?"

"I was just wondering," Buzz rasped, "what Hitler's brain would taste like."

"Probably nasty," Luke pointed out.

"I'm willing to take that chance. So . . . when are we going to go and look for him?"

"Not now, that's for dang sure."

"But you said–"

"Sshh!"

The ringing of a distant telephone came through the device. A chair was pushed back, and then Janice's voice could just be heard, rising in excitement. When she returned, her tone was transformed.

"Hello?"

"Yep, I'm here."

"Okay, I have Jody on the line, and she wants to talk to you," Janice said.

"Jody?" Luke said, squeaking a bit with emotion.

"Luke? Is that you?" He could barely make out his sister's voice. The equipment was, to say the least, lo-fi.

"Yeah," he said.

"What about Fred the Bacon King?" she challenged him.

"He was your guinea pig in sixth grade, Jody."

"Okay, describe him," she said shakily.

"He was all white, except for a red patch on his butt," Luke said. "And he died when we went on vacation, and you left him at grand-dad's. You kept a picture of him in a locket."

"Oh my god. Oh my god. Luke? Is it really you?" Jody sounded like she was crying. "I didn't even know you knew about it. Whatever happened to that locket?"

"I stole it," Luke admitted. He was crying too. "I was going to give it to a girl at school, but it was so hilarious, I kept it."

"You little bastard," Jody laughed, and Luke laughed too.

"I love you, Jody."

"I love you too, Luke. It's so good to hear your voice. I'm so glad . . . you're safe and sound."

"How's Charity? How are the kids?" Luke was grinning through his tears.

"They're fine, well no, not really. Everyone is so goddamn mad

at you, Luke. Why? Can you just tell me why?"

"What do you mean, not really? Is there something you need to tell me?"

"What do you expect? Ded Leper *(crackle fuzzzzz)* circus! And now this private investigator–"–the connection kept on fuzzing out–"questions about your will. He–*(zzzz-bzzzzzz)* Charity!"

"What? Say that again," Luke cried. But just then Buzz took the transmitter in her beak, and crushed it to pieces.

"What the hell are you doing!?" Luke grabbed Buzz by the neck. Pieces of the transmitter flew in all directions. Buzz gave a strangled croak. Luke was furious.

"Why did you do that?"

"Rules. Don't interfere!"

"It's important! Those fucking bastards are trying to frame my wife!"

"What do I care?" Buzz replied. "What's in it for me?"

"You–you vulture! I oughta pulverize you!"

"Yeah, but you won't."

"Why the hell shouldn't I?"

"I'm your ticket outta here, Luke."

"Outta here? Yeah, that's it. I'm gonna get outta here all right." Luke plunged into the gloom and down the steep slope, yanking Buzz along by the chain.

"Where are you going?"

"Back to where I started." Luke skidded down a pile of scree on his heels. "I'm going to pay the goddess a visit."

"You're going the wrong way."

"That's what you think. I've got it all figured out."

"You? You don't know–"

"I know one thing, I got here by going *in*," Luke halted before an opening to a dark tunnel that led down into the mines, "and now I'm gonna dig my way *out!*"

"Don't be an ass, Luke. You can't–wait!"

Luke strode into the tunnel mouth, and Buzz flopped in after him.

"This isn't going to work," she squawked.

*URK urk . . . urk . . . rk . . .* echoed the darkness ahead and all around them.

"Shut up!" *UTUP utup . . . utup . . . up . . .*

Luke's sneakers crunched a few more steps while Buzz scuffled and dragged behind. "Come on, bird, get going!" Luke hissed.

"How am I supposed to do that?" Buzz hissed back. "There's no room to maneuver in here! And walking ain't my style."

"Didn't you see the track?" he whispered. "We'll ride one of those carts."

"Why are we whispering?"

"Sshh! I hear something!"

The distant squeak-squeak and clatter of wheels was gradually approaching, and they waited, listening. All at once the squeak sped up, becoming *sqeesqeeesqueesqeesqeee.* The cart was headed down a hill. The sound grew louder and faster, KWI-KWI-KWI-KWI-KWI. It was a steep hill, by the sound of it.

"*Luke!*" screeched Buzz.

"Ohh, shit!" Luke yelped and turned to run. The condor toddled along ahead of him on her short legs. In the blackness Luke blundered into her, and the two of them tumbled into a thrashing heap.

The clacking and squealing of the cart was deafening as Luke struggled to his feet, and then BAM! The thing hit them, ejecting the two forcefully from the mouth of the mineshaft.

As they hurtled through the air, Luke saw the sloping skirt of the mesa spread below them. The stones looked sharp.

For a split second he hung in the sky, wincing.

Then he felt his stomach drop as he swooped upward, while his arms instinctively knotted around Buzz's neck. Each mighty stroke of the gigantic vulture's pinions made his innards lurch as the wind beat at his ears.

A full moon was rising above the hills, shedding its silvery light across the desert. Luke looked back down to where the miner's cart had come to rest against a wooden stop.

"Luke, Luuuke!" A figure seated in the cart was waving up at him. "I'm sorry Luke! I couldn't stop!"

"It's Billy!" Luke cried. "What's he doing?" The cart was filled with rubble.

"Don't squeeze my neck!"

"Oh, sorry." Luke slid his arms down a bit. "Better?"

"No! I need those chest muscles to fly, Bozo!"

"Where do I hold on then?"

"Hold on with your knees. Not too tight!"

Luke tried to, nearly falling off, which made Buzz curse him until she was breathless. After a while he got the hang of it, and was able to look around him again.

Buzz had wheeled about and the opening to the tunnel was far below them now. Out ahead, beyond the mesas and the marching hills, was something he would never have seen from the ground: a gigantic canyon. At the bottom of it a ribbon curved, glinting in the moonlight.

"Whoa, look at that!" he shouted. "A river!"

"Well hallelujah," Buzz grated.

"Can we go there?"

"Humph!"

"Please?"

"Look who's acting all polite now," she muttered.

"Hey, I didn't know . . . "

"That I could fly?" Buzz snapped.

"That–that you could carry me like this!"

"You never asked."

"Aren't I kind of heavy?"

Buzz clacked her beak, which Luke interpreted as a disdainful snort. "Look at you. You weigh nothing."

"Fantastic! So where are we going?"

"Wouldn't you like to know."

Luke couldn't get anything more out of her than that. Anyway he had no choice but to go along with her, wherever she decided to take him. A warm breeze bathed his face, and as the condor's sinews rippled between his knees, stars appeared one by one in the heavens.

*At least we're flying toward the river.* Luke felt sure, somehow, that the waterway would guide them to the goddess's throne room.

It was a long flight to the canyon, even for a condor with a ten-foot wingspan. The moon was high by the time Buzz landed on the edge of the precipice. Below, the river sparkled. Luke did a few creaky squats to stretch his legs,while Buzz put her feathers in order.

"I hear music," Luke said.

"Let's go check it out," Buzz agreed.

"Naah. I don't feel like seeing anybody."

"You wanna go down to the river, though."

"Certainly."

"Climb aboard, Bozo."

Luke straddled the vulture and she pumped her wings, then flopped over the edge of the cliff and dropped like a stone.

"Cripes!" yelled Luke, but after a few strokes of the vulture's wings their altitude stabilized, and they began a gliding descent into the canyon.

"The music's getting louder," Luke called. "I thought we weren't–"

"You wanna see the river, we're going down there."

Luke could distinguish percussion and guitar, a wolf howling, and a human voice singing, mixed with some unusual sound effects.

"But aren't you getting too close to–"

"I'm catching a perfect updraft," she cackled, swooping around a rock pinnacle and gliding toward the concert.

"Buzz, I don't want to–"

"Tough tomatoes, toots," Buzz rasped. Below them the river gleamed like abalone inlay on an ebony fretboard. She headed straight into the midst of the performers, backed her wings and dropped onto a moonlit platform of stone.

It was an unusual line-up. Beside the lone guitarist, Luke glimpsed several jackrabbits and some chipmunks, scattering like leaves in the gale of the raptor's gigantic wings. A doe shied back with a clap of her delicate hooves, and the wolf flattened both himself and his ears with a snarl. The man stopped playing his instrument and turned, stepping forward as if to shield the smaller animals. But when he saw the condor his face lit up.

Luke had managed to jump off at the right split second, which was necessary for a graceful landing, since Buzz had such short legs. He held his hand out to the stranger.

"Welcome," said the youth softly, taking Luke's hand. "Did you come to join in the music?" He offered Luke a shy smile.

"Wait–River? River Phoenix?"

The youth nodded gently.

"Hey, fancy meeting you here!" Luke felt oddly pleased to see him.

"I don't think we've met," River began, then squinted at Luke. "I'm not wearing my glasses but . . ."

Phoenix scanned Luke's face, and a stricken expression rose in his eyes. "Luke? Luke Mandrake? What– are you–?" He caught himself, bit his lips. "Sorry. I'm so sorry. I didn't know."

Phoenix held the acoustic guitar out to Luke like an offering. "What–what am I thinking? You take this. You play."

"No, no," Luke said hastily. "You sounded great. Please. Don't let us interrupt."

"Oh god, no. I absolutely could not–I mean, Luke! I'd be so honored."

"Errrm. I'm actually a bit . . . tied up at the moment." Luke lifted his right arm to show River the chain connecting him to the condor. River's eyes widened.

"Oh, the poor bird, I mean, how unfortunate for both of you! How did–er–?"

Luke shrugged. "Beats me. We just arrived this way."

"Don't use me as an excuse, Luke," Buzz croaked. "I won't get in your way. Go ahead and play."

"Yeah, come on, Luke. Give us a tune." Phoenix urged the acoustic on him once again.

"Okay," Luke murmured. He sat down cross-legged, accepted the instrument and strummed a few tentative chords. "So . . . you were putting on a show for the bunnies and the chipmunks?" he asked Phoenix.

"More like a rehearsal."

"You mean . . . the wolf is in your band?"

"Totally. And the rabbits, the frogs. What did you think?"

"It was unusual, interesting. I liked it."

"Hear that guys?" River cried, looking around at the creatures gathered in the moonlight, predators and prey together. "He likes it! The great Luke Mandrake likes our music!" River pumped the air with his fist. Aside from a croak from one of the frogs, the animals were silent.

"Quiet bunch," Buzz remarked.

Phoenix gave Buzz an appraising stare. "Unlike you, Madam Condor, these creatures do not have the power of speech. But they understand me very well."

"Ha!" Buzz grated. "How did you know I'm female?"

"I know my endangered species. *Gymnops Californianus*, am I right? The largest flying bird in the Americas, and the female is larger than the male."

"I like this guy," Buzz cackled.

Luke had been strumming away softly, finding the voice of the acoustic. It had a smoky tone he liked, and the action was high enough to do some nice bending. He'd worried that his ragged fingers wouldn't be up to manipulating the thick steel strings. But somehow with the guitar in his hands he felt less fragile, more put together.

"Where did you get this?" he wondered. "It's pretty nice."

"Woody made it for me. Not bad, eh?"

"Play something already," Buzz commanded.

"Okay . . . how 'bout this. It's a new one." Luke attacked the strings with a thundering salvo and began to sing:

> *You ate your dirty bread*
> *Your poverty was criminal*
> *The demons in your head*
> *Devoured the subliminal*
> *Jewel made of paste*
> *Your muddy boots were crude*
> *Genius in the waste*
> *We envy you for being rude*
> *You'll never get approval*
> *You're scheduled for removal*
> *Pig in a poke, pig in a poke*
> *Pig in po-o-o-oke!*

As he played, the wolf began to howl tunefully, while the deer stamped her hooves on the stone. Soon the rabbits were thumping away with their hind legs and two bullfrogs glumped out a wild bass-line. Luke launched into verse two:

*Your caustic ice inferno*
*Branded you with malice*
*The giant caterpillar*
*Gave the clap to Alice*
*You had a loaded carbine*
*Pointed at your spleen*
*You dove into the Seine*
*Your fluids washed the river clean*
*You'll never get approval*
*You're scheduled for removal*
*Pig in a poke, pig in a poke*
*Pig in po-o-o-oke!*

Luke stumbled through an irascible guitar solo, then flamed out. "It's not finished," he said, embarrassed.

"Man, that was something else!" River enthused. "Is it about animal rights?"

"Sort of. It's about a young French poet, a whore's son from a little village, who goes to the big city and becomes an overnight sensation. But ultimately the intelligentsia are only looking for novelty, for someone from the lower classes to consume, co-opt and condemn."

"Oh. So how does that relate to pigs?"

"Well, they treat him like one, I guess."

"Man, I can totally relate. Me and my sister used to perform in the street for money when we were kids. People treated us like we were cute little organ-grinder monkeys that they could adopt as pets. *Oh, you poor kids. Don't you have parents?* And we'd say, *Sure we do, they're right over there at Tiffany's buying us diamond watches. They'll be right back.*"

The rabbits lopped away to nibble at the orange poppies growing from the cracks in the rocks, and the chipmunks frisked and scattered.

"Okay, rehearsal's over," River announced. "See you guys at the next full moon!–That's the only way they can remember when to come," he added, turning back to Luke.

"Well I guess I'll be going–" Luke began.

The wolf whined, and River petted him vigorously. "That's a good boy, Lars!" Lars barked three times in sharp warning.

A low rumbling seemed to emerge from the earth itself, and the rock they were sitting on vibrated. A thunderous noise was echoing through the canyon. River leaped up and shouted, "Flash flood! RUN!"

"What the fuck?" Buzz croaked.

"Go on, Lars! Git!" Phoenix shooed the wolf forward, and it bounded down from the stone stage and took off. "Get to high ground!" he yelled back at Luke and Buzz. "Hurry!"

"Hop on, Bozo!" Buzz squawked. Luke hastily shifted the guitar around so that it hung on his back, threw one leg over the vulture's bony middle, and she rose into the air in great, labored strokes.

They had gained altitude none to soon. Below them tossed a sea of horns, hooves and fur. A vast herd of buffalo stampeded down the canyon, grunting and snuffling, clattering over the stones and splashing through the shallows. Beyond the pounding and lowing of the beasts, a deeper thunder echoed from the canyon walls.

As they rose higher, Luke could see the foaming flood approaching, huge and white, smashing its way down the canyon, from one wall to the other, destroying everything in its path. And looming above and behind it, there appeared an enormous dark cloud in the shape of a man.

But where was River? Luke searched the cliffs with his eyes. He spied a figure clinging to a column of reddish stone.

"There he is!"

"And?"

"We have to help him!"

"We have to help *us*, Bozo!" Buzz retorted. But she flapped over to where Phoenix was struggling to clamber up the smooth sides of the rock formation. Buzz lighted on the top of the pinnacle as Luke jumped down.

"I'll be all right here," he shouted over the roar of the mountain of water that was swiftly bearing down upon them.

Buzz squawked something that sounded like it could have been "Probably, not!" as she dropped down toward Phoenix.

There wasn't much to hold on to, but Luke was able to sit, sort of, on a spot where the formation narrowed a bit. Still, if the flood reached this high he would be swept away. He had no idea what would happen to him then. *Can zombies drown?* he wondered. The biggest danger, no doubt, was being dashed to bits.

Luke wrapped his legs around the stone pillar and extended his manacled right arm down as far as possible. Phoenix had grabbed hold of Buzz's feet and she was straining to pull him along as he scrabbled up the side of the formation. Luke grabbed River's sleeve, hauling on it with all his might. Then the younger man was up beside him, clinging to the summit of the rock as best he could. Buzz perched once more on the tip of the pinnacle.

"Luke, hurry! It's almost on us!" she screeched.

Less than fifty yards distant now, approaching faster than an express train, an airborne lake pounded the canyon walls well above the height of their tiny spit of rock.

"*Luuuuuke!*" Luke thought he heard Buzz skrawking up there, before the thunder of the deluge overwhelmed his ears. He wrapped his arms and legs around both the rock and River Phoenix, who gripped him tightly. Then the flood slammed into them like a raging mammoth, and Luke felt his grasp torn free. He was blinded, deafened, water filled his mouth and nose. River had surely been swept away, and he had no idea whether Buzz was beside him or if they'd been ripped apart. The deluge battered him, he spun and snapped, slammed into stone, felt his bones shatter.

*Why the hell was I trying to be a hero?*

Luke had lost any sense of up or down. Pain seared him where jutting splinters of bone speared through his flesh. The broken bones ground together excruciatingly as he was flung to and fro in the waves. Then he collided violently with an obstacle, and the fragment of his brain still able to think was eradicated in a blast of agony. Everything went dark.

*April 2, 1994* –Brooklyn, NY

*I dreamed I was looking at a photograph of Luke Mandrake, who was resting his arms on the edge of his pit-like grave. He had long hair. Someone was strangling a small, cartoonesque dog beside him–Chevy Celica, I think it was. Two other guys were digging deep into the soft, loose, dark, rich earth. As I looked at the picture I knew that he had been buried alive for three and a half hours, then dug up, still alive.*

*I tossed and turned after that, with the phrase "three and a half days" repeating in my head.*

Rosetta got up at dawn and quickly noted the dream in her journal. She was out in the studio, planning on painting for a few hours before everyone started arriving.

The imagery in the dream made her think of bog mummies. There were photos of them in *Bodies in the Bog* by P. V. Glob, the book she'd borrowed from Phil last month. They were so wonderfully preserved, those two-thousand-year-old corpses.

"Bog-by-Glob. Bog-by-Glob," Phil had said when he handed her the book.

"Yay!" She had seized the paperback eagerly.

"You have to return it, though!"

After a session of painting, Rosetta needed more coffee. She went upstairs. And there was Phil, sleeping on the couch, with a half smile like a naughty little angel.

There was something so lovable about that guy.

She tried to make the coffee quietly. But by the time the milk was ready, Phil was sitting up.

"Want some coffee?"

"Sure, thanks!" he said. Phil really had a very sweet grin.

"Did Aron tell you I dreamed about you the other night?"

"No, what was it?"

"I dreamed you went back in time to save Luke Mandrake's life."

"Oh shit–he's dead?"

"No, it was just a dream." Rosetta reached up to the shelf above the sink for another mug.

"Oh, that's good." Phil blinked his amphibian eyes.

"I was like, 'Phil! Oh no! Don't risk yourself!' How do you take it?"

"Lots of milk and sugar."

"You got it." She emptied the espresso pot into the mugs, and topped them off with warm milk.

"Why didn't you come out with us last night?" asked Phil, spooning sugar into his cup.

Why, indeed. Rosetta was tired of partying with the boys. Aron was as a rule a jolly drunk, up to a point–but if a certain line was crossed, he could be obnoxious. Lately he'd too often insisted on taking a quart of cheap ale with him on the train. Needless to say this was more likely if he was already drunk. She constantly worried he'd get fined, or arrested, or even beaten up. She'd been with him when he got ticketed for peeing on the tracks. He kept shouting "Blimey!" at the cops, which was really embarrassing and also scary.

*This is New York. You don't fuck with the cops. This isn't your privileged Hong Kong boarding school world.*

She had begged him not to drink beer on the train. It was a bad idea in every way. No telling how long you might have to go without peeing.

He wouldn't listen.

She always had to just hold it. But if the N/R train was delayed for an hour, as often happened late at night due to construction, Aron had to whip out the old hose.

"You'll electrocute yourself on the third rail," she'd warn him.

"They should have restrooms in the train stations, like every other civilized country," he'd snarl. Which was true, but surely beside the point.

If he was going to go for the dark side when he drank, let him do it with a friend like Phil. She just hoped that the smooth-talking Jamaican would steer Aron clear of trouble. And vice versa.

"Oh, I was painting," Rosetta answered Phil. "Did you have fun?"

"Yeah, of course. It was fun. What are you working on?" Phil asked politely.

"My picture book. I'll show you before you go."

Just then Perry, compact and vibrating, arrived early to collect Antoine. "Wanna go out for waffles?" he yelled at the door to Antoine's room.

Antoine answered, "Yeah!"

"Well then, hurry up and get ready," said Perry. He interacted with his son like a lion tamer trying unsuccessfully to train an incredibly lazy mole. He was always cracking the whip, but there was no reaction. Antoine stayed in his hole until he was ready to come out, which only increased his father's urge to shout commands.

Strangely, they all got along very well. Perry's usefulness outweighed his irritating qualities. He was like an efficient but insistent robot butler. The Jeeves 5000.

"I'm going to the store now," Rosetta said to him. "When are you coming back?"

"Lunchtime. I'm heading out to Staten Island after the game."

"Perfect. And tomorrow night?"

"I'll probably want to pick him up around five."

"Okay, no problem. We'll be done with all the Easter festivities by then. Bye, Antoine!"

"Bye, Mom! Dad, I can't find my other shoe." To Rosetta's surprise, Antoine was already dressed. He loved waffles.

"Don't forget to take a W with you, if you're gonna eat a waffle!"

"What?"

"Without the W, it's just awful!" Rosetta laughed.

"Ugh! Go away!" said Antoine.

"Hahahaha!" Rosetta cackled.

Perry looked at her, shaking his head.

An hour later, Rosetta was unpacking shopping bags filled with Easter egg supplies and some provender: pecan coffee cake, salad fixings, fresh potato pierogies, cheese and tomato sauce. Virgie arrived shortly after with the gardening gear, which needed to be carried into the back yard. Phil went down to help. Rosetta made more coffee, and put the eggs for decorating on to boil.

Even Aron couldn't sleep through all this. He plodded upstairs and lit a rollup at his usual post by the window.

Virgie showed Rosetta the plans for the garden. The coffee cake was brutally murdered. Rosetta made a fruit salad.

Meanwhile Virginia took stock of the weeding and clearing tasks in the garden.

Jessie showed up, tall and majestic, a marvelous feathered hat set atop the floating veil of red-gold tresses that framed her china-doll face. Her large blue eyes peeped at Rosetta between long lashes, all sadness mixed with love. The two women embraced with the cooing cries of greeting universal to the human female.

Rosetta led the guests to the studio and they admired the paintings.

"Remember when you posed for this picture?" Rosetta asked Kimberly, age three. The pretty tot ran up to a painting of two fairy children, and pointed at them.

"Faiwies!" she said.

"That's you, and that's me," said Alice.

"There's a song that goes with this painting, do you remember it?" said Rosetta.

"The fairy song! Can you please sing it?" Alice asked.

"Will you play it, Aron?" Rosetta asked.

"Sure," the guitar god nodded benevolently. He picked up the acoustic and lovely music came out of it. Rosetta sang the graceful lullaby, and her husband harmonized. The girls listened, enraptured. They called for another song.

There was a tune taking shape in Rosetta's heart called The Joy of Finally Spring, and there were friends to share their table. It was going to be a great day.

Upstairs, Jean-Baptiste sampled a small slice of the pecan cake, just to make sure it was safe for human consumption. It was freshly made, from Merino's Italian bakery on Court Street. It was delicious.

He made his way downstairs. The kids were jumping up and down and dancing around with Rosetta as she proclaimed,

*Teacher I hate you! Teacher I hate you!*

*Teacher, I assed you a question!*

Then Rosetta's husband launched into one of his own numbers, *Harlequin Town.*

*We do look alike,* Jean-Baptiste observed as he watched Rosetta gaze admiringly at Delgado's profile. *Just shrink my schnozz, add a good cleft chin, and voilá, I'd be just as handsome.*

Aron warbled and glowered self-consciously over the jangling of his guitar. He was technically good, yet there was something lacking in his performance. *Authenticity?* Jean-Baptiste muttered. *Or perhaps a kind of generosity . . . Whatever it is, the children know.* The adults listened politely, and Rosetta chimed in on the harmonies, but after a few bars the kids lost interest and wandered off. Jean-Baptiste could see and hear them through the window that opened onto the sun room from Antoine's bedroom.

"I'll be the teacher," Alice was saying, "and you guys are the naughty kids."

Kimberly took Antoine's hands in hers and started to pogo, crying "Teacher! Teacher!"

"No dancing in the school!" Alice yelled in a supercilious tone.

Giggling, she flogged the other two children with a stuffed toy duck. She chased them up the stairs. Their laughter and footsteps flitted above, filling the duplex with the magic of childhood games.

Aron meanwhile launched into another intellectual ditty with complex harmonies. Jean-Baptiste sighed. He recalled a time when Rosetta was an art star, and Aron was merely her accompanist.

"You should start up your band again," she had urged Aron. "I'll sing backup."

"I can't do that. Everyone will ask why I don't let you sing," Aron had objected.

Rosetta had only laughed. "I don't care about being in the spotlight," she had said.

*Which is exactly why she is the one who belongs there,* Jean-Baptiste thought.

*April 2, 1994* –Los Angeles, CA

The high-heeled shoe on the nightstand was ringing. Charity turned under the covers with a mumble. *Come on! Don't wake up the kids,* she thought, annoyed at the phone. But it kept on burbling.

The cordless stiletto fell silent. Charity dozed.

Then the clangor began again. Who was calling her this early? Groggily, Charity ticked off in her mind the people who had this number. Luke, Kaylen, Luke's Mom, Violet, Jody, Rick . . . Luke!

She sat up and grabbed for the shoe.

"What?" she said thickly. "Who is it?"

"Charity, it's me, Jody."

Charity checked the radio alarm clock. It was 9:37 am. Last time she looked, it read 7:32. Two hours of sleep. Woo hoo.

"Sorry to call so early," said Jody hoarsely.

"It's okay. I–ah . . ."

Charity was confused. Why were there no children here, laughing, whining, climbing, attacking her lovingly with their little pink fingers and mouths? She checked in with her brain.

The kids were at Grandma's. *Right.* "I had a hard time getting to sleep last night, is all. What's going on?"

"Jesus Charity," said Jody in a falsetto, jokey girl voice. "You sound like a wreck. Are you gonna be okay?"

"You kidding? I'm having the best fucking time of my life," Charity croaked enthusiastically. She shouted like the world's tiredest cheerleader: "Go, life!"

"Charity," Jody said forcefully. "I just had a really fucking weird experience. Listen to this."

"Okay, shoot." The red-headed rocker babe said. She thrust her toes into her bunny slippers and stood up, reaching for a sheer wrapper with fluffy pink faux-fur trim.

"Well, I got a call from my ex-girlfriend Janice this morning. And she put me on the phone with Luke."

"Holy shit. Where is he?"

"That's just it . . . nobody knows."

"He wouldn't say?" Charity opened the fridge and extracted a coffee tin.

"We got cut off before I could ask. But Charity . . . he told Janice he was dead."

"What kind of bullshit is that?" Charity slammed the coffee can down on the counter. "I mean, god damn it. Luke! What's his problem?"

"I have no idea," Jody said. "I don't know what to make of it. It wasn't–I mean, apparently, he was talking to us through a transmitter that was attached to the wing of some endangered bird."

"What do you mean?" Charity placed a Pyrex measuring cup of water into the microwave and punched a couple of buttons. "Some kind of walky-talky thing?"

"Not really. Janice says it's just a one way transmitter, that's used to track the bird's location. It also picks up sounds, but it's not–not–"

"So you could hear him, but he couldn't hear you?" She scooped coffee into the filter.

"No, what I'm trying to say is, he could definitely hear me. That's what so weird–Janice says that it doesn't work that way."

"So he somehow modified the device?"

"She can't see how he could have done that. What happened . . . isn't actually possible. There's a recorder in the wildlife monitoring station, but the microphone's not even connected to the transmitter. Normally the signal just goes straight to tape."

"Okay, what?" Charity's hand waved a lobster oven mitt. "I don't get it. Is Janice shitting you?"

"No, no. You don't know her. She's like, a straight arrow, fucking Smoky the Bear."

"But you definitely talked to him."

"Charity, yes! And oh–Janice listened to the tape afterward, and you could hear her voice, and my voice, all the things we said. But Luke–Luke's voice wasn't on the tape at all."

"Uh huh," said Charity. She couldn't help being skeptical.

"It's too weird, I know. Janice is mystified. Luke–Luke apparently claimed he was in some afterlife kind of place. Someplace called Famebeau. She called me to confirm that it was really him."

"So what are you saying?" Charity demanded. "Are you trying to tell me that you just had a conversation with Luke from beyond the grave?"

Jody made a helpless squeak. "I don't know, Charity. I don't know. It was . . . really strange."

"It had to be a hoax."

"It was him! I know when I'm talking to my own brother."

"Well, then he was playing a trick on you. You know Luke has a pretty sick sense of humor."

"I sure hope it was a trick." Jody sounded distressed.

Charity blew a raspberry. "Of course it was. Christ, it's classic Luke-dom. What did he say?"

"We didn't get to talk for long. He asked about you . . . about the kids. He seemed worried about you guys. Then we lost the connection."

Charity chewed her lip. "Didn't Janice know where the bird was?"

"That's what they're trying to figure out. She said they couldn't pick up a location. The readings were all over the place."

Charity took a deep breath. "And you're positive it was him?"

"Yeah. He–he knew stuff. About when we were kids." Janice sounded a bit defensive.

Charity's hand shook as she poured water from the Pyrex cup into the filter. The holder tumbled from atop the mug, splashing hot liquid everywhere. "Ow!" she hissed. "Shit, shit!"

"By the way, I got a call from a private investigator last night," Jody said.

"Oh, Defoe? I hired him to help me locate your darling brother."

"He works for you? Well, he had an annoying Police Inspector routine going–he acted like he was investigating a murder. He was asking some pretty pointed questions, especially about you."

"About me?" Charity's foot, which had been moving a towel around on the floor to soak up the puddle of coffee, froze. "What kind of questions was he asking about me?"

"Like how well do you guys get along, is there a will, that sort of thing."

"Mother *fucker*," said Charity, throwing the towel in the sink. "Just what I need. Thank you for letting me know, Jody."

"Yeah, the guy is a real loose cannon. I'd keep him on a short leash, if I were you," Jody said.

"Noted. I'll give his chain a yank."

"Are you going to tell him about this, uh, call?"

"Oh god. Let's hold off on that, and see what else turns up." Charity rinsed out the coffee filter holder. "I just wish I knew where to tell him to look."

"So I guess you still haven't heard back from Luke?" Jody said wistfully.

"Not a peep," Charity growled, wiping the counter. Jody sniffed, blew her nose with a honk. "Look, Jody. I'm sure that phone call was just a joke. It's gonna be okay. We'll find that bum–we'll find him all right, and then, boy oh boy!" she said with relish, "he'd better watch out for us! We'll get 'im. You and me, and Haddy and Cherry, we're gonna pin him down, and tickle him until he howls for mercy!"

"That sounds like a plan," Jody said. "Well, talk to you soon, Charity."

"Yeah, sure thing, sweetness. I'll let you know the second I hear from him."

"I'll do the same." Jody hung up, and Charity refilled the Pyrex measuring cup and put it back into the microwave.

*I'd better tread carefully with old Detective Defoe,* she thought. *If he's going to be any help to me, I'll have to provide him with very specific assignments.*

Charity twisted the sopping towel, ran water over it, wrung it again.

Why did they always do this? Did she have some kind of fucked-up karma, that people were always stabbing her in the back?

*Everybody but Luke,* she used to say. *My best fucking friend.*

She walked into the bathroom, snapping the towel flat, and draped it over the handrail inside the sliding shower door.

*What's your game, Luke,* she demanded of her absent spouse, *and why the hell should I cry over you? Again?*

She stared at her reflection in the mirror. Her fiery hair was matted. She was getting pimples on her forehead. Her eyes were puffy. There were huge black mascara circles around them.

"Daaahling, don't liiieeee! You look faaabulous!" she admonished her reflection.

She looked like a sad raccoon. A hedgehog bandito. A punched-out leprechaun.

She turned on the tap. She favored herself with an angry pout.

She caught water in her hands and splashed her face.

*Please call me, Boo! . . .* begged her aching heart. *Please, please come home!*

"Naturally I searched the whole house." Liam Moore was small and slender and wore a lime green goatee. "I looked high and low. Wherever Luke is, he's not here." The Mandrakes' longtime friend and self-proclaimed butler blinked rapidly when he said this.

Dennis Defoe, Private Investigator scowled at Moore suspiciously. He knew a defensive tone when he heard one. Furthermore, the squat, balding man in the plaid blazer did not enjoy the deprecating lilt of Liam's voice–*possibly a fairy,* Defoe surmised, although he seemed to have some sort of disability as well. Liam walked with a limp, and held one bony arm curled up against his chest . . . *do the gimps have gays?* Or rather, *do the gays have gimps?* Defoe was pretty sure that you had to have big, rock hard muscles to be allowed into gay clubs.

Still, he considered offering to share a few drams with the kid, in hopes of loosening his tongue. Although experience had instructed him repeatedly on the dangers of playing the dime novel detective with a suspect, drinking during investigations . . . Defoe felt for the flask in his pocket, wondering if he dared to take another swig. Drinking during investigations was a given, an indispensable part of the whole Bogie mystique of which he, a forty-seven-year-old bachelor, was passionately enamored.

Sometimes, it was true, he forgot to turn the tape over and recorded on top of important testimonials. Once he left his keys on the seat of his trashcan-colored Ford Pinto, and had to smash in the window with a flashlight. All in all, indulging in the hooch while on a case invited incidents that were awkward to explain to clients. Defoe knew this.

But when he was on a case, he was on it twenty-four-seven. He prided himself on that score. Defoe was generally on the bottle twenty-four-seven as well, and he took special pride in his tolerance for alcohol after the fourth or fifth shot.

Defoe pulled his hand out of his pocket, though not before caressing the brass Jack Daniels logo on the hip flask with his fingertips.

*Soon, my friend,* he promised.

"What?" Liam asked, giving the gumshoe a sharp look. Defoe must have been moving his lips a bit. He compressed them humorlessly.

"None of your business," he snapped.

Defoe detected a whining voice at the back of his mind, reminding him that he ought to take notes, and that he should probably conduct his own thorough search of the premises to confirm whether the green-bearded weirdo was hiding something. He throttled the voice. The chump he was supposed to find could never be hiding here, no-one would be that moronic. And there was no way he was going to waste an evening of all-expenses-paid snooping doing unnecessary legwork.

Defoe leaned in toward Liam. "Any young ladies of Mr. Mandrake's acquaintance, that he might have paid a visit to?" he leered, with what he imagined to be a confidential wink. Liam stepped backward, rubbing a finger under his nose.

"No," Liam responded. He seemed to be holding his breath. Suspicious and uncooperative, that's what this kid was. Why didn't he invite Dennis in, offer him a gimlet or at least a beer? The douche.

"Well, you'll let me know if you happen to remember anything you want to tell me?" Defoe wondered.

"Sure, of course."

"Number?" Defoe pulled a grubby business card out of his pocket, but Liam's phone number was already scribbled on the back of it, so Defoe added *knows something* underneath. He started to hand the card to Liam, then stopped, felt around in his pockets. He found a car window repair shop's card, wrote his phone number down on the back of it and handed it to Moore.

Just then the cordless phone in the front hall rang, and the butler picked it up.

"Hi," Liam began. Turning his back on Defoe and lowering his voice, he made his way slowly up the stairs, leaving the detective to stare disdainfully at a plant perched on a wrought iron stand near the banister. It was in a lavender glazed pot–one of those plants with pink and green leaves, that girls like to distribute all over the place. Defoe strained his ears to catch whatever he could of the conversation.

"Yeah, he's here," was what Defoe thought he heard. It was probably Charity, calling to check up on him. Well, he sure didn't want to talk to that woman. She scared the bejeezus out of him, frankly, with her tough girl act and her smeary mascara and the piercing candor of her enormous brown eyes as she strutted around swinging her shoulders like a pirate. She was the kind of trouble he couldn't afford to get into, and he would have blown off this assignment after their first meeting, if it wasn't for the stink over shooting that black kid in Bakersfield. Suspended permanently without pay–the injustice of it still rankled. So what Defoe really couldn't afford was to turn down the kind of money he had asked for, and was getting, to work on this case. He was living the life of Reilly.

No, he certainly did not wish to speak to that woman just now. He was already clicking open the door of the red Mazerati he had rented with Mrs. Mandrake's money.

Defoe slid into the leather seat and downed a few gulps of Jack. Then he looked at the grubby card, turned it over, and began to dial a number on the car phone.

"Hello, is this Sophie? Sophie Henderson?"

"Yes it is. To whom am I speaking?"

"Detective Defoe, Portland Special Investigations," Defoe lied. His real name was Dennis Terence, and he was no detective. Not anymore.

"He's getting into the car. Should I go out and try to stop him?" It was Liam's voice, coming out of the red telephone shaped like a high-heeled shoe.

"No, let him go." Charity took a bite out of the polished nail on the middle finger of her left hand, and muttered a curse. She had just gotten that manicure done an hour ago. And it was her best flipping-off finger, too.

What was she doing? She was coming unglued. She had to pull herself together, stay rational about all this. *Everyone is depending on me.* She spat the salmon-pink strip of keratin at the phone.

"That incompetent freaking douchebag. He's spending my goddamn money like piss, and he can't even return my calls."

"What log did you turn over to unearth that guy?" Liam wondered. "He's quite the specimen."

"Oh my god. He couldn't find a toupee at a televangelists' convention," Charity quipped.

"–Yeah, and his breath reeks of whiskey."

"Well, to hell with him, I'll see him in court. Anything new to tell me, *please god*, about my *darling* husband's whereabouts?"

"Not as yet," the voice responded from the red stiletto. "I'll let you know when I have any news."

"Bill from Ded Leper is breathing down my neck right now. They're calling every fifteen minutes over here."

"Sorry you're having such a tough time."

"I found out that somebody tried to use Luke's credit card again this morning."

"Shit, you canceled it right?"

"Yes of course, I canceled it as soon as they called me to report that somebody tried to take out a ten thousand dollar advance."

"But they have no idea who it is?"

"Nope. I'll keep you posted if I hear anything useful. Don't forget to water the coleus."

"What?"

"The coleus. Please check and see if it needs water."

"Oh, right. I'm on it."

"Okay, bye."

Charity clicked off the shoe and, even though it was barely past noon, she poured herself a tall flute of prosecco and St. Germain, and drank most of it in a few gulps. She sat down on the bed, let herself fall backward, stared up at the white lace of the canopy, and coughed from the bubbles. She had to try and follow her therapist's advice. Just observe what happened: the gut-wrenching spasm of rage, the torrent of obscene recriminations that crowded in her throat. It wouldn't do to have a tantrum right now. She needed to look her best for the video shoot that was starting in less than two hours.

She sat up and stared out of the window. A half moon hung low in the sky, pale orange and ghostly, sinking into the brownish haze that rose above the Hollywood Freeway. Charity stood, opened the drawer of her escritoire, reached all the way inside, and pulled out a small mushroom made of polished wood. She unscrewed the top of the mushroom from the stem. From inside the cap she removed two white lozenges, and quickly swallowed them with a draught of champagne.

It was going to be a trying day.

*April 2, 1994* – Brooklyn, NY

The three women had finished clearing away the cups of dye and rainbow-stained napkins, the spoons and food coloring and crayons. The dishes were washed. The children were arranging their pastel eggs in baskets and cartons, and chattering.

Downstairs in the sun room Aron plunked on a guitar, frowning at his notebook, his beer and ashtray beside him.

Above, Jean-Baptiste watched as Rosetta opened a bottle of Cabernet.

"I've been saving this," she said, "for just such a gathering."

"Hey, thanks for a wonderful afternoon, Rosetta," said Virgie, as Rosetta filled her china teacup with wine.

"Thank you for sharing it with me," said Rosetta.

"It's so nice to be here," said Jessie.

"You guys are the best ladies in the world to spend the day with," said Virgie, beaming her dimpled smile.

"For we are–" said Jessie, raising the toast:

"*The Unsquelchables!*" they all chorused, clinking. "Wooo! Wooo hoo!"

"Those fairy paintings are amazing," said Jessie.

"And the song is so beautiful," Virgie added. "I could tell the kids loved it."

"Thanks." For some reason, Rosetta was blinking back tears.

"Are you going to record it?" Jessie wondered.

"I wish. I had some ideas for orchestrating it. But–"

"Too elaborate?" Virgie asked.

"Not exactly," said Rosetta, "I showed the score to Aron and he said he would *never* record a children's song."

"What!?" said Virgie.

"Plenty of great bands do children's albums," said Jessie.

"Not the Windup Teeth, I guess," Rosetta said sadly.

The children approached with their baskets. "Mom, may we go outside and hide our eggs?" Kimberly asked.

"Wait 'til tomorrow," Jessie said. "We're going to have to go home soon. I've got laundry piled up to the ceiling."

"Awww!" the little girls cried.

"Don't worry," Rosetta said. "You're coming back in the morning for our Easter party."

Jean-Baptiste stood by, listening to the women talk, and taking the temperature of Rosetta's melancholy. On the one hand, the kindness of her friends was soothing to her injured pride. On the other, it was a sharp reminder that the man she had married was less than kind.

For an Unsquelchable, Rosetta was feeling a bit squelched lately.

Liam watched the Mazerati pull out of the driveway, then gently placed the phone on the carved antique bureau under the window. He stared at nothing for a long while, then sat down heavily on the lace coverlet of the bed.

How could he tell Charity the truth? He had been so close to confessing over the phone, but his courage had failed him. It's wasn't that he didn't trust her. She could be bad-tempered, but she was loyal to her friends, and Liam knew he could depend on her. She and Luke had been there for him when nobody else was.

Besides, she had a right to know.

*I'll write her a letter,* Liam decided. He sat down at the small mahogany desk, removed a pen and a piece of paper from the drawer, and started writing.

*Dear Charity,*

*I have a confession to make. When we spoke on the phone, I wanted to tell you everything that has happened in the past week, but I've been afraid to. Afraid of how painful it's going to be for you, to hear this. Afraid you're going to be mad at me for not telling you sooner.*

Liam pinched the bridge of his nose and grimaced. How could he begin to describe the sad tableau he'd stumbled upon in the third floor sun room this morning?

*Luke is . . .*

What was he thinking? It would be foolish–no, it would be *insane* to put in writing the details of Luke's reckless and highly illegal scheme. Liam sighed. He crumpled the letter and tossed it into the wastepaper basket.

He was going to have to tell her, though, sooner or later.

What to do? He needed more time to figure things out. There had to be a way to fix this, to change the narrative. There had to be a way to protect Charity and the twins from the consequences of these terrible events. Maybe the less she knew about them, the better.

As for himself, Liam couldn't afford to get caught up in another investigation. This time, there would be no leniency, no chance for Daddy to step in and smooth things over. This affair was going to be big news, international news. *If everything comes out, they could put me away for a long, long time.*

*And prison's no place for a gimp like me.*

He needed to think. He needed a plan.

Standing at the top of the steps to the veranda, Charity clutched at the telephone as if it could keep her from falling.

"Are you sure? I mean, he's been out like that for a couple of days before."

She stood and listened for a while, hunched protectively around the phone, elbows drawn in tight over her chest.

"Why didn't you–" she began angrily. The voice on the other end of the line whined and shattered and scattered in broken pieces. Charity continued to listen, pacing and occasionally cursing, but gradually becoming calmer.

"Look, forget it," she finally said roughly. "What's done is done."

Charity continued to stride from one end of the porch to the other, occasionally remarking "crap!" or "ohhh, crap." She finished off with "that goddamn . . . augh!"

Then she switched the phone to her other ear.

"Better give it another day. Okay. I'll . . . I'll throw him off the scent. What?"

The voice on the other end of the line spoke rapidly and urgently.

"It's in my jewelry box. Yes, the wide drawer. Yes." Charity drew in a long, trembling breath.

"Be careful," she said. "Call me."

Charity clicked the cordless phone off, and sat down on the porch swing. She looked at the handset. It was buzzing. The incoming caller's ID was sliding across the little LED screen.

"Bill from Ded Leper," she said. "No way am I freaking talking to you right now. You can go to hell. And voicemail." She watched the phone like it was a poisonous snake, her lips pursing and unpursing, until the message light began flashing. She closed her eyes for a long moment. Then she dialed a number.

"Dennis? I was hoping you'd pick up this time. Anyway. Listen, I got some news. Luke's bank has reported that somebody attempted to use his credit card in Olympia. I think it's worth looking into, so please head up there as soon as you get this. I'm going to call you back with a couple of phone numbers, people you can talk to. Okay?

"Thanks so much Dennis, you're a real hero."

Charity clicked off the receiver, and rose to her feet. She stood there on the veranda for a long time, quite still, like someone waiting at a street corner for a walk signal.

It was a bright Spring day in Echo Park, but on the wide porch a soft gloom reigned. A gust stirred the branches of the pair of enormous old cypresses that barricaded out the sun. Gray-green needles squeaked against beams of hewn redwood.

The breeze died down, changed direction, and Charity breathed

the dusty tang of the trees, heard them whisper of loneliness and long summer days to come. Their writhing starfish arms swayed, reached toward her, twined shadows around her. In the spaces between, Charity could see blurry gleams and flashes.

She blinked. Was she losing consciousness? *No, look . . .* it was only the windows of the cars glinting, as they passed in the distance, down Beverly Boulevard. As Charity watched, a street walker in a pink teddy emerged into view and minced down North Toluca on zebra spikes, disappearing, then reappearing beyond the screen of cedars.

At last Charity lifted her shoulders, squeezed them up against her neck, and let them fall. She wiped a drop of mucus off the tip of her nose with a knuckle, and sniffed. There would be time enough to cry later. Right now she had things to do, things that couldn't wait.

Charity picked up the phone.

*April 2, 1994* – Brooklyn, NY

Aron was downstairs in the studio, plucking on a mandolin when Rosetta came in. She was a little bit tipsy.

"What a fun day!" she exulted. She wanted to pounce on Aron and kiss him, but she didn't dare. Not when he was holding an instrument.

Aron glanced at her, squeezed his lips together, and continued picking at the strings, and she began to sing along in her rich coloratura. *Somebody's Darling* was a Civil War tune that they were rehearsing for the introductory music to a friend's play.

It was a sad, soaring song. The morbid lyrics obsessed over the features of the beautiful dead, in a paroxysm of maternal necrophilia.

> *Somebody's darlin', so young and so brave*
> *Wearing still on his sweet yet pale face*
> *Soon to be hidden in the dust of the grave*
> *The lingering light of his boyhood's grace . . .*

Under the influence of the song's gloomy imagery, Rosetta's thoughts turned toward Luke Mandrake.

"I told Phil about that dream I had," she said.

"You know what's odd," Aron remarked. "That very night, Phil told me that he used to do heroin."

"What?" Rosetta was horrified. "That's disturbing." Why had her nightmare associated Phil with a known addict? Heroin use had long carried a stain, but since the rise of AIDS it had become, along with male homosexuality, the most stigmatized of conditions.

And yet, her worries about Phil made more sense now. He said he used to do heroin . . . and that meant he might go back to using. Maybe he still was, secretly.

Rosetta felt a wave of sadness wash over her. She swallowed a draught of wine, emptying the teacup in her hand.

*Life is such a precarious venture, there's no time to waste. What could possibly be more important than showing the people you love how much you care? Why must Aron's rampart of reserve hold them apart?*

"Do you realize," she mourned, "that you've never even told me that you love me?"

Aron sat by the sun room windows in silence, smoking another hand-rolled cig. His wife came closer, touched his shoulder pleadingly.

"I love you so much! Please, Honey? I need to hear you say the words."

"I married you, didn't I?" he said, as if that settled things.

There would be no talking about feelings of any kind, apparently, except in jest. Aron came from a family that traditionally drank away their emotions.

Rosetta blinked at him quietly, then turned away. "I'm going to get Antoine ready to go," she said.

They were taking a five-fifteen train to see Aron's Dad. Gil Delgado was a retired officer who had flown black ops missions in two wars. Now he sang in a Barbershop quartet. Quiet, every bit the Colonel with his full head of white hair and luxuriant mustache, he lived out in Hempstead, in the house his own grandparents had built. Long divorced, he shared the ancestral home with Irma, an actress he had met on the set of an amateur production of *Hello, Dolly!*

Arriving at six, Aron and Rosetta headed straight for the fully stocked bar in the pantry. It was the only way to get through these visits. Gil knocked back the vodka, poured from a plastic gallon bottle into a tumbler with a splash of tonic, at a rate of one per hour all night long. He had probably started at noon.

After dinner the Colonel dragged out his projector and put on a slide show of his sojourn in Phnom Penh. There were several photos of a pretty young lady who he said had worked at the officer's club.

*She looks, like, fourteen years old,* Rosetta thought.

"And this was Dung, her name was Dung," Gil chuckled. In the awkward silence the ice rattled in his cup, and Aron fingered the paper label on his beer bottle.

They excused themselves after the second carousel. Antoine's bedtime was approaching, and it was a long trip home.

On the train ride back to Brooklyn, Rosetta guarded Antoine's basket of candy, a present from Gil and Irma. Antoine sprawled against her, reading *Small Gods* by Terry Pratchett.

Aron spoke of how as a young boy, he had longed to be an air force pilot like his Dad. "But I was flat-footed, and colorblind," he said, his voice heavy with resentment.

"Oh, dear," said Rosetta cheerfully. "Still, maybe it's for the best."

She wasn't being very sympathetic. She was thinking about other things.

Last night when Aron came in and fell heavily onto the bed beside her, he hadn't spoken a word. His back was turned to her. Rosetta had stroked his arm, but he hadn't touched her hand, hadn't reached for her. She had lain there in the dark, burning. It had been more than two weeks since they'd made love. What was wrong? Why was he rejecting her?

Rosetta knew by now the kind of woman her husband admired most: a petite, firm five-foot-two with hourglass curves. Rosetta was an amazon with big mommy tits, her wide feet sprouting bunions. Truth be told, her boobs were slightly cross-eyed. Did Aron still find her beautiful?

Maybe her husband was having second thoughts. It had been so improbable that they would end up together. Whenever she looked over at him, riding the subway beside her, draped with his guitars and musical equipment, her heart stopped. It was a kind of madness, she supposed, her wild adoration for him.

Maybe now that Aron had what he wanted, there would be no more spats over the band. They would be happy together again.

At Atlantic Avenue Station they transferred from the Long Island Railroad to the N/R subway line.

"Don't forget your jacket," Rosetta reminded Antoine as they rose to exit the commuter car.

"Do you have the basket?" the boy wondered.

"Basket? What basket?"

"Mom."

"Oh! Here's the basket. But I ate all the candy."

"Mom!"

"Well, I ate a peep."

"You can have as many peeps as you want."

"You don't like peeps?"

"Not the purple ones."

"They all taste exactly the same."

"Nuh-uh. The purple ones taste like dirt."

"Fine, more for me. Want a purple peep, Aron?"

"Maybe later," said Aron.

He was so taciturn lately. He used to be light hearted, ready to keep a joke going. Had Rosetta done something to make him unhappy, without realizing it? How she longed to bring back the laughter, and the pleasure that they once shared.

She couldn't get out of her mind the image of Aron in the bathroom, hucking up his guts into the toilet, the night before their wedding. It was a thing that Rosetta couldn't remember him ever doing before. It wasn't on account of too much booze. Both of their mothers were staying in their apartment at the time, and he'd actually had rather less to drink than usual.

*He's just nervous,* she'd concluded. Now, she wondered if there had been some deeper problem, something inside him that was struggling to escape.

*I married you, didn't I?*

That was his answer?

They had to try harder to make it work. She knew they could find a way, if only he would open up to her. It was high time for him to talk to her about their problems, problems that they had to work together to overcome. But whenever she asked him to discuss something with her, he reacted as though he were under attack. The only problem he could see was Rosetta, thinking there was a problem.

What would become of their marriage, if they didn't communicate?

Rain was slashing down when the family emerged at the Seventeenth Street Station. The traffic was heavy on this holiday weekend, and a line of cars was turning left into the Prospect Expressway entrance, which was right across from their building. The little family crossed Fourth Avenue, then cut across Seventeenth. Just then a motorist trying to catch the light charged around the corner at forty miles an hour and accelerated toward them. The car honked.

"Fucking Hell!" said Aron. They all shrank back as the red Honda swerved, narrowly missing them, before zipping up the on-ramp.

"Oh! That was scary," said Rosetta.

Half an hour later, she sat down on the bed next to her husband, tried to snuggle up to him. Aron ignored her. Grabbing his coat off of the floor, he felt around in the pockets for a lighter. "I'm going for a smoke," he said.

Rosetta trailed after him. While he rolled a cigarette, she waited nervously on the margins of his reserve, hoping for a sign. Finally she decided to just say what she wanted to say.

*I am unsquelchable,* she reminded herself.

"Aron," she announced, keeping her voice firm but cheerful, "I've been thinking . . . it would be so nice if you would say sweet things to me sometimes."

Silence.

"You never pay me compliments on how I look. It feels a little bit strange."

Silence.

"How do you think I feel when everywhere I go, people tell me I'm beautiful, but my own husband won't say so? It makes me wonder if maybe I'm not to your taste. Do you feel like you made a mistake marrying me?" Rosetta's voice caught and her eyes stung.

Aron cleared his throat. "You want to know how I feel about you? I'll tell you." He lit a cigarette before going on. "Last week, when you came and met us at the Continental, I looked across the room and caught sight of this sexy woman with enormous, ah, bosoms coming toward me. And I thought, *wow, who's that?*

"And then I realized, *oh! That's my wife.*"

Rosetta didn't know what to say. The anecdote certainly conveyed information.

"I was, of course, terribly relieved," Aron concluded.

Rosetta wondered whether to tell him about her late period, and decided against it. Instead, she went to bed. Aron followed a while later.

Jean-Baptiste stood by the dining room window, and rolled himself a cigarette from Aron's tobacco pouch.

That had been a close call earlier. The driver of the Honda had been extremely drunk, and had sped up blindly just when Rosetta decided to cross the street. If Jean-Baptiste hadn't been there to seize the wheel of the vehicle, things would certainly have gone very badly.

Rosetta might not know it, but she was very lucky tonight, that she had a guardian angel. And so were her husband and son.

Jean-Baptiste was going to enjoy this cigarette. He needed to calm his nerves.

So, lately, seeing that I find myself at the point of
screwing the final pooch ! It occurred to me to search
for the key to that long-lost party, so that maybe I
could get back the old gusto.
Charity is that key. That revelation proves I was
dreaming!


*A Season in Hell*
*Arthur Rimbaud*

***Eternity* – The Island of the Damned, Famebeau**

She was close to him, stroking his brow, brushing his hair back out of his eyes with tender fingertips. He could feel her breath on his cheek and neck. Bliss enveloped him with her caress, triggering in turn an instinctive response, which in Luke's case was generally a spurt of anxiety.

"Sshh," she soothed, seeming instantly to divine the shift in his emotions.

Through half-closed lids he discerned that he was lying beneath a soft blanket on a sofa. He relaxed, and as she bent over him and kissed his forehead, he almost surrendered to a sense of well-being and delicious anticipation. Almost.

*Goddess!* He yearned for her languidly, struggled to lift his arms. *Stay near me.*

She was receding, shrinking.

*Don't go!*

Luke woke up. Buzz was gently nibbling his brain.

"Get off me, Buzz! Christ."

Luke rolled over onto his back. He'd been cast up on the sandy slope of a beach. The waves washed the shore gently some twenty paces downhill of his feet. Coconut trees arched over him. Seagulls swooped mournfully across the sky above, raging at one another in high-pitched voices.

"So you finally decided to wake up," Buzz remarked.

Luke groaned. If only he were still dreaming. He stared up at a seagull and watched it land on the white sand near his legs. Buzz lunged with a skrawk and the gull flew off.

"Everybody wants in on the action," Buzz remarked.

"Where are we? Is this an island?" Luke fretted. He was feeling very fragile.

"How do I know? You want me to fly around and check?" The vulture croaked.

"Yeah, could you?" Luke responded weakly.

"Bozo!" Buzz rasped in an irritated tone.

"Well you know, if you want me to be, ah, mentally sharp, maybe you should stop eating my brain."

Luke felt himself for broken bones. He ached all over, but whatever parts of him had been battered and crushed in the torrent, he was on the mend. Still a bit muzzy though.

Buzz pecked at the sand. "Looky here," she said, "a cowrie shell."

Luke took it, turned it in his hand. The seashell was smooth and glossy with a pink-lipped opening and brown spots on its back.

Luke looked up as a shadow covered him. It was River Phoenix.

"I believe this is the Island of the Damned," River said.

"That doesn't sound too promising."

"It's a land of rebels and misfits. You'll fit right in." River removed a joint from his shirt pocket and lit it with a snap of his fingers. "Smoke this," he said. "It'll fix you right up."

"Where the hell did you get that?" The pungent smoke brought back a rush of pleasant memories.

"Doobie tree," said River. He handed Luke the doobie, and the zombie boy took a long draw, holding in the smoke. A little bit of white vapor seeped out from among the rags that covered his jutting ribs.

Luke passed the joint to Buzz.

"No thanks," she rasped. "I don't smoke."

So Luke handed it back to River, who took another couple of hits before passing the joint back to Luke. "Yeah, that's the ticket," he said. "I don't know how long I would have been able to stand being dead, if I didn't have the kind weed to keep me sane."

"I hear you," Luke agreed. "Where is this doobie tree?"

"Oh, up over yonder," said River, waving his arm vaguely. He lay back on the sand and gazed up at the sky. "It's so beautiful here," he sighed. "Much better than I would ever have imagined. And yet, I miss Rain, my sweet sis. I miss the family. And Sam. I was just finding out what it really meant to be in love," Phoenix sighed. "How 'bout you? Any regrets?" he wondered.

"Tons, of course. I mean, look at me. I obviously got screwed royally in this deal. There are things I would have done differently, sure." Luke sat up, put his arms around his knees and rested his head on top.

"I don't mean that. I mean, anything you wish you'd done that you never did?"

"I dunno. Be a better dad, I guess." Luke was wondering if River was going to light the joint again. Thinking about the way he'd failed Cherry and Haddy made his stomach roil.

"Well I wish–I wish I'd gotten good, really good at cunnilingus," River went on. "You know? I mean, I was such a spoiled brat in my first relationship. I really couldn't be bothered. And now . . . now I think about it. A lot."

"Eating pussy, uh huh. Definitely preoccupies my mind. It's the second best drug on earth."

"Totally. And the funny thing is, I half thought I was gonna grow up to be gay. The way guys were always after me, I figured they must see something in me that I didn't."

Luke laughed. "Yeah, I know what they saw. They saw a real nice-looking kid that was kinda lost, and vulnerable."

"You're right. And then, it was so easy just to reach out, get what I wanted. I guess I got so used to being the one that everybody was after, I never bothered to go after what *I* really wanted."

"And what was that?"

River turned and propped his head up on his elbow, fixing a gaze on Luke that was intensely passionate, yet pensive. Luke felt a bit unnerved by it. "I guess I always just wanted to be able to go home–

if and when I needed to. And the problem was, I didn't even know what or where home was–someplace safe, sure, someplace where you're loved . . . but I could never untangle the urge from a sense of responsibility, from the role of being the one who had to make sure everything was okay. I was so sure I was, like, the only one who really could." He lit the joint again. "I think I just wanted to have had an actual childhood," he remarked as he passed the doobie. "My parents were so fucking clueless."

"I hear that. When I was in high school, I wanted to go home so bad, but my Mom–" Luke lifted the joint to his lips and the chain clanked, "she always had some boyfriend, some total jerk. I couldn't stand it." He sucked smoke in thoughtfully.

"So you stayed away?"

"So I'd make myself such a pain, my Mom would give me marching orders."

"Oh shit. That's harsh." They were both silent for a little while, smoking.

"There . . . there *was* this girl–woman, I should say, she was older than me–" Luke ventured.

"Oh, *now* here it comes," River laughed. "The one that got away."

"One? Call it dozens. I'm the worst at getting laid, ever," Luke said with a painful breath of a laugh.

"No way, you? You're like, a god." River insisted.

"Me? I was always sickly, I had a lot of stomach pain, starting from way before I began doing dope. And this may sound strange, but I'm kind of introverted, and too intense, especially toward girls. All that made it difficult to be, you know, casual about stuff. The more I like a girl, the more likely I am to scare 'er off."

"Damn. I didn't know."

"I guess I could have had plenty of shallow-ass pussy. But the nice girls, the really cool girls, they have built-in junkie radar, right? They sensed how fucked up I was, and they always gave me an elbow in the face–so to speak."

"That's gotta hurt, dude."

"I try not to complain, but–anyway I could hear them whisper-ing about me. I have good ears that way. *Don't go out with him. He's bad news.*"

"But Charity wasn't like that, I guess."

"Charity was a hero. But I always knew she was putting up with a lot from me. Because I was such a huge success, I suspect, she was willing to deal with my problems. And . . . and she was also into getting high, so she didn't look down on me for it." Luke sighed quick and deep, took another hit.

"But–there was one woman you regret not hitting on . . . or something?"

Luke was quiet for a few beats. "Rosetta was her name. Rosetta Stone."

Phoenix chuckled. "For real?"

"Maybe it was a stage name, who knows. First time I saw her perform was at this community art center in Atlanta, when we were on tour, maybe it was in '88." Luke lay back beside River. "Man, she was gorgeous. In that Laurie Anderson, that David Bowie way, you know? Short hair, a dancer's body, green eyes . . . that cut right through you, thoughtful, deep. But with a sweetness too, all nerdy and, you know, real." Luke inhaled deeply, let it out slowly. "She had this super cute kid, about three, who was dressed in a homemade, five-pointed star costume. He went around the audience, pulling silver paper stars out of the little pocket in the front, and handing one to each person. I kept mine," he said softly.

"So . . . she was, like, a performance artist?"

"Yeah, really good. Reminded me of a few of the feminist artists I knew who'd influenced me early on.

"She'd brought a humongous Styrofoam tray, and these two guys with dog head masks sealed her onto it using a huge roll of saran

wrap. Not nude, she was wearing a body suit. There was a video playing, footage of a stream and rocks, with her voice saying, *take, eat,
this is my body, this is my blood, poured out for you.*

"A couple of people got up and walked out, saying *she thinks
she's Jesus Christ!* But most of us stayed, and it was a pretty full house.
Slowly, she cut away at the plastic wrap with a pair of scissors from
a Swiss army knife, and finally popped out. Then she announced she
was washing everyone's feet."

"Did she wash yours?" River wanted to know.

Luke stretched his arms, fetters tinkling. "Naah, I couldn't stay
for that, we had a gig that night, and had to go get ready."

"But you saw her again."

"Yeah." Luke had thrown his arm around Buzz, and was rubbing
the cowrie shell between his fingers. "A couple years later, after she
had moved to Brooklyn. It was just before our second record came
out, you know the one–"

"Somebody's coming!" Buzz interrupted.

Voices rose above the sound of the sea. Male voices.

"Who's that?" Luke asked.

"No idea," the condor replied, "but they're on their way over
here." And she seized the cowrie shell from Luke's hand, and swallowed it.

"We haven't checked Castaway Bay since yesterday, don't you
think we'd better have a look?" one of the voices shouted.

"What should we do?" Luke wondered.

"Maybe we should get out of here," River said lazily, not moving.

"Too late," Buzz screeched. The strangers could be seen making
their way along a path that led down the cliff. The leader was pointing
at them and exhorting the others to follow.

Luke lurched to his feet, but by now the three men were running toward them slowly over the soft, fine sand.

"You are under arrest!" cried the foremost runner, a tiny man who was wearing a bowler hat and oversized shoes.

"Come along quietly," puffed the second fellow, who had a bulbous head and enormous ears. He sported a dark mustache, a white undershirt and khaki shorts.

"For god's sake, don't make a fuss," the third man grumbled, lagging behind the others. He was the tallest and heaviest of the three but loped along gracefully, clad in knee breeches, a velvet jacket, a voluminous cloak and a broad-brimmed hat. He pointed a weapon at them that looked an awful lot like a novelty store dildo, the brightly colored sort made out of translucent gel. The object emitted a glowing purple ray, that enveloped first Luke, then River.

Luke felt all his muscles relax. He could barely lift an arm. It was like being stuck in soft taffy.

The vulture was fluttering around out of reach, as the three men surrounded them. They shot Buzz with the dildo ray, too.

"Get it!" cried the first runner. He took hold of Luke and the other grabbed River, while the tall one seized Buzz.

"In the name of DWOG, you are ordered to appear before the Discriminatrix," announced the mustachioed man.

"She is wise and merciful," the guy in the clown shoes assured Luke.

"She'll set you to rights," drawled the large fellow. "I advise you to cooperate."

Luke and River were half-dragged across the beach and then hoisted up a set of steps carved into the cliff face, to the palm grove above.

They stumbled like drunks up the hill through the coconut grove, and out to a long flagstone walkway that bisected a lush lawn. As the cavalcade moved along, onlookers gathered. Soon throngs lined the path. The fans waved and shouted:

"Charlie! Charlie!"

"Gene! You scurvy dog!"

"Oscar! Oscar Wilde!"

Sometimes the fans reached out, trying to seize the clothing of the celebrities. Buzz hissed and pecked at their arms and hands. But nobody tried to touch Luke or River. Nobody called out Luke's name, and this filled him with an unpleasant mixture of emotions. He had always loathed the mindless, fame-crazed rabble, yet now he was jealous. Why did he even care?

At last they reached broad marble steps leading up to a magnificent edifice like a Greek temple. Guards held back the crowd as the procession mounted the stairs, then Luke's captors turned to face the people.

Eugene O'Neill was the first to address the fans. "You mustn't feel sorry for me," he cried. "Don't you see I'm happy at last — free — free! — free to wander on and on — eternally!" The crowd cheered.

Wilde stepped forward next. "Every great man nowadays has his disciples," he announced, "and it is always Judas who writes the biography." The voices of the throng rose in a mighty roar.

Chaplin, who had been waddling about on the marble pavement, turned to the crowd and bowed, flipping up the tails of his coat. Then he turned to face the temple and bowed again. When he flipped up his coattails his shorts could be seen.

The tumult was deafening as the two other icons bowed as well. Then they dragged Luke toward a pair of gigantic iron doors decorated with bronze reliefs depicting Hollywood idols. The sea of faces took up a chant that swelled louder and louder as the doors swung slowly open, then shut behind them.

*"Bette! Bette! Bette!"*

The tumult was audible even after the massive portal clanged shut. The three celebs hustled their captives along a wide corridor hung with tapestries. Luke couldn't help staring at the dramatic hangings celebrating the lives and works of various stars of the stage and screen.

They halted before a tall set of double doors decorated in the Louis XIV style. The wood was painted white, with ornate gilded decorations swirling about on the surface.

Eugene O'Neill entered first, River Phoenix sleepwalking beside him. Luke remained outside with Charlie Chaplin and Oscar Wilde. They waited for some minutes in silence. The dildo ray was starting to wear off, and Luke could move a little more freely now.

Something on a nearby console table caught his eye: the head of a rat peered from the top of a ceramic vase emblazoned with the visage of Judy Garland. The rodent stared directly into Luke's eyes, then winked.

Before Luke could do more than wonder what the hell was going on, he was ushered into a magnificent chamber, gilded and painted. There were two long L-shaped tables, and in the center of the room on a blue velvet divan lounged the immortal Bette Davis. She was dressed in a low-cut gown of gold tissu, and on each side of her stood a handsome young man stirring the air with a large feathered fan.

"Madam Discriminatrix," Chaplin intoned, "Here are the other castaways we apprehended."

"Bring them closer," Davis commanded with a regal curl of her finger. Luke was hustled up to the diva, his arms held tightly by Wilde and Chaplin. Buzz flapped along above, then settled docilely onto Wilde's broad shoulder.

"And who–or what–are you?" she asked Luke, her nostrils flaring and then pinching as if he emitted a foul odor. Luke wondered for the first time if he did in fact smell bad, and just didn't know it. This seemed likely.

"Answer me!" Davis barked, fixing him with her enormous, terrifying eyes. He felt as if he were about to swoon. "What is your name?" Luke was swimming in those liquid eyes, sinking, drowning. As the waters of Lethe closed over his head he felt a rising terror of oblivion, of losing himself in its dark anonymity.

"Your name?" the movie star repeated more loudly.

"Lu-luke Mandrake," he stammered.

"Never heard of him," she replied dismissively.

"He is a popular musician of the current day, O Discerning One," Chaplin offered.

Luke wrenched his gaze away from the diva's hypnotic peepers and turned it to the fanboy beside her. Dressed in little more than a loincloth and heavy bracelets, he seemed awfully familiar.

It was River Phoenix.

"River!" Luke cried.

"Silence!" cried O'Neill, stepping up and giving Luke a violent shove.

"Hello Luke," River said gently, never shifting his regard from the queenly figure on the divan. The Discriminatrix was losing patience.

"Why is he a zombie? And what's this horrid thing?" she asked, pointing to Buzz. The vulture snapped at her finger and she pulled it back hastily.

"Ugh! Get it away from here!" she shrieked.

"Madam Discriminatrix, they are inextricably linked," Wilde pointed out, displaying the chain that bound the condor to Luke's wrist. "Do you wish us to remove the prisoner?"

"Yes, for goodness sake. Take him to the grinder. I have no use for him."

"The grinder?" Luke yelped. "What the fuck–let go of me!" He struggled fruitlessly in the grasp of the two writers, who dragged him unceremoniously out through a side door. He stared back over his shoulder at the elongated form of Abe Lincoln standing guard by the door.

"To the grinder it is, then," remarked Wilde. "One can survive everything nowadays except death."

"I wish you would stop quoting yourself," O'Neill snapped. "It's not becoming."

"I never quote myself. I leave that to others," Wilde objected.

"Insufferable peacock," O'Neill spat.

The other playwright shrugged. "I'm certainly not myself anymore, you must admit that."

"We all quote ourselves, friends," Chaplin remonstrated gently. "What else can we do?"

"Thanks for the philosophy lesson, *Dad*," O'Neill retorted sarcastically, then subsided into a mutter. Wilde turned his head up and to the side. There was something unnerving about the gesture, about the way they all fell silent at once, as if listening to a distant voice. As a matter of fact there was something odd about all three of Luke's captors, a dreamy, robotic manner. It reminded Luke of the way River had gazed at Bette.

*It's like they're under a spell.*

Luke was dragged away and out behind the Parthenon-like building to a hangar-sized, lichen-green quonset hut. Upon entering, the first thing Luke observed was the pulsing glow that rippled across the walls and ceiling. They approached the source of this phenomenon. It was a round hole fifty feet across, that contained a whirlpool of light, as if the aurora Borealis had been employed as illumination inside a titanic hot tub.

"What will it do to us?" Buzz asked their captors.

"Grind you up, of course," Chaplin replied cheerfully. "This is Famebeau's only ectoplasmic vortex accelerator, invented by Madam Discriminatrix herself. No spirit can survive passage through its portal."

Luke stared down into the vortex, in which laser-bright particles swirled so rapidly that they appeared to the eye as streaks. A rotating galaxy viewed in time-lapse velocity, it was a breathtaking sight, but ominous.

"Will I just . . . disappear?" Luke wondered.

"Don't you mean *we*, Bozo?" Buzz interjected.

"Energy never really disappears, of course," Wilde explained. "Your ectoplasm will be recycled. But you as beings will cease to exist."

If Luke had been told this not so long in the past, he might have greeted the prospect of annihilation with relief, or at least a certain equanimity. But ever since his conversation with his sister Jody, his perspective had altered. He had a mission now. He had to learn what was happening with Charity, to protect her and the kids from any harm. From the fragments of Jody's sentence, he gathered that his wife was being investigated on account of his disappearance. He had to find a way to dispense with any allegations that might be leveled at her, clear her of any suspicion in his death. Their children could not be allowed to lose their mother into the bargain.

But now it was looking like he would never get the chance to champion his family. His captors were lifting him up, along with Buzz, to cast them into the cosmic blender. It churned below, a humming abyss, a tunnel to nothingness.

"Wait!" Luke cried.

"What is it?" O'Neill uttered gruffly.

"I–I can be useful to you. I know things!"

"Really?" Chaplin said politely.

"Yes!" Luke shouted. "Put me down!"

"Everyone knows things," Wilde drawled. "What do you know that's of use to us?"

"I know–" Luke wracked his brains, "I know how to ease the pain of the living with frequencies of sound. I know how to make music that can knit together a miscellaneous collection of misfits into a cohesive band of love-infused, blissfully confused worshipers of everything accidental."

"Well, why didn't you say so?" O'Neill chortled. "Golly, that's something else again."

"Maybe we should spare him," Chaplin mused.

"Maybe we truly should," Wilde agreed. They all looked at one another.

"Nawww," said O'Neill.

They hurled Luke into the pit. As he fell, dragging the vulture down with him, Luke could hear their mocking laughter rattling around in the corrugated arc of the quonset hut.

"Fall slower!" Buzz croaked, tugging upward on his wrist.

"What? How can I?" Luke objected. But the moment the idea was suggested, he could actually feel his rate of descent slow a bit.

He concentrated his thoughts on braking, and soon the swirling cone of particles was no longer rushing toward him.

*I'm a leaf floating in the air,* he told himself

Luke felt a burning prickle in his right foot. He was too close to the vortex! Luke withdrew the foot from the stream of particles and the sensation stopped.

Then Buzz was under him and Luke eased down onto her back gently. She pumped her pinions, and he looked up.

"Don't cry. The damned don't cry." It was O'Neill's voice echoing up above, very melancholy.

"Indeed, if you want to tell people the truth, make them laugh, otherwise they'll kill you," Luke heard Wilde reply.

Luke's captors had their backs turned to the incandescent pit. If it was their job to make sure that he and the condor were consumed in the grinder, they weren't very conscientious employees.

"If we can just stay down here a little longer," he whispered to Buzz.

Buzz had flattened her wings, riding the updraft, the tips extending into the humming funnel of particles that surrounded them, where she held them steady. Over the thrumming of the ectoplasmic accelerator, the footsteps of the captors could be heard as they made their way out.

"OK, now!" Luke urged.

"I have perfectly good hearing," Buzz grumbled. "Better than yours!" She flapped her wings and in a few seconds they emerged from the pit.

Buzz landed on the cement floor as Luke lightly leapt clear. *We're getting pretty good at this,* he remarked to himself with a certain satisfaction.

"Are you OK?" he asked Buzz. "Nothing dissolved, I hope?"

"Fine, Bozo. Thanks for asking though."

"So whaddaya say we get out of here?"

"What about us, Luke?" said a tiny, squeaky voice.

Luke looked around but couldn't tell where the voice was coming from.

"Down here!"

By Luke's sneakers was a golden hamster, and the rat that had winked at him from the vase.

"Oh, hello," said Luke.

"It's me, Luke!" said the hamster. "River!"

"Wait, what? No way."

"Way." The fluffy rodent and the rat were joined by a mouse and a large cockroach. "My proper form's been taken over, turned into a robotic slave, but my will migrated to a hamster."

"Lucky fellow," said the cockroach.

"All right, I'm totally confused," Luke said.

"Allow me to explain," the cockroach offered. "I and my comrades Eugene and Charles," here he indicated the rat and the mouse, "were once members of DWOG, otherwise known as Down With Our Goddess. We came to this island to plan an agenda in our fight for a change of regime in Famebeau."

"I can dig that. I'm not exactly thrilled with the way she runs things either," said Luke.

"I am, however, distinct from my colleagues," the roach continued, "in that I was, and am, a double agent."

"I knew it," the rat hissed.

"Oscar! I'm shocked by this revelation," the mouse piped.

"So sorry, I forgot to tell you," the cockroach went on, "I was sent by GAFF to infiltrate DWOG."

"GAFF?" squeaked the rat.

"The Goddess Alliance Forever Force," the mouse supplied. "I should have known."

"I thought you guys were called OGG," the rat remarked.

"No, no, that's another group. They've never gotten past the fundraiser stage," the cockroach protested. "We've nothing to do with those pathetic Our Goddess is Great poseurs."

"Aherrm," Luke put in.

"Anyway," the cockroach went on, "The committee began as part of a democratic reform movement. But as a hierarchy began to take shape, the agenda shifted. Fearing reprisals, a task force was appointed for defense. Soon the conversation was no longer about representation, it was about power, and how to accumulate large amounts of it. We at last decided to go off in a rather risky direction. We would bolster our defenses by taking over an Earth satellite, one that, er, broadcasts classic films, and use it to capture star power from the noösphere."

"That was your idea," the rat objected.

"I was merely pointing out the obvious, dear Eugene. Bette had already been planning this for some time."

"Bette Davis had a tendency to dominate the discussions," the mouse remarked. "But we didn't realize that she had another agenda entirely."

"I knew, of course." The cockroach preened its antennae. "Perhaps I should have tried to stop her. I had no idea she would be capable of doing so much harm."

"She's an egomaniac," the rat hissed. "Worse than Persephone!"

"Exactly my point," the cockroach murmured.

"She's a monster," the mouse, who was certainly Charlie Chaplin, exclaimed, "and she's been tapping the satellite's energy to run the grinder, which she uses to dematerialize her enemies, and then to manifest ectoplasmic succedania–"

"Please don't let him go into the technical aspects," the cockroach, who appeared to be Oscar Wilde, interrupted. "Once he gets started, he'll never shut up."

"–In other words, she replaced us with exact duplicates," the rat, who was obviously Eugene O'Neill, summed up hastily.

"So she had all of you thrown into the grinder?" Luke prompted.

"Not just ourselves." The rat reared up on his hind legs. "Anyone she doesn't trust, anyone who can be of little use to her she simply erases, and absorbs their energy. The rest she remakes as slaves."

"How loathsome it is to see my poor abject form stumbling about, attending to its infernal tasks. What a travesty!" the cockroach bemoaned.

"So . . . but now you're in the body of a cockroach. How'd you manage that?" Luke wondered.

"Accident, my dear boy," the cockroach said. "As my being was disintegrating in the vortex, my will transmigrated into the nearest living thing, which happened to be a cockroach."

"I'm of the opinion," the mouse put in, "that the new shape is manifested, albeit unconsciously, by the will. The nature of the form is representative of a psychic state. I didn't have enough energy to manifest a large body, so I manifested a small one. I was thinking of the need for silence and secrecy, so I manifested as a mouse."

"Be that as it may," the cockroach interrupted, "only a few of us, those most accustomed to the act of creation, persisted in some diminished form after our executions, dwelling unnoticed in the interstices of this place."

"So you want me to help restore you guys to your true selves?" Luke asked.

"That would be ideal," the mouse said. "But that's not why we are appealing to you, Luke."

"We suspect that Bette Davis has another source of power besides the satellite," said the rat.

"Her most dreadful weapon is her eyes," said the cockroach. "She uses them to immobilize her victims, and to maintain control over her slaves."

"She does have incredible eyes," Luke agreed.

"She is a gorgon, a basilisk." The mouse said, its whiskers trembling.

"She has a secret, lad, and we need you to help us discover what it is." The cockroach straightened its antennae emphatically. "Not for our sake, but for the sake of all Famebeau."

Luke shook his head. "Forget it," he said. "I never joined your stupid revolution, and I never will. I'm an anarchist!"

"Come, Luke," said the mouse. "I know you're a courageous fellow."

"Hell no, I'm a coward. I can't wait to get off of this messed-up island."

"If you don't stand up for your ideals now, you may regret it come tomorrow," said the rat.

Luke laughed bitterly. "Come on, Buzz. Let's go." But when he tried to walk off, she pumped her wings and pulled against him. Luke wasn't unwilling to simply drag her off, resisting, but he suspected that she was in fact far stronger then he was.

"Buzz! Come on!"

Buzz hopped up onto Luke's shoulder and hissed, "You know, Bozo, that dame intended to disintegrate us."

"Exactly! That's why the sooner we get outta here, the better."

"If we can cut off her power source, we should try to do it."

Luke just stuck his chin out without saying a word. Buzz hopped down with a flutter to the floor. "I'm with the rodents," she said stubbornly.

"Come now, gird on your manhood, boy, and help us!" the cockroach said briskly.

"Pfft!" Luke retorted. He lunged at Buzz and folded his arms around her fiercely.

"At least hear us out," the rat added, "before you decide."

"I have decided," Luke snapped. "But this darn bird won't cooperate." He had succeeded in trapping one of the vulture's wings, but Buzz was beating the other wildly in his face.

"Don't–you–" Luke grunted, hurling himself down on the raptor and pinning the creature beneath him.

Luke felt suddenly dizzy and closed his eyes. Surely there was a woman in his arms, he felt soft lithe curves turning beneath him. His arms locked around her waist, her fingers in his hair . . . desire washed over him in a heady wave.

*Kissing her . . . the goddess . . .*

"Grawk!" screeched Buzz. "Get off me, Bozo!"

"What the–!" Luke wrenched himself away, opening his eyes to the sight of the condor rising into the air before him. Buzz puffed her crop and hissed, darting at him with her hideous head.

"Christ!" Luke ducked and staggered, nearly squashing the small creatures at his feet. He threw himself backward to avoid them, hit the ground inches from the edge of the pit, and almost rolled in.

The rodents exchanged looks. "Tut tut!" said the roach.

Luke shook his head, dazed. He had completely lost control of the situation, that was for sure. Where was his sanity? Had he finally given in to that cursed scavenger?

Luke put his head into his hands. He was getting nowhere. It was the goddess he needed to find, not the secrets of a power-hungry diva. But he was stuck with this rebellious vulture!

"So," Buzz rasped, "what's the plan?"

"Not long after I took this form," the cockroach began, "I happened to be creeping late one night along a passageway in the basement, when who should I see pacing the corridors alone, but the Discriminatrix."

"Our cruel deity of perfection never sleeps," interrupted the rat.

"I made myself as insignificant as I could as she passed, but my curiosity being aroused, I followed her." The cockroach waved its antennae gracefully. "She marched up to what appeared to be a blank wall at the end of a hallway, whispered something into a sconce lamp, and then walked through the wall and disappeared."

The cockroach sighed. "In vain I tried to enter, but without the password it was futile."

"We can't hear it from the floor," the mouse put in.

"I crawled up and hid near the sconce," the roach continued, "in an attempt to learn the secret. The next time she passed by, I was seen. I barely escaped with my life!"

"So what am I supposed to do?" Luke demanded.

"You, dear boy, simply have got to let her think you're an empty vessel for her to control." The cockroach looked around at the others, and the all nodded in agreement.

"You're shitting me," Luke said.

"Let her use your body like a puppet," urged the rat.

"No fucking way."

"We've got to get that password, my boy. And you are our only hope!" The mouse jumped up onto Luke's knee. "You were able to resist her the first time, and you can do it again."

"This is crazy," Luke protested. "Buzz, please!"

"If you ask me, Bozo, you gotta do it."

"Look, you've got the wrong guy. I'm not cut out to be a spy, or some sort of action hero."

"What's the risk? The second things get too hot for us, off we fly."

Luke shook his head. "This is a ridiculous plan. She'll see right through me."

"Please, Luke?" River said. "If we can get in there and cut off Bette's power source, I might be able to get my own body back."

"Luke, they need us," Buzz rasped in his ear.

Luke heaved a sullen sigh. "I see that I have no choice. But the plan sucks, and I'm cooperating under protest."

"Don't strain yourself, kid," the rat said sarcastically.

"Just keep on playing the fool," the cockroach counseled, "Exactly the way you've been doing."

"Remember, never look into her eyes," the mouse advised.

"When all else fails, improvise," the cockroach added.

"She'll catch on," Luke pointed out, "the second I fuck something up."

"Just let her take charge," the Hamster said. "We'll do the rest."

"That's so reassuring," Luke seethed. "Exactly how am I supposed to get in touch with you guys?"

"Easy," the rat O'Neill said. "We're coming with you."

A few minutes later, Luke strolled past the guards and through the side exit of the main building, trying to appear dazed and robotic. One of the guards looked a lot like Jack Kerouac. He shot Luke a hard stare, but said nothing.

Now Luke stood at the open doorway to the committee room. Bette Davis lounged on the blue divan, getting a foot rub from Errol Flynn, while she argued with Clark Gable.

"Madam Discriminatrix," Gable said, "there have been three more attacks on women since our last session. Surely you will permit me to authorize a posse of vigilantes?"

"Attacks on women? What kind of attacks?" Bette barked, flicking her cigarette.

"Two ravished, Madam, and one carried off."

Davis gently fluffed her sculpted coiffure. "Carried off? This is a small island, Clark. Carried off to where?"

"Madam Discriminatrix, we do not know."

"Not so hard!" Madam Discriminatrix whacked Flynn smartly on the temple with her toe.

"Forgive me, O perfect one," Flynn whined.

"You're a bore," Bette said, and Flynn slunk away.

"Clark, fetch me my feathered slippers," she directed crossly. Gable retrieved the slippers, knelt down and carefully shoed her pretty little feet.

"Now tell me all about the victims," she drawled, looking at him from under languorous lids. "I want every juicy detail."

"Ah, Madam Discriminatrix, the two women were both seized from behind, and sacks were immediately popped over their heads. So neither saw their attacker, although they report that he seemed to be quite large and powerful."

Davis moistened her lips. "How were they found? Were they injured at all?"

"Madam, one was found tied to an upholstered chair. She was unhurt but sadly, had been force-fed a three pound cheesecake. Another turned up in the lily pond, bound hand and foot and floating on an inflatable banana."

"A banana?"

"A very large banana, yes Madam. She had been made to consume eighty packets of rollos and, ah, chastised with a leather strap, and required medical attention."

Davis leaned back, narrowed her eyes and stretched herself like a cat. "Whose fans are they?"

"One Judy Garland, and one Lucille Ball." Gable thrust out his lower lip. "The third victim, the missing girl, was not a fan, but one of our celebrity castaways, Evelyn Nesbit."

"Nesbit? Not the Gibson Girl! How simply awful." Bette dragged on her cigarette, not looking particularly sorry. "But how do you know she was carried off? Did anyone witness the crime?"

"Not as such, Madam, but she was rooming with one of the others, who heard her crying out as she was borne away."

"Hand!" said Bette. The golem River Phoenix, still at his post as fan-flopper, instantly obeyed, and she stubbed out her cigarette on his palm. The lad stared straight ahead, unflinching.

"Well, it could have been anyone I suppose. Men are beasts, as you have every reason to know," she said, fixing Gable with an accusatory look, "and I can't control everything that goes on here. Perhaps Lord Zeus has paid another visit to our island." She furrowed her porcelain brow.

"Organize a patrol to examine all the female fans, and select the ten prettiest. Better round up any girl celebs you find, too. I'll place all of them in protective custody in my private chambers. That ought to discourage the predator," she asserted.

Gable still stood there looking at her, wearing an irritated pout.

"Well? Are you waiting for something?"

Gable cringed. "Madam Discriminatrix, we've collected some evidence," he ventured in a near whisper. "The rope used–"

"To hell with your evidence. I tell you, whoever it was, he got away with it. We have to focus on prevention now."

"Yes, Madam Discriminatrix," Gable bowed.

"Take Charlie and Oscar with you," she called after him as he marched out. "They have excellent taste." That was when she spied Luke peering in.

"You!" she burst out. "I thought you were recycled. What are you doing here, may I ask?"

Luke merely stared carefully at her knees with his mouth open.

"Can't you hear me, fool?" Bette sneered.

Luke felt a sharp pain in the vicinity of his right nipple. The rat, who was concealed inside his ragged flannel shirt, had bitten him. This cleared his head momentarily.

Luke cocked his head to one side and let his mouth hang open, hoping he looked suitably moronic. "Please forgive . . . uh–stupid me–Madam!"

"Oh lord. Somebody please put this mistake back in the grinder." Fred Astaire and Abe Lincoln, who had been standing like statues at either side of the door, moved toward Luke to seize him.

Quick as lightning, Buzz struck out with her powerful beak. She snipped off Lincoln's nose, swallowed it, then chomped down on Astaire's ear.

"Step back," Bette ordered. The two slaves returned to their positions, but now each was missing something. Blood streamed forth from the wounds, but there were no screams of pain from the two guards.

Bette rose deliberately from her divan and gazed at the condor. Raw power beamed out of her eyes like white hot lasers.

"How did you do that?" she hissed between gritted teeth. "Nobody bites off bits of my creations. Nobody!"

"Better start begging for your life!" whispered Oscar from behind Luke's ear. Luke threw himself onto the floor and began to moan.

"Forgive, forgive! Bird is wild, bird is vicious! Bird eat Luke's brain! Forgive Luke, Madam, save Luke!" He looked up for a moment, holding his hands in a prayerful pose, and caught a jolt from the diva's eye-beams. But they weren't directed at him. Bette was striving to control Buzz, their eyes were locked, and the vulture's neck and wings were twitching as though she were being electrocuted.

All at once Buzz went limp, and the actress smiled. She lit a cigarette and stepped toward Luke. Buzz flapped into the air, dragging Luke's arm with her, and landed gently on Bette's shoulder.

"I want the bird," she said. "Chop this thing off," she waggled the chain and Luke's hand, "and dispose of it."

Lincoln stepped forward, holding his cane, and drew out a sword hidden inside the walking stick. He looked warily from the bird to Bette, and seized Luke's arm.

"Please Madam, goddess, beautiful one, please!" blathered Luke, crossing his eyes frantically. "Spare Luke for take care of bird. Bird very hungry, bird can eat brain!" Buzz fluttered over to Luke and politely nibbled at a bit of his cerebellum.

Bette stood looking at Luke, sneering, her hands on her hips. Luke felt her eyes drilling into him; first she narrowed them and then opened them wide. He couldn't help himself. The moment he looked into her eyes, he felt paralyzed.

Her brute strength bore down on his mind. He wanted to close his eyes, but he couldn't. His will broke like a rotten thread.

Luke bowed his head. Let her do with him as she pleased. He would no longer resist.

Again he lifted his eyes to her, willy nilly. She hit him with the full force of the hypnotic orbs, and he trembled. Hot bolts of ecstasy shot through him as he groveled on the floor at her daintily shod feet. His mind emptied of everything but her: the oversized eyes dominating the china doll face, her perfect starlet form, her flawless rouged lips and skin, the sensual texture of her gown. At the same time, he saw himself through her eyes: a greenish scrap of rotten flesh, organ meat and brittle bone, a bloodshot monstrosity, chained to a mindless scavenger.

There was something about the monumental narcissism of the diva that reduced everyone in her vicinity to quivering, obedient slabs of meat.

Bette's lips curled up. She was changing her mind, not because she was merciful, but because she was getting an idea, he realized with horror, an idea about what she was going to do with him, now that he was utterly in her power.

Suddenly she cast a benevolent smile upon him, peeping over the ruff of fluffy white feathers that adorned her collar. She turned abruptly, then looked back at him again over her shoulder.

"Well, you're an ugly creature, but harmless. And you just might be useful after all. Come along," she said and stalked out of the room through another of its four doors.

Luke felt his arms and legs moving of their own accord as he rose to his feet and followed her. His hands hung at his sides, heavy as lead, as he paced along. Buzz sat quietly on his shoulder, taking bite after bite from the open dish of his cranium. He didn't even try to stop her.

Luke had surrendered. He could hear nothing but the mind of the Discriminatrix.

"LOOK AT THAT SKIN!" the voice yelled. "DISGRACEFUL! AND THOSE CLOTHES MUST BE BURNED! –TURN LEFT, IDI-OT! PAY ATTENTION TO WHAT YOU'RE DOING!" And so forth.

Bette walked down a long corridor and then up a broad stair-case carpeted in blue. At the top were heavy double doors guarded by Beethoven and Helen Keller. The actress put her lips close to a carved rosette near the door that held an oil lamp. Luke was still conscious enough of his mission to wish he could have gotten closer, to hear what she was about to whisper, but he was not in control of his limbs.

Whatever it was, the doors opened and Bette Davis stepped through. Luke followed.

Inside the doorway stood two female guards, clad in Roman gear: skirts made of short strips of studded leather, horsehair-maned helmets, and inlaid disks of bronze for brassieres. The sentries un-crossed their long spears, saluted, and Madam Discriminatrix passed into her private apartments, her newest slaves trailing behind.

Bette led Luke through a maze of corridors, tunnels and stairs, built with pale, roughly dressed stone blocks for walls, ceilings and floors, and with decorative metal sconces, wrought in a mandala shape and containing flickering flames, positioned every few yards. At last she stood before a large white metal panel. Here she paused and began to run her fingers across its slick surface.

Sensing an opportunity to escape, Oscar, who had made his way down to Luke's shoe, lost no time in jumping off and scuttling behind the draperies that covered the stone walls of the entrance hall. The rat, the mouse and the hamster, all of whom had been nestled among the rags that hung from Luke's gaunt frame, swarmed down his body and into hiding.

No sooner had the four creatures concealed themselves than the panel slid open, and Bette entered a large room filled with technology of mysterious purpose. She drew on a lab coat and rubber gloves, then seized Luke's face, turning it this way and that, and staring at him intensely.

"We'll have you back in bloom in no time, my dear," she remarked. "I don't know what you did to end up in this sorry shape, but I believe that once we reset your ectoplasmic pattern back to the default, you'll be tolerably good-looking . . . of course, we'll need to make some changes." She winked in a knowing way that made Luke's skin crawl, and pushed him toward the opening set in a sloping wall of polished basalt. Luke marched inside the chamber, carrying Buzz with him, and heard the door slide shut behind them, enclosing them in blackness.

After some time had passed a pale glow began to shed a barely perceptible light on the interior of the chamber. As the light intensity increased, Luke realized that it was a single beam that bent and scattered into iridescent colors. They were beneath a huge crystal prism that was suspended within a pyramidal chamber ten meters high.

A broad beam of light moved through the chamber, from ceiling to floor, passing through Luke like a bank of lasers.

In the absence of the Discriminatrix, Luke was beginning to recover his own will, and he whispered, "Buzz!" He thought he felt the weight of the condor on his shoulders, but she didn't answer. He turned.

A curvaceous female form stood near, lit by a penumbra of flame. It was the goddess, clad in a misty web of fresh green, here before him in all her heart-stopping beauty. Jeweled pomegranates hung from her girdle, and tongues of fire, blue and yellow, played about her head. Around her neck was a silver collar, and at the other end of the chain that was affixed to it, a bracelet encircled his own wrist.

Luke stared at his hands, his arms. They were noticeably un-decomposed. He put his fingers to his face and felt boyishly smooth skin and firm flesh.

He was healed. He was whole again, and here, where there had been a vulture just a moment ago, here was the goddess, sweet and soft as apricots, and just his size. Attached to him like a pet, no less. He blinked a few times, feeling woozy, but the vision remained.

His heart lurched with a deep and satisfying pang, and his eyes moved over her as she gazed at him tenderly. Luke breathed in her scent, yet he remained utterly unable to accept that she was anything more than an apparition. Surely this fantasy would evaporate in a matter of seconds, as the others had.

If the goddess's expression was one of impassioned joy, his own adoration evinced a hopeless yearning. After a few moments her look became more poignant, as she absorbed the depth of his preemptive despair. Her mouth formed an O, and her eyes filled with tears as she gazed into his own. She reached out and seized his hand, pressed it to her lips.

Luke's sluggishness melted away at her touch. He felt a wave of excitement that stirred him, so that he unfurled his wings quite rapidly, bruising them on the sides of the prism.

"Ow!" he murmured.

"My lord, stand closer the wall," she whispered. "Bette cannot be allowed to see your wings."

"Where–where's Buzz?" he stammered.

"Shh! Bozo," she murmured fondly, and kissed his nose. Luke's hands darted around her waist. It was like embracing a waterfall, she seemed to vibrate softly in his arms, and as he pressed his mouth to hers he tasted spring water, refreshing and delicious.

Suddenly he stopped kissing her, and looked at her in puzzlement.

*Wait–did she just say . . . my wings?* Luke looked up at his pinions, and she stroked the feathers that were golden brown, soft and warm.

Her touch tickled and Luke shivered. *Bette Davis gave me wings?*

He opened his mouth to ask all the questions that were crowding his thoughts. But the goddess placed two fingers over his lips and whispered, almost soundlessly:

"Know that she cannot destroy you, nor change your form against your will. I may not say more."

Luke placed his hand over hers, kissing the fingers she'd laid against his mouth. He searched her eyes with his for a long moment. *What does she know about me?* he wondered. She was gazing at him with infinite compassion.

It was enough.

*Keep your secrets, then. I'll seal your lips,* Luke thought, *with a kiss.* He proceeded to demonstrate his plan, and would have devoured her with kisses, but she pulled back with a warning look.

"There is no time," she mouthed, disentangling herself from his embrace. "You must assume the shape that she is expecting."

Luke sucked in his breath, suppressing an urge to wrestle the divine creature to the floor, and folded his arms instead. He scowled, then immediately wished that he hadn't been so bad-tempered. But the goddess only pointed to the screen set into the pyramid wall, where a wireframe model flashed and turned.

*Just open your mind to hers,* the goddess enjoined, communicating by signs. "Let her thoughts shape you," she breathed.

Luke understood, and although he disliked the idea, as with the fall into the vortex, all it took was a suggestion for the change to begin. He craned his neck to look at his wings as they began to shrink.

"What about you?" he hissed.

Wordlessly she placed her hands over her heart, then held them out to him. *I am with you.* She reached behind her neck and unclasped a fine chain that hung there. On it was strung the cowrie shell Buzz had swallowed on the beach. This pendant the goddess hung over Luke's heart.

He seized her hand, kissed it, and looked into the divine creature's anguished face. Was the goddess weeping? He shot her a questioning look. *Are you okay?*

She cast her arms about him and buried her wet cheeks in his neck. "My lord," she whispered.

"I don't even know your name," Luke murmured, knowing even as he spoke that he would get no answer. He closed his eyes, crushing her to him.

"My lord," she breathed again and he felt her lips pressed against his eyelids, one by one.

When he opened them, she was gone. Buzz stared back at him from the other end of the chain, and combed the feathers at her breast with her beak, then spoke in a barely audible hiss:

"The password is, *all men are scum.*"

Luke couldn't help it. He let out a tiny squeak of laughter. At least it would be easy to remember.

"How did you find out?" he whispered. Buzz only looked at him with her head cocked to one side, and preened.

The door to the prism-pod slid open.

"Improvise!" the vulture hissed as the Discriminatrix commandeered Luke's body once more.

"Come on out you two, and let's have a peek at you," Bette sang out cheerily.

Luke felt desperate to fight back, to take control of the prism, and restore himself and the goddess to the forms they had taken moments ago. But he wasn't even in control of the movements of his own limbs. Out the door he marched like a puppet, with Buzz on his shoulder.

"Turn around," Davis ordered, and he slowly spun about so she could examine his new appearance. He was clean-shaven, wearing a long, belted black jacket, close fitting but with wide sleeves. He had on pointy shoes, dark red tights, black bloomers and some sort of hat.

"Remove the cap," commanded Bette. He obeyed. The hat was a three-cornered creation in black felt, with a red feather held in place by a jeweled pin, and without it he felt air hitting his exposed brain. Luke's mind raced, as he tried to appear blank.

"Put it back on. I want the vulture to have a good appetite, so you'll wear it at all times, unless you have orders from me to let her feed. Do you understand me?"

"Yes, madam."

"Come here. What did you say your name was?"

"Luke, Madam."

The Discriminatrix took his chin in her hand. "Look at that darling dimple. What a pretty face you have, Luke. As pretty as a girl's. Too bad your mind is gone, but then if you hadn't been a fool, I'd never have brought you in here." It seemed, Luke thought, that she could project her thoughts into his mind, but she could not read his.

She released him, compressed her lips, tapping the philtrum with a finger. "The ladies will fight over him, no doubt, but I've made sure he can't do them any harm." She clapped her hand between his legs, and that's when he realized that she had not made him, as it were, anatomically correct.

He was no longer a man at all. He was a eunuch, a walking,

talking Ken doll.

"Good enough," said the Discriminatrix, shedding the lab coat and gloves, "come along." Luke followed her with the steps of a sleepwalker, Buzz on his shoulder. Externally he was a docile automaton. Inside, his mind was screaming, screaming. Exactly what his mind was saying he could not make out, because the onslaught of orders, criticisms and judgments broadcast from the control center of the Discriminatrix's mind boomed in his thoughts like a sonic cannon:

"STAND UP STRAIGHT! EYES FRONT! WALK FASTER! DON'T SLUMP!"

She led him along a stone-flagged corridor, and stopped at a beautifully carved oak door.

"Wait here," she ordered, and went inside.

When Bette Davis emerged, she had changed into jodhpurs and a fitted jacket, and she held a riding crop in one gloved hand.

They continued along the hallway until they arrived at stairs that spiraled down and down, issuing onto a doorway of heavy oak slabs banded in iron.

She must have mouthed the password, though the words were inaudible to Luke, for suddenly the door swung open.

Within, two more Amazons stood at either side of the portal. These saluted Bette Davis, tapping their spears on the floor.

Luke was expecting a basement or underground chamber, but they entered a large stone-paved courtyard enclosed on three sides by gracious porticoes. A bright flower garden surrounded a plashing fountain, and soft music was playing. Everywhere there were women: sitting, standing, lounging, talking, jogging. All were scantily dressed, like the nymphs in a Maxfield Parrish painting: a piece of cloth knotted round the waist, a scarf draped coyly, a garland perched on a curly head.

All the women had pretty faces and many were decidedly plump, while others were frighteningly thin. None of the girls appeared to be a normal, healthy weight.

There was a volleyball game going at the other side of the enclosure by the high wall, a match between fat and thin, with much jiggling and bouncing on the fattie side of the court.

There was not a single male face to be seen.

As soon as Davis entered, a number of the females crowded up to her, calling out her name and hoping to claim her attention. Several noticed Luke and began to regard him with interest, but Buzz warned them off snappily.

"Girls, girls," Bette cried above the clamor, "Thank you, thank you for your loving tribute, but we must continue with our socializing later. Right now I'm calling an emergency meeting in the chapel. Come along," she said, and strode forward.

At once some of the women began banging on gongs and announcing, "Emergency Meeting in the Chapel!"

Davis crossed the courtyard and passed through an arched opening in the wall, entering a small theater with rows of marble banquettes set one above the other. Luke followed her closely down the stairs, and a throng of ladies filed in behind them, while Amazon guards rounded up any stragglers.

Davis made her way to a bench of carved black marble that stood on the stage, bedecked with flowers, and piled with red silk cushions. Here she leaned back, sighed, and after taking a sip from a pink cocktail decorated with a paper umbrella, she placed the glass on the ebony occasional table beside her, and spoke in a theatrical tone.

"My dearest ladies, you see why I work so hard. It is for you, you who are the last bastion of civilization in this mad, frightening place. You who know what it is to love, to be caring and thoughtful. You, who are not merely my fans, but my devoted wives!" Clutching a lace handkerchief, Bette brushed a tear away.

"Is everyone present?" she asked, searching the crowd. "Where is our newest spouse?"

"She is here," announced an Amazon, pulling Evelyn Nesbit forward by the arm. Evelyn was a petite woman with the face of a fairy-child, and wide eyes filled with fear.

"Evelyn," Bette said softly. "Come here, my girl."

The lovely creature approached timidly, and Bette reached out and drew the girl to herself, embracing her with cries of pity.

"Oh, my poor, poor child. Are you better now, my dear?" Bette asked.

"Yes, Ma'am," said Evelyn, not looking up. "That is, I–"

"Thank goodness, for that," Bette interrupted. "Now, we are all ladies here. So you must never fear to share with us, here in this safe place, the horrors you experienced out there in the world of food."

The girl merely shook her head fearfully. The Discriminatrix took her by both shoulders and looked her sternly in the eye.

"It is important to get this off of your chest. Tell us about the bad man who abducted you."

"It–it wasn't a man, Ma'am."

"Not a man? What do you mean?"

"It was a . . ." she buried her face in her hands, "a monster!"

"A monster?"

"A man, ma'am, with the head of a bull."

"Ah." Bette pressed her lips together "So. The monstrous beast that is Man has once again taken its true form in that hideous creation, the Minotaur." Bette took Evelyn's hand in both her own. "Tell me, child, what did this monster do to you? I want all these women to hear the truth of your tragic trials."

"I–I–" Evelyn stammered. Tears poured down the poor girl's face and she shrank away from Bette, but the Discriminatrix held her hand in an unrelenting grip.

"Go on," urged Bette. "Did the Minotaur harm you?"

"Oh, Ma'am, he–he tied me up, and made me eat a banana," stammered the girl.

"And?" Bette urged.

The girl shook her head, and hung it in shame, as the tears dropped to her bosom. "I don't–" she whispered.

"I see that you are too distressed to speak, so I will speak for you. Ladies," Bette addressed the company fiercely, "the fiend forced her, in the most brutal fashion, to eat a dozen large unripe bananas, and then to consume twelve boxes of ice-cold profiteroles. He left her lying in the coconut grove with a terrible stomach ache and a debilitating case of brain freeze. That is where my servants found her." The Discriminatrix strode up and down a few times before returning to the trembling girl and throwing an arm around her shoulders.

"Poor dear Evelyn has been given the mystical healing potion that has restored her virginity, her beauty and her health. Still, I shudder to think of the violence and agony she suffered."

The crowd murmured sympathetically.

"Ladies, my news gets worse. The same monster has assaulted two other women on the outside, since yesterday."

The group gasped in horror and pity. "Shameful!" cried one.

"This tragedy has caused me to ponder anew the question of preserving the women of Famebeau from obesity. You privileged few, my loyal wives, are protected here in our blessed cloister, and yet–" here Bette looked sternly around at the group, "and yet, especially among the newcomers, there are those who grumble, there are those who may even think of leaving us, and venturing out into the dangers of the world of food!" Bette put her hand to her forehead in an anguished gesture.

There was a flutter of protest. "Oh, no, mistress!" and "Not I!" cried many in the congregation. As Luke looked out over them, he saw some eyes filled with fear, others with sly calculating glances, and still others brimming with tears.

"The rule against straying beyond these walls exists solely for your safety," the diva went on. "Yet some among us have been complaining about a lack of freedom. Freedom! It is your freedom that I protect so jealously! Think: do I use my great powers to take command of your minds or bodies, as I so easily could do? I do not." The Discriminatrix looked up toward the heavens for a moment in mute supplication. "I do not, although it would be infinitely easier for me to protect you if I did." She shook her head, gazing at her harem of eating-disordered girls with tearful indulgence, as though they were spoiled children who had brought their mother to ruin.

"But although you make it so difficult for me to care for you, I must persevere. I fight on, only for the sake of your happiness, and your love–" her voice caught, and she touched the napkin to a delicate nostril, "–and love by its very nature must be freely given!"

By now, sobs and wails could be heard among the throng, and scarcely an eye was dry.

Bette rose once more from her couch and faced them fiercely, pointing up and out of the walled chapel. "Out there in the world of food," she cried in ringing tones, "I have done my best to control the forces of brutality! But as this latest incident proves, I cannot always prevent evil from bursting forth." Bette, still holding Evelyn's hand tightly, swung her arms up toward the sky in a prayerful gesture. "These evil forces are rallying against us, the darkness is rising around us, and I cannot keep it back forever!" The women had fallen silent, except for a cough and a few scattered sniffs.

Bette put her arm around Evelyn and gripped the girl's shoulder. The Discriminatrix appeared stricken now with terrible grief. "To leave this place and my protection is . . . is, I fear, to betray the most solemn of vows. For have we not all promised to protect one another? And yet those who wish to leave us are even now spreading dangerous lies, encouraging their sisters to make the same perilous mistake as they themselves are ready to make. I cannot allow catastrophe to threaten our bower, our refuge."

"This is why I have brought you a new guardian," she gestured to Luke, who stepped forward. "Chained to this eunuch is a vulture with a beak like steel pincers. If any of you," and she raked the group with accusing eyes, "were so foolish as to attempt to depart from our safe haven, it is from this vicious creature that you will face the justice you deserve! It is to the cruel beak of the condor you will answer!" Bette whipped off Luke's hat and Buzz, snapping her beak viciously, took a huge bite out of his brain and swallowed it in several messy gulps. The audience of women gasped.

"It is better to be eaten, my dears, than to eat. You may lose a nose, an ear, a finger or an eye," the diva went on coldly, "but the value of these things is slight compared to your greatest treasures: your virtue, your svelte physique, and ultimately, the safety and beauty of all our sisters here."

Not one among the group gathered there in the chapel spoke, but over the crowd rose a collective sigh, a sound like a gust of wind rushing through the branches of an olive grove.

"But there is an even more serious threat to every maiden here," Davis went on, seating herself again on the divan, and pulling Evelyn down to sit beside her. "And I say maiden truly, because every one of you has taken the vow. Every one of you was made a virgin when she arrived, when her sacred throat-hymen was restored by my elixir, and has sworn never to willingly allow a bite of food to pass her lips." Bette, who had her arm around Evelyn, caressed the exquisite girl's cheek.

"How about you, dear Evelyn?," she asked, trailing her finger down Evelyn's creamy neck. "You are our fresh lily, our maiden from the midden, transformed by grace into a new perfection. Will you share our vow?"

Evelyn trembled, looked up at the diva fearfully. "Must I swear?" she asked piteously.

The Discriminatrix's grip on the girl's waist tightened, and she said sternly, "You do not wish it? You do not wish to forswear the sin of gluttony? You–you whose shame is here for all to see?"

The Discriminatrix gestured to the Amazons that stood one at each side of her divan. Forward they came, moving like puppets. One pulled up the nightgown Evelyn wore so that the other wives could clearly see the brand that scarred the girl's ever-so-slightly plump belly. It was in the shape of a bull's head. "No! No!" Evelyn sobbed. "That wasn't–"

"The Mark of the Minotaur!" Bette intoned dramatically. "Only the flesh shall expunge the shame of the flesh!" The guards seized the poor child by the hair, and bent her over Bette's knee.

"Only the flesh shall expunge the shame of the flesh!" chanted the women as one.

Standing like a statue behind the Discriminatrix, Luke watched as one of the Amazon guards placed a huge wooden salad spoon in Bette's hand.

"With this chastisement I expunge the shame of the flesh so that the child, Evelyn, may be pure and reborn!"

"P-please Ma'am! I will swear the vow!" Evelyn whimpered. "I will swear it!"

"Too late for that!" Bette snapped. "You must be purified of your unclean desire!"

The ladies on the benches sat frozen as their mistress, eyes ablaze with rage, brandished the spoon, and brought the rounded end down three times, *smack, smack, smack!* across the girl's bottom.

"Don't! No, no! Please, mistress! No!" Evelyn shrieked and sobbed, squirming in the iron grasp of the Amazon guards.

"Where were you when he seized you?" Bette demanded.

"I was in bed," Evelyn moaned.

"What were you doing there?"

"Please, mistress! I was reading!"

"And what were you reading?"

"I don't remember!" Evelyn sobbed wildly. *Smack, smack,*

*smack!* went the spoon, and her sobs crescendoed again into frantic protests and screams, and tears streaked her childlike face.

Bette lifted a book in her hand. "Evelyn, were you reading this?" she demanded. "*The Joy of Cooking*?"

"No!" Evelyn cried. *Smack, smack, smack!* went the spoon.

"Yes! Yes, I was reading it," she wept. "Please mistress, I didn't mean it!"

"This filth," sneered the Discriminatrix, "this unholy bible written to glorify the disgusting habits of mortal beings, solids who wallow in the hideous muck of physical pleasure!" She threw the cookbook to the ground, kicked it, and plied the spoon even more energetically upon the piteously weeping girl's derrière. "This *(smack!)* is how you summoned the demon, *(smack!)* the beast *(smack!)* who even now may be ravishing some poor girl! *(smack! smack! smack!)*"

The girl's cries were so heart-breaking that Luke could hardly bear to witness the beating, but the Discriminatrix was not finished. She punctuated her words with repeated blows that caused her victim to twitch, shriek and blubber.

"This has filled your mind with evil thoughts, *(smack!)* thoughts of cheesecake *(smack!)* with cherry pie filling *(smack!)* and whipped cream! *(smack! smack! smack!)* You, Evelyn, are a fattie! *(smack!)* A harlot! *(smack!)* And a traitor to your sex! *(smack! smack! smack! smack! smack!)*"

At this last attack the spoon broke in the Discriminatrix's hand. Bette tossed the pieces aside, put her hand out palm up, and an attendant slapped a large wire whisk into it.

Evelyn saw the whisk, and screamed and whimpered, begging Bette to have mercy. The women sitting on the marble benches watched quietly, some with their hands over their mouths, some clinging to each other and moaning softly. The Amazon guards stood like statues, their hands clamped tight on the wailing prisoner's arms and legs. Bette raised the implement and began to whip the poor child with passionate ferocity.

For a long time nothing could be heard but the zing of the whisk, and the shrieks of the victim as it made contact with her fanny. Even after the girl had stopped struggling to escape, and her hysterical weeping had become no more that a weak moaning, the sound of the whipping continued. Evelyn lay limply across the Discriminatrix's knee, and at every blow, a tiny whimper escaped from her lips. Bette had beaten the poor girl into abject surrender, but she continued to inflict the whisk upon her like a terrible machine. At last she gave a guttural, orgasmic gasp, lashed at the child's torn flesh a few more times, and flung the whisk aside.

"Only the flesh shall expunge the shame of the flesh!" the Discriminatrix uttered hoarsely, panting. Her bloodied victim swooned across her lap.

"Only the flesh shall expunge the shame of the flesh!" responded the congregation in reverential tones.

The Amazons lifted Evelyn to her feet and gripped her by the arms.

"Evelyn, alas, is not fit to be a part of this company of ladies. It was she who called up the demon with her unclean thoughts. It was she who shrank away from the holy words of the vow. She is no fit wife among wives. Shame!"

"Shame!" cried the women.

"Shall she be shown mercy?" Bette called out, "or shall she be given to the beast?"

Silence fell. The Discriminatrix, as fascinating as she was terrifying, seemed to absorb the energy of everyone in the chapel. Luke, frozen in place, could only watch the diva in helpless horror as she played out the dreadful scene. Bette walked up and down the stairs and aisles of the little amphitheater, holding each of the women's eyes with hers in turn, searching their hearts, challenging them to defy her.

"Shall she be shown mercy?" she called out once more, "or shall she be given to the beast?"

The women of the congregation remained silent, eyes down, but stole sideways glances at one another. Finally a whisper rose from their midst: *the beast!*

*The beast, the beast, the beast!* rustled through the congregation as the Discriminatrix stood triumphantly watching them.

Bette picked up the cookbook and held it aloft. "By her sinfulness she has brought the beast into our very sanctum." She tore the book in two. "The beast must be fed with the wicked, or it will destroy the innocent!"

"The beast must be fed! The beast must be fed!" chanted the women again and again.

"Very well, ladies, since you have decreed it. I will choose her consorts for the ceremony."

The hall fell silent as Bette prowled hither and yon, indicating to the guards one plump and shapely woman after another. The others avoided looking at those she had selected. When at last the twelve unfortunates had been assembled, a wave of nervous giggles and chatter rose through the rest of the group.

The Discriminatrix proceeded from the chapel behind two guards who bore Evelyn along between them. Her chosen handmaidens followed her up the aisle. Not a few of these hung back fearfully and had to be drawn along by their fellows, while two more guards brought up the rear to ensure that the consorts did not attempt to shirk their duties. Luke and Buzz straggled after them.

The small troop of helmeted guardswomen, athletic-looking and anonymous, conducted Bette and her entourage through a maze of corridors, until they arrived at a large underground chamber that contained what appeared to be an old-fashioned carousel. This merry-go-round had no roof, the poles of the horses being affixed to a massive disk set in the lofty ceiling. At the center of the ride, instead of a pipe organ, rose a large clear tube. Inside the tube hung a long chain that terminated in a pair of shackles.

"Stay here by the door, and don't let anyone in or out," Bette ordered Luke and Buzz. She pressed a lever and the tube moved upward so that the Amazon guards could secure the victim within it. Evelyn's hands were fettered, and she hung there, balanced on tiptoe, eyes wide with anguish. Luke couldn't help staring at the girl's body, for her form was resplendent in its perfection. *She doesn't look fat to me,* he thought.

"No, no!" Evelyn cried out. "What are you going to do? Please, please mistress! No!" The tube was lowered, so that her wails of terror were silenced by the thick layer of glass.

The voluptuous consorts were helped into rubbery catsuits that had two oval openings, one for each buttock, and a similar opening for each breast. Then the guards lifted the women one by one up onto the high, sculpted horses that decked the carousel. There was much buckling and adjusting of straps, as the girls' hands were bound securely to the necks of their carven mounts. The guards next slipped a padded leather helmet over each head, which covered the upper part of the girl's face in a protective, opaque shell so that only the lips could be seen. The helmets were buckled on under the chin, and then the tops of the helmets were buckled to the yokes of the rubber catsuits so that the women's heads were drawn sharply back.

*Christ,* thought Luke, looking around at the parted lips of the bound consorts, contorted and arched on their mounts, bosoms and bums bulging from their vinyl packaging. The spectacle was calculated to get him a bit heated up, willy nilly. But Luke could detect no movement in his man-hosen. There was nothing there to move.

"A wild ride is in store for you, my darlings," Bette announced as the guards were securing the leather buckles that kept the helmets in place, and she glanced at Luke smugly for a moment, "and this measure is to protect you from injury, and keep you from biting your sweet tongues."

*Is she doing this for my benefit?* Luke wondered. *No, that's impossible.* But he still felt sure that this entire exercise was intended to make an impression on some captive audience.

All seemed to be proceeding smoothly when one young lady began to thrash about. Bette was forced sternly to chastise her with the wire whisk.

"No struggling!" the Discriminatrix snapped as she applied the whisk with vigor to the girl's backside, protruding in two quivering mounds from the rubber. The poor girl continued to flail in her fetters, with tiny cries like a frightened animal.

"Sit still and surrender to your fate!" her mistress ordered, now plying the whisk with gusto on the exposed bosoms as the girl yelped louder and louder, driven in her panic to struggle on against her helplessness.

But the Discriminatrix was determined, and she always won in the end. After what seemed like an eternity of ruthless flogging, the captive began to tire, surrendering to and embracing her torment. Her movements quieted down to a hopeless twitching, her vocalizations became weakened till they sounded like a bird twittering, and she slumped on the wooden horse, resigned. All around were quiet, and Luke divined that there would be no further struggling among the captives.

The Discriminatrix directed the guards to bring chains heavily loaded with large round jingle-bells of brass. These were fastened to the feet of each of the consorts, and connected together below the tails of the carousel mounts. The poor captives were now bound both hand and foot into jockey-like poses, while their slightest movements caused a cascade of chimes. The Discriminatrix remarked approvingly upon the cavalcade of upturned mouths, ready to be fed.

Then Bette herself went round the carousel stage, checking

that all the straps were secure and adjusting the buckles so that they were tight, but not too tight; making sure that each girl was positioned on her steed just so. She watched as the guards pushed a half a dozen large marshmallows one by one into each consort's mouth. If it seemed that the prisoner could still chew, she had her helmet buckles adjusted. It was thus that the Discriminatrix ascertained that the blind captives were one and all helpless to refuse the force-feeding, nor able to bite the fingers of their keeper. It delighted her as she made the rounds of her hapless harem to smartly smack the girls' bottoms and breasts at random with a ping-pong paddle, causing them to vellicate with strangled yelps and grunts.

An Amazon followed the Discriminatrix on her rounds with an ice chest, which contained a quantity of chocolate truffles, ranging in size from that of a ping-pong ball to a softball, and chilled until firm. The mistress herself chose one of the round confections and inserted it into each maiden's mouth. To make doubly sure that the victim swallowed the treat, she would then take the ping-pong paddle and soundly spank the girl's haunches with it for at least twenty strokes. This exercise generally produced involuntary choked cries, which were instantly smothered when one of the attendant Amazons clapped a hand over the girl's mouth, pinching her nose shut so that she was forced to swallow the truffle whole. Upon the next visit the attentive mistress chose another chocolate of greater circumference, which was duly crammed between the captive's parted lips. And then out came the paddle, which she applied to the unfortunate woman like a cook giving a sound whipping to a recalcitrant bowl of meringue. The Discriminatrix proceeded thus from one of her wives to the next, darting about energetically, tucking ever larger sweetmeats into the women's mouths, and relishing the quivering, writhing movements of her victims as they struggled to swallow the frozen desserts whole.

"There, my dear. Gulp it down. I know, I know. Just try and surrender to the experience as best you can. It will all be over soon," she frequently cajoled. But if the poor girl gagged or coughed, failing to dutifully swallow her treat, if she held it in her cheek, or especially if any particle of food was allowed to escape from between her lips, the mistress became filled with righteous fury. As this was almost invariably the case, the smacking of the paddle against reddened flesh was to be heard incessantly.

"Bad, bad girl! Greedy floozy! Pig!" she would shriek as she plied the paddle ruthlessly. "Lazy, worthless hussy! Hog! Is this what you want?"

An attendant now positioned herself beside each one of the unfortunate harem-girls, and began to force bonbons unrelentingly into her mouth. These Amazons had set aside their weapons and helmets, and Luke found himself staring at one of them, who looked familiar.

*Is that Janis Joplin?*

The Janis look-alike was administering chocolate to her prisoner with the same robotic movements that characterized all the slaves, himself included. He stared around surreptitiously and noticed Jean Harlow, Marilyn Monroe and Grace Kelly all tending to the carousel-riding brides.

The Discriminatrix continued alternately to paddle and admonish the captives into a docile receptivity to the intrusion of the treats. At last she was satisfied that not one of the moaning, trembling creatures possessed a remaining iota of any refractory impulse.

And so when there was not a single orifice to be found upon the carousel platform that could accommodate her ministrations further, when all mouths were filled to bursting and all was at last perfectly, quiveringly ready, the Discriminatrix stood beside the glowing tube containing the sacrificial victim, and looked at her with devouring eyes. All around her she could hear the soft sobbing, coughing and tinkling of the women, so chastened, so ready to obey her will, and so bountifully stuffed with candy, and she listened to the sound with pleasure. She knew that all, all of them were utterly in her power, all were there to be used, consumed, fed, remade, punished or cherished, just as she chose. Even the little harlot, Evelyn, was at last hers to do with as she pleased, for there was no-one here to stop her. As she mused on these things, the Discriminatrix was filled with a magnificent and lustful ecstasy. These emotions and thoughts of the mistress flooded Luke's mind against his will.

"Today you, my dear, brave wives, offer yourselves to be used by terrible powers, but never forget that you fight against the coming night. As you reach the heights of ecstasy, as you plunge into the depths of agony, remember that I am with you. Your suffering will summon the beast from the depths to feed. Because of your pure and innocent sacrifice, your equally pure and innocent sisters will be spared untold pain and humiliation. I salute you!"

Not one of the consorts replied. But the muffled moaning, gasping and gagging emanating from the group was as music to the ears of the Discriminatrix.

Bette Davis stood with her hands on her hips, surveying her helpless prisoners with a satisfied snigger.

"Many of you must be worried right now, that as a result of this orgy of desserts, you will become a fattie. I'm sorry to say that this is inevitable. You are already damaged goods. That is what brought you here to me. You have no self-control." The Discriminatrix looked around at her wives. One of the wives was choking loudly and Bette stepped closer to smack with her paddle the ample teats that spilled from the captive's vinyl suit. The woman coughed violently at this and unfortunately a glob of chocolate hit the Discriminatrix on the cheek. Bette rounded on her now with her riding crop, beating her so furiously that Luke began to feel queasy. If he had ever been even a little bit turned on by bondage and sadism, he thought, he was cured now. This really wasn't erotic at all.

At last the Discriminatrix tired of inflicting pain on the pathetic girl, called for a towel, and wiped the blood and chocolate from her face.

"Damaged goods, I say, and in need of a firm hand to keep you from falling into error. But I want to reassure you that no matter how unattractive you become, I will not abandon you. Most likely no man will ever want you again, it is true. But you will have no need of men, just as you have no need of food. So long as you have me to care for you, to love you, to reward you and to punish you, you will have a reason to continue. And that is all we need in the afterlife, in the end: a reason to go on."

She raised an arm signaling that the attendants were to force a new round of treats down the women's throats: cream-filled cupcakes, and sugary fruit pies. The ladies could do no more than twitch and squirm in their seats as they gulped, overcome with the apparently endless glut of rich desserts from which they were helpless to escape. The captives stirred involuntarily in their fetters, their ankle bells tinkled, and the music of the bells was now a loud and steady chiming.

But the torment of the twelve lovely consorts had only just begun.

Bette flipped a switch, and the lights went out, all except a single spotlight upon each of the maidens, and the illumination inside the tube where sweet Evelyn still dangled, nude, lacerated and awaiting her fate. Luke could see now that the walls of the upper two thirds of the lofty space were in fact tinted glass that had concealed rows of seats, which were filled with the remainder of the Discriminatrix's harem. All eyes in the theater gazed upon the diabolical carousel at center stage, which was slowly grinding into movement to the accompaniment of tinny, wheezy mechanized music.

The troop of Amazon keepers had strapped themselves to the horses behind the helpless consorts. There were capacious saddlebags secured to the horses' rumps. The carousel music had begun and the platform began slowly to rotate, and the horses to move smoothly, conveying the captives and their keepers up and down along the polished poles. The Amazons reached into the saddlebags and continued to force-feed the wives. Everywhere Luke looked, an entire coconut snowball, Twinkie or cream puff was being shoved into a captive's mouth.

Then Luke noticed that the floor under Evelyn's feet was slowly sinking away. Before this she had just been able to touch it with her toes, but now she was hanging by her shackles in the tube, and though her cries were muffled by her prison, it was plain to see that she was wracked by tormented shrieks. Before long the floor rose up again, bringing with it, as if riding in an elevator, a sandy-haired man in an Edwardian suit and bowler hat. No sooner had Evelyn set eyes upon this gentleman, than her visage became distorted by renewed terror. She knew him, and his arrival filled her with panic and despair.

"Fuck," Luke whispered. "This is so not cool."

With a cruel smile, the man in the bowler hat seized one of Evelyn's tiny feet in each hand

"We've gotta help the poor kid," Buzz remarked.

"Um . . ." Luke replied. He realized that he could move his arms and legs freely. Looking around the room, he couldn't see Bette anywhere. It was odd that she would be missing this, after all her careful preparations. Surely she was watching from a hidden vantage point. Still, her mind-control over him had unaccountably ebbed. "Yeah, come on!"

They had to get the poor girl out of there. Who knew what that man was planning to do to her, but whatever it was, this had to be stopped.

But how? Luke glanced surreptitiously at the Amazon guards standing two on either side of him, and scratched his head. That was when he noticed that his body was changing. Released from the power of the Discriminatrix, he was turning into a zombie again.

The tempo of the mechanistic calliope tune was increasing, as were both the speed of the carousel, and the number of high-calorie snacks that the riders were required to consume. Some of the harem-wives arched and writhed as they rose and fell on their mounts, some contended fruitlessly against their bonds, and others shook with spasms as the cream-filled cakes were stuffed rapidly between their reluctant lips. Sparks of red light gathered around them all, moved up the poles. Within the glass tube, the man in the bowler hat seemed to be in a place of stillness at the center of the vortex. He had swept his victim up in his arms, where she lay limp and lifeless, wrapped only in a gossamer scarf, while his eyes raked over her with implacable hunger. Her eyelids fluttered, and she shrank away from him. He unhooked her fetters from the chain, leaving her hands bound together.

Luke pointed his chin toward the lever by the door that raised and lowered the glass tube. "It's that one," he muttered to Buzz. "Do you think we can get away with it?"

"Not likely," said Buzz, "unless we can get the guards on our side."

The carousel spun ever faster, so that the wooden horses seemed to gallop madly around in circles. The twelve figures strapped to the carven saddles choked and thrashed, the bells clanged, and the robotic melody was deafening. Scarlet bands of energy danced all about the unfortunate captives, passing in waves through them and up the poles along which the mounts plunged madly up and down at an ever greater speed. It was apparent that the agony of the women was being channeled up the poles, and as Luke watched the extraordinary machine, he saw that the energy waves were passing down into the glass tube. There the man in the bowler hat stood, bathed in a red glow like the Devil caught in the act of snatching a sinner to hell, clutching Evelyn while lightning played all about him and passed up his arms and legs. The man was clearly absorbing power from the suffering of the captive women who had been offered to him as fuel, to be consumed in the furnace of his wickedness.

As the carousel spun faster still, the consorts tensed their limbs and bodies into arcs, or writhed wildly against their restraints, desperate to avoid not only the punishing glut of sweets, but also the bruises, abrasions and broken ribs that seemed an inevitable consequence of striking against the brass poles along which their bodies were drawn, up and down, with ever increasing speed and force.

It seemed that the greater the terror and agony of the harem-wives, the more power the sandy-haired man derived from them, for now he was incandescently lit in the red glow. He began to expand to an enormous stature, his shoulders and neck thickened, and his head swelled to a disproportionate size. A broad snout sprouted upon his face, and horns emerged from his forehead. He had become a giant, half man and half bull, hellishly powerful and dark, with a single red eye.

The Minotaur had been summoned.

The carousel continued to pick up speed. The mechanical mounts now pounded like pistons on their brass columns, and the Amazon attendants hung on tight to the captives as cakes whirled in the air, carried off by centrifugal force.

The Minotaur began to fondle the girl in his arms with a rough brutality, like a chef kneading bread or a priest readying his victim for the knife. Luke watched as Evelyn shrieked inaudibly, writhing to escape. She somehow slipped out of the grip of the monster's huge hard hands and, seized in the powerful centrifugal force generated by the carousel, slammed suddenly into the side of the tube. Evelyn whirled around, plastered to the glass. The Minotaur snatched at the girl as she whizzed by.

Meanwhile, flung up and down like sacks of flour, the tormented riders had begun to vomit. Food was hurled through the air in every direction. Strangling on the undigested contents of their stomachs, one by one the girls surrendered to unconsciousness. Pinned within the violent, infernal machine, their heads lolled to one side and the other while the bells clamored on their limply flopping ankles. Had they not already been creatures of ectoplasmic form, Luke supposed, they could surely never survive this brutality. But as the captives fainted, the energy that powered the carousel dissipated, and the mechanism began to slow down.

Luke decided that this was the moment to act. He leaped toward the lever on the wall and pushed it, and instantly the glass tube rose. Seconds later he was on Buzz's back, and in the air.

The Minotaur was sinking out of sight in the center of the carousel, the musical machine whirling around him still. He carried Evelyn over one shoulder like a wet rag.

First a coconut snowball knocked off Luke's hat, then a flying devil dog hit him in the eye. He threw himself instinctively backward and almost fell off of Buzz's back, but he had the presence of mind to imagine himself back in balance and a split second later, he was.

The vulture hurled herself into the space which moments before had been enclosed by the glass tube. They plunged down into the pit, and swooped out through what appeared to be an elevator door, and into a corridor, just as the Minotaur was turning a corner up ahead.

Luke leapt off the condor's back. There was no room here for her to fly, so he held up his arm and she landed on it. He saw that the arm had shriveled and turned green. Bette's control over his appearance had completely vanished.

*At least I have my dick back.* But how useful was it going to be to a rotting zombie?

He took off down the corridor, turned the corner and pushed his way through a pair of double doors into what looked like a hospital room. The woozy plonking tune of the carousel filtered down from above as Bette Davis, dressed as a nurse, bent over the swooning Evelyn. Bette looked quickly up.

"He went that way!" the Discriminatrix cried, gesturing urgently toward the open doorway on the opposite wall.

Luke hesitated. The girl who lay sprawled over the hospital bed lifted her head.

"No!" she cried weakly. Bette smacked her hand over Evelyn's mouth.

"Hurry!" she hissed, fixing her gigantic blue eyes on Luke's. He fought the urge to turn toward the door.

*"Go to hell, bitch!"* screeched Buzz, launching herself at the Discriminatrix. Luke was jerked off balance as she lunged straight at Bette's face with her hooked, razor-sharp beak.

The transformation was nearly instantaneous. Bette flung up her arm and a moment later, the Minotaur reared enormously where she had been. He was more animal than man, with a huge hairy chest, a tufted tail and gigantic hooves at the ends of his bovine legs. The beast bellowed and swung an enormous fist at the condor. Buzz pumped her wings to avoid the blow, which unfortunately caught Luke on the side of the skull. A queer sensation, exactly like his head was a watermelon that had just been struck by a sledgehammer, overcame him as he dropped to the floor, dragging Buzz down with him.

The Minotaur combined his two hands into a massive ball and hacked down at Buzz, striking her breast where the left wing joined it. Buzz's body was smashed down onto Luke's chest. The monster lifted the club of his double fist again to deliver a crippling blow to the stunned vulture. Just then a white-and-red medical tin hit him between the eyes, exploded open, scattering cotton balls in all directions. Evelyn, who had recovered consciousness enough to rise and make her way around behind the cabinet that stood beside the sickbed, was pelting him with any object she could lay her hands on.

Luke's head injury was painful, but less so that one might imagine. The brain itself feels little physical discomfort. He closed his eyes for just a moment and envisaged his skull whole again. Nothing much seemed to happen, but he could think more clearly now. He saw the Minotaur lurching toward Evelyn, who held a glass canister filled with long cotton swabs above her head in her raw-wristed, still-manacled hands. The Minotaur was both enraged and inflamed, he was naked and hairy and sported an erect phallus of Brobdingnagian proportions. He looked like a devilish creature from the walls of a secret garden in Pompeii, with little Evelyn as the nymph about to be ravished in the next frame. One thing was apparent to Luke: if he let that happen, the gigantic beast would surely rend her limb from limb.

Luke and Buzz lunged together at the monster, and Luke leapt up high like an acrobat, landed on the thick shoulders, and clapped his hands over the Minotaur's eye, while Buzz sank her beak into his wide, damp nose. Blood spurted from the nostrils, and the Minotaur tossed his head, hurling Buzz up into the air. She narrowly missed being gored by one of the beast's long, sharp horns. Luke meanwhile had managed to avoid being thrown off. Buzz hung in the air for a moment, then she stooped, hawk-like, to slash at the Minotaur with her cruel beak.

A fountain of gore erupted, but the creature somehow got its hands around Buzz's neck. Luke watched as the thing twisted her head off in a single motion. The vulture's body dropped to the floor, and her head bounced after it, while the collar that had bound her to him jangled on his wrist, empty.

"Buzz!" Luke screamed.

*April 3, 1994* –Brooklyn, NY

*Room with art in it. Rich white men. Photographs of deformed women–one legless, one thin and ugly.*

*A picture of someone has another piece of paper taped over it. It says* NO HISTORY.

*Idea for comic strip about my own death:* Woman's Body Found.

*A mentally disabled child wants to help by fanning her while the autopsy is going on, as if to wake her up. Actually he's driving the doctors crazy on purpose.*

*Doctor's verbal description of the woman's injuries makes it clear that she is dead.*

*Police come to a wealthy house.*

*The "idiot" child is actually clever– he continues pretending that a murder has been committed, and that he's trying to cover it up. All the family members are flustered.*

*Cops are amused–let the kid go.*

*Violet knots spiral macramé button covers . . . ?*

Rosetta frowned at the scrawls in her journal. She could barely decipher the words, jotted in the dark while half asleep. Who was Violet? Anyway, it was just another weird death dream.

Eager to get into the studio and work, Rosetta closed her journal.

Some hours later, she and Antoine were striding through the Brooklyn Botanic Gardens. Rosetta was wearing an antique slip of black satin, high laced-up black boots, black stockings that were really a network of runs and holes, and a slightly unraveled thrift store cardigan of white cashmere, densely embroidered with artificial pearls.

The weather had cleared up just in time for the outing, and cottony clouds billowed swiftly across the blue. Rosetta raced past the conservatory, while Antoine sprinted lightly ahead, then trotted back. Rosetta remembered being ten, complaining about how slow grownups were. Still, for a grownup, she thought she moved pretty fast.

She was supposed to meet Jessie at the pagoda on the pond, and she was a few minutes late. Still Rosetta didn't want to miss a single petal of the lovely Spring blossoms. As she speed-walked, she gazed from side to side to take in the yellow and white clouds of narcissus that bravely peeked up between the leftover patches of snow. Oblivious to a group of tourists who had paused to snap photos of the flowering magnolias, and were pleased to incorporate her statuesque form into their compositions, she craned her neck hoping to glimpse the first of the lilacs shimmering off to the left. They would not be blooming yet, but she peered all the same.

When they entered the Japanese Garden, Jessie was with a woman Rosetta had never met before. Alice and Kimberly ran and played up and down the paths while the women talked.

" . . . Liam saw him on Wednesday, but then he disappeared again," the woman was saying to Jessie in a low voice. When Rosetta approached, she fell silent.

Jessie introduced her willowy companion, whose short black hair was accented in a loud fuchsia, as Violet Ball. She was married to Fester Finkle, Jessie said, formerly the bass player in *The Peter Principle,* Jessie's soon-to-be-ex-husband's band. Violet and Fester, Jessie explained, had recently moved back to New York to start a new musical project.

"That's so fantastic," Rosetta said with a welcoming smile. "Nice to meet you."

Jessie looked at Violet, and Violet turned to Rosetta. "I wish I could say I was enjoying New York, but things have just been crazy since we got here," she said with a big sigh. She was dressed à la 80's redux, wearing a long black tee shirt dress that had been cut to ribbons, then reassembled using pink plastic safety pins, over a fully armored purple bra, spangled carnation leggings and spike-heeled boots.

The children found Violet fascinating. Rosetta could see them, over there next to the dwarf cherry tree, the one that always bloomed before the others. The first pale petals already speckled the dark wet branches. Nearby Antoine and Alice stood staring at Violet and talking.

"Just crazy!" Violet looked back at Jessie meaningfully.

"You heard about Luke Mandrake, of course," Jessie began.

Rosetta was reminded of the unaccountable way Luke had been haunting her dreams, and began to feel rather queasy. "I . . . no, what happened?" she replied. "I haven't been following the news the past couple of days."

"He's been missing for almost a week," Jessie confided, smoothing back the tendrils of red hair that had escaped from under her flamboyant hat bedecked with netting, faux gems and silk flowers. "It was being kept hush-hush, but now that Shambala has canceled out of playing Lollapalooza, everyone knows."

"Oh my god," Rosetta said. She was feeling decidedly nauseous.

"Let's not talk about this here," Violet said. She looked a bit like an armadillo, hugging her little quilted bolero jacket around herself to keep out the chilly breeze as she peered around at the crowd of week-end stroller-pushers. She exited the observation deck and proceeded along the path encircling the lake. Jessie and Rosetta followed, with Antoine, Kim and Alice laughingly running back and forth ahead. "Charity Ball is her stepsister," Jessie whispered.

"We're all worried sick about him," Violet went on in a confidential tone. "Charity hired a private investigator and everything."

"I'm so sorry to hear about your trouble," said Rosetta to Violet. "I hope they find him soon, safe and sound."

As they strolled, Rosetta's eyes hungrily sought out the crocuses that nodded along the track, and noted with satisfaction the swollen tips of twigs. After the long, unusually bitter winter, Rosetta had come to the urban garden to fill a physical need for proof that Spring was on its way. She stopped to snap a few photos of the bursting pink buds, carefully framing the dark pattern of the branches against a backdrop of opalesque cloud.

When Rosetta caught up to the others, she considered mentioning her recent dreams, but she was reluctant to bring them up to Violet Ball. The poor girl had enough to worry her, without adding macabre visions to fuel her imagination.

They wandered the upper paths to look at the artificial waterfall, the miniature temple. The subject of Violet's missing brother-in-law was not brought up again.

"Should we walk around to the cherry esplanade?" Jessie asked.

"Sounds great," Violet responded.

"There should be some bulbs blooming up in the Osborne Garden," Rosetta offered.

"Rosetta's in a band, you know," Jessie said to Violet.

"What do you play?" Violet asked.

"Singer-songwriter," she replied shyly. She suddenly felt embarrassed, ambivalent; she refrained from telling her new acquaintance any details about the project. "How about you?" she asked.

"Keys," said the resplendent girl. "And vocals, of course." Violet appeared so confident, so unfettered. "It's all about improvisation, really."

*Didn't I used to be daring and free, like her?*

"What's it called, your band?"

"We haven't decided yet. I'm leaning toward *Two Left Ears*."

"Cool!" said Rosetta.

She had almost forgotten how it felt, to really be herself onstage. How did she get to this point? How was it that she had somehow lost herself along the way?

*       *       *

Jean-Baptiste was having difficulty containing his frustration. What was the problem? Oh, please. She knew very well.

She had married a pompous, controlling, ungenerous fellow—ah, that was it!

"Open your eyes, Rosetta!" he pleaded silently. "You miss performing on your own terms, being able to express yourself freely. You long for the excitement of extemporizing in front of an audience. If you pine for your lost self, it's because you've betrayed yourself, and your art, for love."

How easily Jean-Baptiste could have answered Rosetta's questions about her life, if only she would remember to ask him.

In vain Jean-Baptiste made note of the incidents, tallied the times when Delgado bullied Rosetta in subtle and not-so-subtle ways. In vain did he urge her on in his mind, to take a firmer stand, to be more independent. Rosetta did not take action. She did not even admit to herself that she was permitting it to happen. She would speak up sometimes about specific grievances, but when her husband ignored her, she backed down. Each time he treated her as insignificant she swallowed her hurt, and forgave, and accommodated.

A man might count himself fortunate, to have married a kind-hearted and beautiful woman. Rosetta was more than that: she was passionate, joyous, intelligent, inspired. And she loved him! Yet Delgado could not appreciate what he had, could not allow himself to unbend.

And so naturally, her forgiveness fell upon him like a reproach.

*Send me your churlish husbands, and I will school them,* Jean-Baptiste grumbled. Hundreds of years had passed since he wrote those words. The crowned heads of Europe had applauded them then. How was it that so little had changed?

178

Doug Clinquant stared sadly into the toilet bowl at the sunken condom. It appeared to have ruptured during its short journey in and out of his anus. He'd failed to remove the object manually, and the music industry giant guessed that he'd torn the condom in the attempt. Clinquant had been disgusted at having to push the drugs out the conventional way, had done his best to avoid dropping any actual turds, but this proved to be beyond his skill. Now that he'd succeeded in excreting his stash into the bowl, the rubber was slowly filling with water.

The joints contained therein were probably already wet, and would no doubt stink of poop. The stash was double-wrapped in sealed ziploc bags, it was true, but those things were notoriously leaky. Anyway the bags would have to be washed now, and where was Doug going to perform that criminal act? At the sink, in the public restroom at the airport? Furthermore, he had forgotten to bring rubber gloves.

Some folks might make the best of it, might try and fish the stuff out of the shitter bare-handed and salvage it, wrap it up in toilet paper and shove it into a pocket or bag. Doug was not one of those sad, desperate people. There was plenty of pot in the world. He could let it go.

Anyway he had a backup plan. He had had his assistant prepare some powdered hash and bud, and pack the mixture into capsules which were hidden among the supplements in a vitamin bottle in his suitcase. There wasn't much, but he could scrape together a couple of doobies, he figured. Not that it was the ideal consistency for rolling. Still, he extracted the bottle from his small suitcase, which he had brought with him into the stall. He sat down on the commode and got to work. He would make do.

As Clinquant sorted through the capsules, trying to identity the ones with weed in them, his mind flew back to the dream that had come to him while he napped aboard the early morning flight from Los Angeles.

He'd seen the stars gather together into an array like an army preparing for battle. They had marched toward him, coming closer and closer. Two chatoyant lights, one blue and one green, had turned out to be the eyes of a black cat that led the forward guard. This creature had jumped into his lap, and he'd woken up with a start.

But there was something else that had happened in the dream . . . It was difficult to be sure of the order of the events, but as the armada of stars had approached, he'd understood that they were marching to the aid of a great kingdom. And he knew that he was the grand vizier, whose wisdom and counsel were required to ensure victory. He'd read about it in the newspapers: how the prince had died, had sacrificed himself in battle, securing the victory. The prince had perished from a gunshot to the head.

When he read the reports, he'd felt a dark pride in the trick he'd played to salvage the reputation of the prince, and of the entire royal family. For the prince hadn't really been killed in battle at all. He'd died ignominiously, falling down the stairs of the castle tower in a drunken stupor. But the family had hushed it up, knowing that if the army found out, morale would plummet, and the war would be lost. And so he, Doug Clinquant, had fabricated a story, a romantic tragedy of the prince's duel with an officer from the other side. He'd claimed to have acted as the royal heir's second in this secret meeting. In reality he had called out the commanding officer of the enemy forces and himself impersonated the prince, shooting and mortally wounding the other man. And then, instead of taking credit for the deed, he'd put a bullet through the head of the Prince's corpse, poor sot, as a proof of his Lord's valor, and his Pyrrhic triumph.

There had been a woman at the duel, a gorgeous redhead with

a green cloak, carrying a black cat on her shoulder. She had urged him on, handing him a silver bullet that was sure to bring victory, she said. But Doug had refused to use the magic bullet against his adversary, not wanting to dishonor himself by resorting to sorcery. Rather than cheating, he had won by his own skill and daring. The silver bullet was instead lodged in the brain of the late drunken prince, a fellow who, now that Clinquant thought of it, had looked quite a lot like Luke Mandrake.

When he rang the doorbell at Luke's Riverwood house, nobody answered. But Doug Clinquant hadn't climbed to the lofty position he occupied in the industry due to a lack of persistence. He was, in all things related to partying, whether booze, coke, weed or the ladies, indefatigable, but when it came to getting to the bottom of things, which is to say, finding and following and guiding and guarding the big money acts, Doug was relentless.

After ringing the bell every ten seconds for five minutes, he switched to using a different finger.

When Liam finally opened the door, still rubbing his hair with a towel, he was not expecting to see the Vice President of Development for Ded Leper Records standing on the doorstep.

"Oh! Doug!" he chirped, not moving from the doorway as he stared at the record exec with fearful, doe-like eyes.

"Doctor Love is here," Clinquant purred as he moved toward the opening. "Well, Liam? Aren't you going to invite me in?"

"Uh, uh, uh," Liam stammered, "Are you luh, looking for Luh, Luke?

"No, I'm looking for Santa Claus," Clinquant replied with a smile, but his eyes glittered sharply when he stared into Liam's. The green-haired retainer stepped back instinctively, and Doug sauntered into Luke and Charity's place with casual bonhomie.

Doug didn't look like a big money man, of course. His uniform consisted of an unbuttoned Hawaiian shirt over nankeen cargo pants worn low on the hip, and Birkenstocks. He tended his long golden dreds, which he allowed to swing free, with care. At home in Santa Monica, Doug nearly always had a half-clad sylph at his side bearing a knapsack pharmacopoeia. But today Doctor Love was wearing a goose-down jacket and an alpaca hat with ear flaps and pom-poms. He had dressed for the arctic chill of a Portland Spring.

A languid manner and cheerily dismissive tone were the Doctor Love trademarks. Liam detected a profound change in the record executive. On the surface Doug was as breezy as always, but there was a strange tenseness to him, a pent-up energy, and now, a sudden directness that was unexpected.

"Bill tells me that Luke was seen around here," Doug began, his chin pointed at Liam. "And, well, I need to speak with him. It's a matter of the utmost importance to his future with Ded Leper, do you understand me, Liam?"

"Sure, Doug, I get what you're saying, but, L-L-Luke–" Doug raised his eyebrows as Liam stumbled along. "Luke is . . . unavailable at the moment."

Doug heaved a sigh. "Liam, Liam, Liam," he shook his head sadly. "I love you man." Clinquant sat down heavily on a rococo divan covered in silk damask, and bounced several times as though to test the springs. Then he removed a doobie from his shirt pocket, and lit it.

"Look at you," he mused fondly between puffs. "Such a loyal friend. That's the thing about you I always loved. You'll do anything for a friend. I wish I had a buddy like you, Liam. I really do." He handed the joint to Liam. Liam swallowed and nodded before taking a hit. But the joint had gone out.

"That's why it hurts my heart to see you doing this. I know you're just trying to help out your friend, but Liam, Luke . . . " and he leaned forward and spoke in a whisper, "Luke is totally fucking up right now, guy. He needs help, yeah, but not," Doug's hand circled and made figure eights in a window-washing gesture, "not *that* kind of help."

"You-you want a beer, Doug?" Liam offered, although it was barely ten AM.

"Sure."

Before long Doug had a Beck's dark in one hand and the lit joint in the other. "Liam, you and I know Luke pretty well, don't we?" he resumed pleasantly. "I mean, of everybody he knows, how many people can he *really* talk to? These days, it's you and me, Buddy, you and me. We're the ones who have his best interests at heart, don't you think?

"Sure, Doug. Of course," Liam replied.

"So what am I supposed to think when he sends me this?" Doug said in an aggrieved tone, as he reached into his pocket and pulled out a small folio. From this he removed several pages of notebook paper, closely written in red ink, and handed them to Liam.

It was Luke's left-handed scrawl. Liam read it all, while Doug watched. In these pages, Luke announced that he was quitting the music business, immediately and for good. And he explained at great length why he was doing so, and what he expected Ded Leper to do in response.

Doug took the letter back out of Liam's hands and looked at it ruefully for a moment before returning it to the folio. "I just haven't gotten any pleasure from playing music in a long time," he quoted in a pitch-perfect imitation of Luke's nasal speaking voice, only just a hair more whiny. "Oh my god!" He tossed the folio on the coffee table and put his face in his hands. Liam watched him in horror as Clinquant's fingers suddenly writhed among the dreds like earthworms trying to burrow home, then pulled frantically at the locks.

"Do . . . you . . . know . . ." he began slowly, scraping hard up and down on his scalp with his nails with each word, "how much *money* we are going to lose, if Luke doesn't record the next two albums he's contracted with us?" Clinquant looked up at Liam and the stress rose into his voice, pushing it half an octave higher. "Do you have any idea how *much* money, how many hundreds of thousands of dollars, Ded Leper has already put into marketing for *Open Womb*? And we," he gave an impatient cough, and wheezed on, "we were counting on Lollapalooza, we were *counting* on Paris."

Clinquant took a long pull on the bottle of Beck's. He appeared distracted. "For two years now, all we've gotten from Luke is one publicity disaster after another. Sales have gone through the floor, Liam. The floor!"

Liam was gazing at Doug the way a man looks at a tidal wave that's towering over his head, and is about to break.

"And now this, this ridiculous, self-pitying breakup letter." Doug flapped his hand tiredly toward the missive in its pouch. "I– Christ, I *made* Shambala. I *made* Luke Mandrake. And now this. What the hell am I supposed to do, Liam?"

Doug stood up and began pacing back and forth. Then he stopped, facing Liam, threw his arms out wide, and tossed his dredlocked head like a crucified man.

"You have to talk to him, Liam. You have to get him to meet with me on this. Bill is chewing glass right now. And you know how he gets." Doug plunked back down on the divan. "I'm afraid even to go back there, unless we can find a way to fix this!"

Liam finally spoke.

"I–I have no way of getting in touch with him right now, is the thing–"

"Well, *find* a way," Doug pleaded, authoritatively, but with a note of panic bleeding into his voice. Liam shut his mouth, and took a swig of beer. Doug also took a swig.

"Listen, Liam," Clinquant spoke more quietly now. "I'm sorry, bro, I'm sorry to put you in the middle of this. You're not the one who created this mess, I know that. It's just that, if we don't fix it, Bill's made up his mind that he's going to sue. And that means, if I know anything about Luke's finances at this point, that all this," Doug indicated the house and furniture with a game-show-host wave, "goes, *poof*."

"Poof?" Liam repeated.

"*Poof*, like it never existed, Liam. Because, you know, Luke spent so much on court costs in his custody battle with the state, that without better album sales, he's gonna be broke. This house, this whole life of yours, is teetering on the brink."

Liam's mind was racing. "Charity–" he managed to get out, but Doug cut him off.

"Charity is not taking our calls at the moment," he complained as he relit the joint. Liam recognized the wounded puppy-dog look as a stock character of Clinquant's. The industry man sucked in smoke.

"Which is why I've come to you. Fuck it all!" Doug cursed. There was a run up one side of the doobie and it was gushing papery smoke. The man was helpless without his pharmacist, and he shrugged and looked at Liam ruefully as if to say, *You caught me, my embarrassing secret is out, for as you see I cannot roll a smokable joint.*

"I'll roll another," Liam stood up and made his way, gracefully swaying on his spaghetti leg, to the humidor where Luke kept his choicest bud. He selected some potent Hawaiian, settled himself on an ottoman across from Clinquant, and began to clip the sweet-smelling green nuggets into tiny bits with a delicate pair of scissors.

What would Charity want him to do? Liam was cudgeling his brain for an answer. *Luke is definitely not coming back. Doug is going to have to find out about it sooner or later.* It was starting to look like disaster was inevitable. Was there a way out?

And if he made the wrong choice now, would Charity ever forgive him?

Liam knew he had to pull himself together, do some damage control, before everything went into a tailspin. He lifted his head and favored Doug with a penetrating stare.

"What is it Buddy?" Doug said gently. "Is there something you want to tell Doctor Love?" Liam looked back down at his scissors. "You know me, Liam," he went on, "I'm the good guy here. I'm the one who can make everything all right. For Luke, for Charity and the kids. Even for you, Liam."

Liam was licking the paper now and after a couple more snips he held in his hands the perfect marijuana cigarette: firm and evenly packed, well-proportioned, tapered at the ends. Liam had learned how to roll from his Gramps, a notorious impresario who during the fifties had held the Detroit music scene in a powerful grip.

"Liam. Where's Luke?" Doug asked.

Liam pointed with his eyes toward the upper storeys.

"He's here?" Doug was on his feet already.

"I'll take you to him. But . . . smoke this first. You'll need it."

"You're still just a hyena, etc. . . ." howls the demon, who'd crowned me with such pretty poppies. "The prize is death, you with your insatiability, your selfishness and all the mortal sins!"

Ah, I can't take it any more : Come on, Satan darling, I'm begging you, a less surly stare ! And while you're waiting for a last few pathetic little squirms, since you appreciate a writer lacking any descriptive or expository skills, how 'bout if I rip out a few loathsome pages for ya from my scratch pad of the damned.

*A Season in Hell*
*Arthur Rimbaud*

*Eternity* – The Labyrinth, Famebeau

The Minotaur bellowed, spewing blood that spattered on the moss-green hospital-room walls. Luke clung to the horns, kicking out wildly at the monster's face. The half-blinded beast put its enormous hands around Luke's head, pulled him off itself, and slammed him to the ground. It raised an enormous foot to crush him.

Just then a sound that had been gradually growing all around them squalled forth so loudly that the monster paused, confused, to listen. He hesitated long enough to allow Luke to scramble out from under his upraised hoof.

The wheezing repetitive nickelodeon music of the carousel had at some point given way to something more cacophonous, less predictable. Luke looked around and the room was crowded with Amazons who, helmets removed, were all familiar to him. Janis was there, banging on a keyboard and scatting an intertwining improvisation with Josephine Baker and Billie Holliday. Others that he couldn't name played instruments, recited poetry or danced wildly. Each one of the women appeared to be making it all up as she went along. Nothing seem to go together, yet there was a weird harmony to it.

There was a distinctly different energy around them than there had been minutes ago. The conviction of inevitable doom that had been imposed upon them by the Minotaur's hideous strength, the inescapable force of his brutality, had ebbed. Bit by bit the brute's dominance was being supplanted by a sense of possibility.

The music was mounting and now the Minotaur blinked, blood running down his nose and dripping on the floor, then shook his head and turned toward Evelyn where she cowered in the corner, still clutching the jar of swabs. The monster lunged at her, she hurled the jar and the swabs exploded in all directions.

Luke had been weaponless but now, to his astonishment, Judy

Garland thrust an electric guitar into his hands. He began to play fierce and triumphant riffs, altogether new, a series of notes that rippled through the room like a swirl of bees, and cracked at the end like a whip.

But the beast had already slung Evelyn over his shoulder. All Luke could see of her now was the heart shape of her fanny above the Minotaur's arm, where it gripped her around the back of the knees. He could hear her shrieks emerging from behind the creature's broad back as, with a prodigious leap, the Minotaur launched himself across the space. He made it clear to the door, scattering the celebrity Amazons who were crowded there.

The monster made a wild grab and managed to get hold of one of them, swinging her around by the arm to fend off the rest, while he kicked the door down with one blow of his hoof. He vanished through it with his two hostages.

The music had fallen to silence. The screams of the two kidnapped women continued for some seconds, then stopped as suddenly as if their windpipes had been crushed. Luke ran to the doorway and looked through. On the other side was a long corridor with doors leading off it every ten feet or so. The Minotaur was nowhere to be seen.

Luke turned back to the scene of carnage with a heavy sigh. The vulture's body lay on the floor in a pool of blood, wings askew, her head some distance away.

"Buzz!" he sobbed, falling to his knees. Tears poured down his cheeks. The Minotaur had actually killed her. Now he would never know her real name.

"Don't be so forlorn, my boy," said a soft voice behind him.

Luke looked up at the tall Amazon with long blond hair.

"Oscar Wilde!"

"At your service, Luke," the poet said with a little bow.

"What—what happened?"

"We followed you into the prism room, and using the device, we managed to regain our old forms," said River Phoenix, who had just wandered over, following by Chaplin and O'Neill.

"While the Discriminatrix was distracted by her ceremony," Chaplin added, "we were able to learn how to disrupt her power source. That's why all her slaves were suddenly released from mind-control."

"The Amazon guards were easily persuaded to join us," Gene went on, "Boadicea and Joan of Arc are guarding the door to the prism room right now."

"You *do* know that Bette Davis is also the Minotaur, right?" Luke wondered.

"What?" said Oscar. "I thought it was Thaw who was the monster."

"Thaw is the man in the Bowler hat?" Luke replied.

"Harry Thaw," said Chaplin, "was a very rich man, and cruel–a murderer. Here in Famebeau he is a predator who succeeds in continuing his existence by sucking out the life force of other, more celebrated souls. Sometimes he steals their very faces and forms. He is wily and without remorse."

"And, he was Evelyn's husband," Gene put in. "Still obsessed with her, it looks like."

"Evelyn Nesbit was the first supermodel," Wilde supplied. "Gibson girl. An icon of fashion."

"Poor girl," Luke shook his head. "She sure married the wrong guy."

"I think we had better go and secure the prism room as soon as possible," Chaplin proposed. "That monster is still out there."

"This way," said O'Neill, beckoning them back out to the long hall with all the doors.

"Wait!" cried Luke, picking up Buzz's head. He then tucked the body under his arm, and ran after the others, still carrying the guitar slung over his back.

"We have him on the run," Chaplin shouted back at Luke as they dashed down one corridor, and then the next, after O'Neill. "The music back there frightened him a good deal."

They made another right hand turn, down a long flight of stairs, and out into another tunnel. All the corridors in this underground labyrinth looked alike to Luke. He had no idea where he was.

*I hope Gene knows where he's going.* Luke increased his speed and caught up to Chaplin.

"Why is improvisational music so frightening to the Minotaur?" he asked.

"Because he can only triumph through fear. Without it, his power melts away. And when one is creating, extemporizing, one cannot possibly be afraid."

"I can see that," Luke answered thoughtfully.

"Also, because panic works through expectation, through the prediction of harm. Destroy the prediction by reinventing every moment afresh, and the mechanism of self-fulfilling trauma can be interrupted," Chaplin added.

"So the Minotaur is the manifestation of trauma," Luke said, with a flash of insight.

Chaplin never had the opportunity to reply, because they had arrived at the white metal panel that was the entrance to the prism room. It was splattered with gore. The Warrior Queen was seated on the floor holding Saint Joan, who rested her head in Boadicea's lap. The Queen was using a wad of fabric torn from her mantle to try and staunch the gore that gushed from the empty socket of Joan's right arm.

"The Minotaur knows the password," she was saying to Gene. "He took Joan's arm in there with him, and now he seems to have sealed the door from the inside."

"Where are Countess Lovelace and Madame Curie?" Oscar asked.

"Inside the control room."

"Shit!" Phoenix said. "What'll we do? He'll find a way to turn the juice back on if we don't get in there and stop him!"

O'Neill pounded on the white door.

"All men are scum!" Luke shouted.

"Oh my. Nothing happened," Wilde observed. "He must have changed the password."

"We have to get Joan's arm back," Boadicea snapped, "she's suffering horribly!"

"He feeds on the suffering," Luke pointed out. "Don't you people have any pain meds here?"

"The Discriminatrix outlawed them," O'Neill replied.

"Of course she did," said Luke.

"Well, if we can't get in there," Chaplin announced, "we will have to wait."

"Fuck that," Boadicea retorted. "You stay here with Joan, I'm going to get in there and destroy that thing. There's got to be a way."

In his mind, Luke was retracing the places he'd already been during that long and eventful day. The Grinder. The Prism. The Carousel. They all seemed to have something in common.

"I think . . . there is a way in," he said slowly. Everyone looked at him.

"Well?" said Oscar.

Luke suddenly felt terribly embarrassed. After all, who was he to make assertions about this bizarre place, he who had only arrived a day ago?

"Buh, I don't know. Never mind," he said.

"No, please," Boadicea was staring at him intently. "You see that we have nothing more to go on. What is your idea?"

"Well . . ." Luke began, "what if the grinder was, like, feeding the prism with energy? What if they were actually stacked, one above the other? I mean, the energy from the grinder has to go somewhere."

"Impossible!" said Oscar. "The grinder obviously goes down hundreds, maybe thousands of feet into the core of the earth."

"So it seems," Luke said thoughtfully. "And yet . . ."

"And yet, time and space are flexible here," Chaplin observed.

"Wow," said River. "So it's all interconnected."

O'Neill sighed. "This is nonsense," he asserted firmly. "Even if the grinder led directly into the prism, what would that accomplish? Anyone who goes through it is ground up into ectoplasmic dust. No," the writer said, shaking his head. "We can't get in that way."

"Not me," Luke said, "I mean, I could. I bet I could get in."

Wilde shot Luke a pitying look.

"No way," Phoenix protested.

"Yup. Though the grinder," Luke said.

"But this is too dangerous," Chaplin protested.

"Luke, no! We need your music to help us defeat him, man!" River cried.

"I will go!" Boadicea cut through the others with her ringing proclamation. There was silence and all eyes turned to her.

"I . . . will go . . . through the grinder!" Boadicea said, panting with rage. She pointed to the sky. "For too long, that sadistic demon from hell has delighted in our suffering. For too long, that creature has preyed upon us, making a mockery and a commodity of the renown that we, some of us, bought with our very lives! And today, he has taken our sweet Evelyn, and Madame de la Pompadour, Madame Curie and Countess Lovelace, and . . . and the arm of my darling Jeanne!" The Queen rose to her feet, wiping her eyes savagely. "If there is any possibility that by going into the grinder I will be able to slice that Minotaur's balls off," she brandished her sword, "and wear them as a necklace, I will go into the vortex, and if need be, I will go alone. Come what may, it is better than a life of slavery and torment!"

The others all applauded at the end of Boadicea's speech. Chaplin was starting to speak when Luke approached Boadicea and looked directly into her eyes.

"No," said Luke. "No, your majesty. Though you are very courageous, the vortex would destroy you. Only I should go."

The circular hole was thirty feet across and seemed to plunge into infinity. Looking down into it, Luke wondered if he had done right to trust his instincts, and the whispered words of the goddess, so implicitly. Could he really survive the journey intact? Not that you could call being a zombie intact, not exactly.

Oscar had offered to conduct him here, and Phoenix had come along, as had Boadicea. Now the three of them were arguing.

"He can't do this! We have to talk him out of it," River insisted.

"Coward! We should all go together," Boadicea yelled.

"He knows what he's doing," Wilde repeated. "He's been in the grinder before, and survived. Let him try."

"Okay you guys," Luke interrupted. "When I get into the prism room–"

"*If* you do," River put in.

"–I'll open up the door." Luke looked over at the Queen. "Please don't follow me into the grinder. I need you all to go straight back to the Prism room and stand by."

"At least let us guard the condor's corpse for you," Wilde suggested.

"No thanks," Luke said. "She's coming with me." He turned, adjusted the guitar that still hung behind him, tightened his grip on the vulture's body. The head bulged in his pocket, and his jeans were stiff with blood. He stared down into the pit, took a deep breath, and plunged in.

As he fell Luke felt a spasm of self-pity. *Maybe this is it, and I'm about to disintegrate.* If he could just get back into the prism! He was sure it was the only way to de-zombify himself, to remake Buzz. To bring back the nameless goddess.

He needed to become his true self. Failing that, he didn't care what happened.

He was falling slowly into the whirlpool of light, reluctant to lose control completely. As the grinder closed in around him, he felt the same tingling sensation. He thrust a hand into the whirling stream and watched the laser-like particles strike it, and pass through it. The grinder did not seem to be destroying it, in fact, the hand seemed to be growing less zombie-like. He let himself slip down into the funnel. Light blanked his eyes, and his ears were filled with whispering, humming and whistling sounds.

And then with a thud, followed by a second, smaller thud, he landed. He was inside the pyramid chamber, directly below the prism.

Before him hunched the Minotaur, bowed over the supine form of one of the captured girls. He was emitting a steady, repeated grunting while the girl whimpered listlessly.

Luke realized that he was naked, no pants, no pockets, no– he looked around. The second thud had been the condor's head landing on the rubbery floor under the prism.

Buzz was still dead. Luke's guitar was gone. Here inside the prism, he was once more a winged angel, but his wings were virtually useless in the enclosed space.

He was desperate to attempt to revive Buzz. Perhaps the equipment in the control room would be of use. He also wouldn't mind figuring out how to retain this angelic form outside the field of the prism. If he could just cast off the zombification for good!

But first, he had to fight the Minotaur.

The monster had Evelyn in his grip, and had been steadily beating the girl with what appeared to be a woman's severed arm. Suddenly he tossed the bludgeon aside and, seizing Evelyn's arm, ripped it too out of the socket. Blood spurted like a fountain as Evelyn screamed horribly. The Minotaur stared at the arm for a moment in surprise. Luke watched in horror as the bull-headed creature pressed the shoulder of the avulsed limb back onto the socket. And in seconds, the arm had grown back.

Evelyn's screaming continued. The brute was torturing her in the most inhuman way, and yet she could not die.

Luke knew it was hopeless to try and take this creature on unarmed. He had to get out of there, get help.

Luckily the beast was distracted by his prey, and Luke managed to slip out of the door. He realized as he did so that he was still carrying Buzz's body. He had left the head inside.

Then he stared around the control room at an alarming scene.

It looked like a charnel house, where body parts were displayed by category. Three heads in a row on the console. A pile of legs in one corner, arms in another. And everywhere the warm, sticky, dripping, oozing, pooling blood.

And the sounds were infinitely horrifying. Evelyn's muffled shrieks could just barely be heard, emanating from inside the pyramid chamber. But a split second later a tinny version of her agonized cries cut in and out on the monitor in the control room. The obscene grunting and heavy breathing of the Minotaur was also picked up, close and loud, on the console.

The video image was askew, so that only Evelyn's hand and head were visible, where she lay on the floor. Her eyes stared blankly as she shuddered and twitched, and her mouth was open. Luke couldn't tell what the monster was doing to the poor girl, but whatever it was, she definitely wasn't enjoying it.

Luke felt a terrible sense of dread. There was no stopping this monster! And the blood-soaked machinery would surely be useless now, destroyed! He dropped his head in his hands in despair.

That's when he noticed that they were still his old hands. He had not turned back into a zombie when he left the prism.

He could just walk out of this hell-hole right now. Just leave and never come back. Stay an angel.

Find an angel to love.

Evelyn's thin screams tore into his guts, and they roiled. His stomach turned and wrenched at the endless scenes of violence here in this hell, here on the Island of the Damned.

But even if he knew how to unlock the door, how could he just walk out? Could he simply tell everyone who was out there waiting for him, that he had changed his mind about destroying the monster, that he was just was going to fly away now on his pretty new wings?

If only he could. But there was no way out of it. He had to face that demon in there, had to find a way to neutralize it.

*Think, Luke. Why does the Minotaur tear people's limbs off? Why has the monster placed all these body parts in separate piles? Maybe that's how he's keeping his victims prisoner, immobilizing them. Maybe he's keeping the body parts away from each other, so they don't rejoin!*

Luke got to work with haste, matching a head, a pretty young thing with blond hair and cherub cheeks, to a torso. As soon as the head was attached a scream started from the lips.

"Shh!" Luke warned, placing a finger on her lips. She stared at him in surprise. A nude angel was the last thing she'd expected to awaken to. He gestured warningly toward the prism, and she nodded.

Luke darted to the pile of legs and hoisted one. The woman shook her head. He noticed a petite leg clad in a white silk stocking decorated with roses. She nodded vigorously when he pointed to it.

It took a bit of time to assemble all three of the women, starting with Madame de Pompadour, the childlike French courtesan, who then helped him revive Madame Curie, the famous chemist, and Ada, Countess Lovelace, author of the first computer program. Madame Curie quickly pushed a lever that opened the door for the other con-spirators, who all stared at Luke in surprise.

"Put some trousers on, Luke," O'Neill complained.

"Sorry," Luke said, "I lost 'em."

Madame de Pompadour rushed out of the door.

"I'll go find a mop," she offered with a winsome smile, and took off down the hall wearing nothing more than her bloody silk stockings and chemise.

"I don't think she'll be coming back," Chaplin mused.

Curie and Lovelace had already set to work trying to bring the central control system back online.

"Where's Joan's arm!?" the Queen demanded.

"Everybody, hush!" Luke hissed. "The Minotaur will hear us!" Just then poor Evelyn let out a wild cry.

"Nononononono! Noooo! Oh my GOD!"

"What's the plan?" Phoenix mouthed as her screams cut in and out on the monitor.

"Puns and improvisation," advised Chaplin in a whisper. "Kill fear, and invent our way out."

"Mind over matter," said Luke quietly. He closed his eyes, and imagined himself a left-handed guitar and an amplifier. The Fender stratocaster appeared instantly, he could feel the weight of the strap on his shoulder

"Splendid!" whispered the Countess. "We've succeeded in restoring the imagimatrix!"

Luke kept going. He dreamed up drums and a tambourine. When he opened his eyes, the musical instruments were arrayed about him, weapons waiting to be deployed.

"We need to repair the rest of equipment," Madame Curie whispered. "Everyone imagine away the pools of gore that soaked them, and caused them to short out."

In a few blinks, the chamber was shiny and clean. A few more, and Luke had pants on again.

Chaplin selected a flamenco guitar, Wilde a lute. O'Neill chose a trumpet, and Boadicea a large frame drum with a big soft beater.

"I'm going to blow him to bits with this!" O'Neill giggled, testing the trumpet with a soft toot.

"Quiet!" whispered Wilde.

"Good, good, keep the wordplay coming," River breathed encouragingly from the doorway. "I'll stay here with Saint Joan, and stand guard."

*Is this really going to work?* Luke wondered nervously. He recalled Chaplin's words in the hallway. He was right–if they tried to engage the beast in a contest of strength and brutality, they'd lose. Their only option was to change the narrative.

"We'll back you up," Madame Curie whispered in Luke's ear. "With us at the controls, you won't be disarmed."

"You're not going to fight the monster without us," cried Janis Joplin, bursting into the control room. Behind her were Josephine Baker and Billie Holliday.

"Sshh!" "Hush!" "Quiet!"

"Fighting monsters is our specialty!" Josephine whispered.

"Right on!" hissed Billie, and the three women bumped fists.

"Let's get in there, while we still have the element of surprise on our side," O'Neill rasped.

"I must say, this is the first time I've ever set out to kill someone with a joke," murmured Wilde to Chaplin.

"Good luck," whispered Countess Lovelace.

Gene opened the door to the prism room, and Luke entered first, playing a series of chirps and twangs on the strat. He was followed by the others, each of them contributing to the improvisation in the most surprising way he or she could.

The Minotaur turned with a snarl from the body of Evelyn. Her hands and feet were now tied to a wooden frame, and he had already removed the skin from much of the torso. It hung at her waist like the flap of a breechcloth. She screeched thinly, without stopping.

The Minotaur bellowed.

"When life gives you turds, you can't make lemonade!" Luke

shouted, plonking a goofy melody.

The Minotaur lunged toward Luke. O'Neill distracted him with a blaring, arrhythmic tantivy on the trumpet.

"When Ford gives you lemons, file a class action suit!" O'Neill cried. The Minotaur knotted his brow, hesitated.

Janis howled, "When life gives you lemmings, make lemming-aid!" while Chaplin plucked the strings of the acoustic in a series of falling notes.

"We are the woooorld . . . we are the rodents!" he crooned.

"Shut up!" bellowed the monster, leaping on him. "You are making no sense!"

"Get a job! Or you make no cents!" barked Boadicea, jumping up and down, and flogging the drum like thunder. Luke was meanwhile stroking and vellicating the strings of the strat as if he were using the notes to tell the story of a rubber duck floating out to sea. Billie scatted to this while Josephine performed a goofy dance, one that involved a lot of kicking and forced the Minotaur to protect his vulnerable bits. Gene added some foghorn bleats, but the Minotaur swiped at him, hurling O'Neill violently against the inner wall of the prism.

"You're not his enemy," Oscar yelped, scrubbing the mandolin, "You're mine-otaur!"

The monster howled with rage, and lurched toward the poet.

"Your grisly rites are just wrong!" Luke called out desperately, playing a limping salvo.

"Row! Row you fuckers!" O'Neill gasped, rising from the floor. Josephine crowed like a rooster and came on, and she and Oscar began to prance about doing the chicken dance, extending their long legs in vicious kicks, while Billie whistled *Home on the Range*. Meanwhile Janis sang, "'Fishy fishy fishy fish! Oh wishy washy widdo fish!"

The bull-man put his hands up and grasped onto his horns, as if his head were exploding.

"Shut up! Shut up!" he roared.

"You would be a drag, even if you were in drag!" Chaplin taunted.

"If you were an elephant, you would still be irrelevant!" Wilde put in. The beast bleated and seized the poet, snapping his neck and removing the head with a single twist. He tossed it across the chamber, but the others still came on.

"Your tale has gone on too long!" Boadicea rejoined, slicing off the Minotaur's tail with her razor-sharp sword.

"Having teeth is such a grind!" O'Neill gloated as he swapped off the Bull's nose with a machete.

"How dare you come before us armed!" Luke laughed, removing one of the creature's arms with a meat cleaver that happened to be in his hand.

"You are about to be de-feeted!" Boadicea whipped off one of the Minotaur's hoofed appendages. The monster bellowed, and blood bubbled from every severed limb.

Madame Curie meanwhile darted bravely in and out, hastily seizing up the monster's body parts and placing them in covered buckets. She also retrieved Jeanne's arm and Oscar's head from the floor, and made sure that both of them were quickly restored by the healing power of the prism.

"You know it's wrong what they say about you," Wilde sneered at what was left of the monster, where it wallowed, moaning, in a pool of plasma. "That you never give head!" And with that he removed the bull's head from its shoulders in a single clean swipe of a broadsword.

Everyone cheered.

Just then little Evelyn, now restored to wholeness, freed from her bonds, and clutching the rags of her nightgown to her bosom, crept up and stared down at the denuded torso of her tormentor.

"You know what I think?" she said in a tiny voice.

"What do you think, Evelyn?" O'Neill responded politely.

"I think . . . I'm going to have a ball," she said, brandishing a knife with a naughty smile. And she did.

While the others finished off the Minotaur, Luke had brought together the parts of the vulture and placed the head back on the long, scabrous neck. But nothing happened. For some reason, he still could not reanimate the bird.

"Everyone else around here gets brought back to life," he muttered. "Why not Buzz?"

"What are we supposed to do with these?" River wondered, looking at the shiny metal buckets, sealed with bolted-on lids, that contained the various parts of the Minotaur.

"Well, better not put them into the grinder," Luke said. "No telling what would happen."

"They must be taken to separate locations throughout the land," Jeanne d'Arc proclaimed, "so that they will never again be reunited."

"And what about the real Bette Davis?" Janis wondered. "Has she been erased?"

"Who knows?" Boadicea answered. "Many of our number may have disappeared, never to return."

"I'd like to meet my doppelganger now," Wilde said, cracking the knuckles of his large, fine hands. "I'd give him a taste of regret."

"It will take some time to sort all of this out," Billie pointed out.

"We're far from finished with our task," Chaplin reminded them. "What about the mysterious power source that we suspected? If we don't know how the system operates, how will we know if we've really defeated Thaw, or the Discriminatrix, or whoever the mastermind who summoned this monstrosity really is?"

"The suffering of the maidens was the power source, no?" Josephine surmised.

"Actually," Lovelace interjected, "We've already discovered the source of the largest energy field in the complex. Look at this." The group crowded around the console where a monitor showed a 3D diagram of the labyrinth.

She pointing to the green circle inside the quonset hut. "Here's where the grinder is, situated immediately above the prism. Inside, the vortex is deep, and from above you can see that, but being multi-dimensional it's actually flat, and it only takes up a micron of physical space, top to bottom. The material from the vortex is transferred down here, and this is where the Discriminatrix has been creating and configuring her recycled slaves," Lovelace indicated the prism room on the diagram, then switched to a view that showed the power grid.

"Here is the satellite that's been modified to collect and transmit star power from the consciousness field of the living, the noösphere. As you can see, the waves broadcast from the satellite are being picked up by this receptor dish here," she traced the route on the on-screen diagram with her finger, "which enters a building behind the quonset hut, here." Ada placed her finger on the rectangular shape. It was marked in the center with a red star.

"Before being transferred to the vortex, however, the energy passes through some kind of transformer. Here the star power is merged with or magnified into a force a thousand times greater, one that can run the vortex and supply energy for the entire island. The transformer is connected to another power source, here." She tapped her finger on a mandala symbol located in the heart of the maze. "We believe that this is the true source of the Discriminatrix's power."

"What is it?" asked River.

"That's exactly what we have to find out," Curie announced.

"So if we want to shut down the grinder," said Chaplin, "all we need to do is disconnect that transformer."

"At the least we ought to get inside and learn more about how it operates," Lovelace averred.

"I'm game," said Oscar. "Er, what's the alternative, lunch?"

"Yeah, does anybody else in this place wanna eat?" River wondered. "I could dig a veggie burger right now."

While the others discussed scrounging up a meal, Luke wandered back over to Buzz's body and squatted down next to it. Why didn't she come back to life? Luke had already met with several fatal accidents, and here he still was. How could he survive, while a goddess perished?

Did she exist in some other dimension now, glad to be free of her vulture form? If so, Luke could hardly blame her. But when he remembered the way she'd wept over him in the prism, he couldn't believe that this was simply a perverse form of escape. There had to be something more to it. Luke couldn't shake the conviction that he was missing some vital piece of information, that would show him how to reanimate the condor.

That's why he didn't want to leave Buzz in the pyramid chamber alone. Who knew what might happen to her? He picked up the vulture's mangled body and head.

Madame Curie approached him with a kind, maternal expression. "If you're going topside, I'll look after the corpse," she offered.

"Thanks anyway," said Luke.

Using the diagram, Ada had found the quickest way to get up to the surface. It was an iron ladder inside the utility closet, that led straight up to a maintenance hatch near the mysterious cube marked with a red star.

"Are you coming, Luke?" River asked as he grasped the rungs. Everyone else had already ascended, but Luke was still packing the condor's remains inside a knapsack. He had to wear it in front, because of his wings.

One by one the assortment of dead celebs emerged behind a clump of cycads next to a dumpster. River immediately went over and started to open up the trash receptacle.

"You don't want to do that," Wilde said dryly.

"Why?" asked River. "Is there likely to be something dangerous inside?"

"No. I just can't bear to fraternize with a dumpster-diver," the poet said haughtily.

"Maybe there's something valuable in there," Luke said. "I found a vintage hula girl charm in the trash once."

"What a treasure!" Oscar enthused snidely.

"Hey, it was solid gold! I sold it for fifty bucks." Luke and the others had been circling the perimeter of the white stucco cube, but there was no door, window or vent on any of the four sides.

"There's the receptor dish," Gene pointed up. "We should go up and take a look–but I don't see a ladder."

"I'll fly up," said Luke. "Be right back."

Landing on the flat roof he observed that the receptor dish was a crystalline structure twenty feet wide, a good five feet wider than the cube, and was mounted on a tall basket-like network of steel rods anchored into cement pylons. Luke squeezed in between these bars. Beneath the dish, there were a number of gray doves walking or fluttering around, and he could hear their mournful calls.

*HooWOO! hoo hoo.*

In the middle of the roof was a rectangular shaped pylon the size of a phone booth, and there was a door in it. Next to the door was a huge spool of rope with a crank. Luke walked up to the door, and opened it. Air whooshed in past him. It was completely black inside.

*There's got to be a light switch.* As he felt around on the wall a gust of wind pushed against him, and he toppled into the space. There was no floor.

His wings were bruised and scratched against the rough walls as he fell, down, down through the narrow hole. There was a force greater than gravity acting on him, as though an enormous mouth were sucking him in through a straw. No matter what he tried, he couldn't seem to slow his descent. The tunnel curved and he shot round a corner, getting stuck in a way that nearly broke his left wing. He extended his bare feet out in order to slow himself down, but the rough walls scraped his skin. He pulled in his arms and wings, straightened out his legs and tucked his head down, trying to imitate a projectile.

After what seemed like ages, but was probably less than a minute, Luke whammed to a dead stop against something, or someone, that let out a grunt. The sucking wind continued for five or ten more seconds, then he heard the sound of a door slamming in the distance. The wind stopped instantly.

He had landed on a person, he thought. But he could see nothing. It was absolutely black. He lay, gasping and whimpering in pain, and listened to the soft sound of air moving through a tube, a sound that was coming from somewhere very close by.

He was lying on someone soft, but there were also some hard objects under him. Luke touched one of them. It was smooth, curved. He should move off the person underneath him at least. He shifted his weight and she made a distressed whimper. Definitely sounded like a girl.

"Sorry," said Luke, "I'm–" Just then he put his hand somewhere that he probably wasn't supposed to, because she bucked and made an infuriated noise, the kind of noise your sister makes when she's throwing something at you to make you get out of her room.

Luke really was trying with all his might to get off the girl, but it wasn't that easy. Even the slightest movement of his wings caused him excruciating agony. The painful bumping against the rough walls indicated to him that the confines of the space were very small. Luke was starting to feel claustrophobic.

It was like being deposited into a grave, and finding out that someone else was already in there. And that the corpse was still alive. And that you just woke her up.

He managed to roll to one side and rest his weight up against the wall, where his wings felt squished, and ached horribly.

He was still pressed up against the creature though, whoever or whatever she was. Maybe she wasn't even human. Maybe she was a vampire, or part insect, or a zombie like he used to be. Maybe she just sounded human, but she was really some kind of alien creature. His skin crawled.

Why did it have to be so dark in here? He needed to see who he'd angered just now. He was starting to panic. He found that he was whispering:

*Let there be light, let there be light, let there be light!*

Nothing happened. Luke was getting more and more panicky. Where was his courage? He needed to think creatively. Humorously.

"I know how we can get out of here," he whispered. "We'll take the tube!"

There was no response.

"No wait," Luke went on, "we can advertise for someone to come and rescue us. All we need is an underground newspaper!"

Still no sign that the creature had heard him. But he could hear her heartbeat, now that his own heart had stopped pounding quite so loudly.

"Sorry to disturb you," he attempted, "I thought I'd just drop in."

That was a pretty lame one. Luke was already wracking his brains for a better jest when he realized that the body under him was shaking. Were those sobs? Or–

Was she laughing? She kept on shaking and making this sort of clicking noise for a little while longer, before she starting coughing and gasping.

And there was a glow coming from her, ever so faintly, but in the utter darkness it seemed like a blaze of light.

She was small, and slight, and there was a tube in each of her nostrils, and one in her mouth. Every orifice seemed to have an over-sized tube inserted in it. There were other tubes that entered her body in places that would not normally have had holes.

Luke had spent enough time in hospitals to see some pretty disturbing things. But he had never seen anyone intubated the way this woman was intubated. She literally could not move for all the tubes.

Her eyes were hidden by some sort of helmet that covered most of her head and had lots more tubes going into it at various points. The tubes all ran together along the tunnel and disappeared into the darkness.

"Christ," said Luke.

*Who is she? Why is she here? And–could she possibly help us find the "power source" everyone's been talking about?*

Luke immediately chastised himself. What was he thinking? This poor girl was in no shape to help anyone.

"Look," he said, "I don't know what's going on here, but maybe I should go and get help. You look like you're in pretty bad shape."

The figure inhaled deeply, the air bubbling and hissing in her breathing tube.

"Okay, well I'm going to try and find a way out of here."

Luke scooted carefully along, trying not to pull on any of the woman's tubes. If he could get past her in the tunnel, maybe he could see where those tubes were going.

She began to make more noises, so he stopped what he was doing. Maybe he was hurting her. But it seemed more like she was trying to communicate with him.

"Hngh! Ngh! Hngh!" she said. She was moving her hand toward him, straining against the needle-tipped thin tubes that everywhere entered her veins, and the cruel thick tubes that pinned her in place.

"Ngh! Hngh!"

"Do you want me to do something?"

"Ngh!"

"Do you want me to . . . take out the tubes?"

"Hngh!! Nhgh!"

"Will you die?"

She was quiet for a few beats. Then she writhed her whole body, from head to toe, as she grunted. "NNgh! NNghh!"

"Okay. Okay." It seemed he was going to have to do this, whatever the results. Who knew how long this poor creature had been imprisoned in here, but he had to set her free, one way or another.

Luke started with the easy ones, the thin tubes with spiky ends. He peeled off the tape and pulled the needles out one by one. There must have been at least two dozen of them. Then, he looked at the helmet. Was there some trick to it? He had no idea what was going on inside there. He was worried about really hurting her by yanking the helmet off.

So he set to work on the other tubes, pulling them out one by one, starting with the mouth and nose tubes. When those had been eased slowly out, she sighed and then started to gasp. Maybe she'd been hooked up to an iron lung, and now she labored to breathe on her own. It was frightening to watch her struggle for air, but somehow she kept breathing.

There were tubes in her stomach, her chest, her armpits, and of course ever so many tubes inserted into the nether regions. Some were empty, others contained a reddish or brownish or yellow sludge. One tube seemed to go right through her body. Every time he pulled one of the tubes out, she groaned.

"Is this okay? Am I hurting you?" Luke asked over and over. And though she never answered a word, she would sigh so gratefully, he knew she wanted him to.

At last he'd removed every medical attachment but the helmet. He paused, trying to think what to do next. That's when he heard her whispering. He put his ear close to her mouth.

"Thank you," she croaked softly.

She put her hands slowly up to the helmet, touched it.

"Please," she whispered.

"Are you sure?"

She nodded slightly, pushing up on the helmet weakly.

"Okay, here." Luke inched his way up along the tunnel, until he could get a grip on the headgear. It was like a sci-fi hair dryer made of smooth aluminum, with a spaghetti of cylinders coming out of it. He yanked it once, twice, a third time. It started to loosen.

She was biting her lips. Luke gave another sharp tug, and the dome popped off. She gave a cry of pain.

He saw her face for the first time. She was hideous.

Her head was covered with sores and scars, and several oozing holes. Her scabby lips looked parched. Luke stared at her with pity and horror. She was a revolting thing, pale and puffy.

Her eyes were still closed. Then they fluttered open, and he saw a flash of bright gold.

She saw him. Her face lit up with tender joy, and suddenly just for a moment, she was beautiful.

The woman licked her lips and spoke in a voice so soft, he had to strain to hear it.

"Is it . . . really you?" she asked. "After . . . after all this . . . time? You . . . ?"

Luke's eyes overflowed. The poor, sad thing. How long had she been down here underground, alone?

"I'm Luke," he said gently. "What's your name?"

She looked puzzled, squeezed her eyes shut. After a time she whispered slowly, "Charlotte."

"Well Charlotte," Luke said briskly, "How are we going to get you out of here? Any bright ideas?" His wings were healing quickly, but it was hard to imagine dragging her along a narrow tunnel that was barely wide enough for a single person to wriggle through.

He opened his mouth to suggest again that he try and search for a way out on his own. But she was speaking.

"Necklace," she said weakly.

Necklace? Luke was mystified. What did she mean? She wasn't

wearing a necklace. Then he felt the little cowrie shell, smooth and cool, against his skin.

"This necklace?" He held up the chain so that it dangled before Charlotte's eyes. She fastened her gaze on the shell.

"Yes," she whispered. She looked up at Luke. She seemed to be fading.

"Follow . . . tubes . . ." she murmured. She was getting brighter, becoming transparent. Suddenly she dissolved into tiny sparks that fell away like the embers of a firework display. Only one glowing kernel remained. This little light zipped round in an arc, then into the cowrie shell. The shell lit up, as bright as a candle.

Luke looked at the cowrie thoughtfully, dangling there on its chain. The light showed him the tunnel ahead in stark relief. Only a few feet from where the girl had been lying, all the tangled tubes he'd removed from her body disappeared together into a larger tube. This larger cylinder was bolted into the cement floor. All Luke had to do was loosen those bolts, and he could probably squeeze through. He tested one of them with his fingers. They were frozen, stuck as fast as the lug nuts on the rims of an old rusted Chevy.

What he wouldn't have given for Buzz's strong beak, to turn those bolts! But Buzz was . . . well, Buzz was in his backpack.

Could he use her head as a pair of pliers? Why not?

Luke extracted the condor's cranium from the knapsack. The bill was partly open and fitted nicely onto the bolts. In no time, he'd gotten all of them loosened and was able to move the cylinder aside. He pushed the tangle of tubes down into the space below.

Luke dropped down into the room, which was dimly lit by the embers in a coal grate. The other ends of the tubes disappeared through an opening in the top of what seemed to be an old refrigerator.

Luke turned to survey the room in the stark beam from the necklace. He was not prepared for what he saw there.

He was in a large Edwardian kitchen adjoining a dining room. The space was crowded with objects. A massive table, a sideboard and a lab bench were laden with beakers and flasks, gloves, pliers, cleavers and knives, rusted meat hooks. And everywhere Luke looked, there was a grisly trophy. There were heads, glittering with salt, hands and other body parts stacked in piles. There were skins made into pillows, lampshades and hats. There were chairs with breasts made of human skin. There were cups full of teeth, bowls fashioned from skulls. There were mummified body parts everywhere, stuffed into boxes, wrapped in newspaper, perched precariously on stools, stacked on shelves or hanging on the walls.

Just then, he heard footsteps approaching. Luke tucked the cowrie shell inside his shirt and ducked behind the icebox, just as somebody entered the room. He peered cautiously around the appliance, and made out a figure standing before the mirror of an antique vanity, admiring himself.

He was nude, except for a bibbed apron made of human skin, and a mask. Luke saw in a flash that the man, for from behind the figure appeared to be male, was wearing a translucent mask of human skin. Breasts and vulva were included in the construction of the apron. As the sickly stench in the room penetrated his nostrils, Luke retched, stepped back, and bumped into a hurricane lantern that was on the floor behind him, knocking it over with a cartoon crash.

The man turned, swiftly taking in the jumble of tubing lying atop the icebox, and Luke himself, who was making a dash for the door.

"You!" shrieked the masked monstrosity and, seizing a pickax, he hurled himself at Luke, swinging a deadly blow at his head. "What did you do to her? Where's *Mommy*!?"

Luke took to the air, grateful that the dining parlor was lofty in height. But he wasn't accustomed to using his wings yet, even in the open air, and the room was an obstacle course from floor to ceiling.

Making his way across it involved getting around a large wrought-iron chandelier, with tiny lampshades decorated with human lips, while avoiding the swinging pickax of the crazed serial killer below. This was going to be a challenge.

*What was the guy's name? Ed Gein?* There was a book he'd read as a teenager describing the man's gruesome murders, and the macabre house of horrors where he'd preserved the remains. It was a sensational story that had spawned many a tasteless riddle.

"What does Ed Gein have in his cookie jar?" Luke blurted, hoping to distract his foe, just as the grotesque figure swung the ax at him with a grunt, barely missing Luke's hip.

"Ladyfingers!" the killer replied. He was grinning behind the skin he'd removed from Bette Davis' face.

"Why did Ed Gein's girlfriend break up with him?" Luke taunted, ducking behind the chandelier.

Luke's adversary palmed a razor from the top of a cluttered bureau. "Because he was such a cutup!" he snarled as he hurled it. A few feathers came floating down from Luke's left wing, and he could feel a warm trickle. Then came the sharp pain. "You can't stump me," boasted Ed, "I know 'em all."

Luke made a dash toward the door. He had to drop to the floor level to escape. As he did Gein lunged at him, the pickax poised above his head. Luke dodged the blow, which struck the door, the point going right through the solid wood with a crunch.

"What kind of beer does Ed Gein like?" Luke gasped. Ed, struggling to extract the pickax from the door, did not immediately come up with the punchline. Luke spotted a huge hatchet leaning up against the wall, and he backed toward it, hoping Gein would not detect the weapon, until he was able to get it in his grasp.

Meanwhile Gein had given up on the pickax, and opted for an enormous meat cleaver that was lying close at hand on a table.

"All body and no head!" said Gein triumphantly, whirling the cleaver through the air as he rushed upon Luke, aiming a vicious blow at his neck.

Rising up suddenly into the air, Luke swapped off Gein's cranium with a single, well-aimed blow of the hatchet. A fountain of blood spurted up, hitting the ceiling.

Luke paused, panting, and watched as Gein's body slumped slowly to the floor, spraying gore in every direction. He pulled the cowrie shell out from under his tee shirt, and whispered into it.

"It's going to be okay, Charlotte. I got him!"

But what to do with Gein's head? No way did Luke want it joining back to the serial killer's body one day. Better to let them send it to some remote spot, like they were planning to do with the Minotaur's remains.

So Luke had to stuff the bloody head into the knapsack with Buzz's body. What a mess! His tee shirt and jeans were dark and heavy with blood. *If I'd known about this in the prism, I would've imagined myself wearing a hazmat suit!*

Luke opened the door, eager to escape the creepy room and its curiously sweet, bacon-like smell. Outside was another of those identical stone corridors with bronze sconces. He felt utterly disoriented.

He held the cowrie shell up. It still glowed warmly from within. He put it to his lips.

"Charlotte?" he whispered. "Are you there?" He held the shell to his ear. Had he heard something?

"Charlotte, we need to get out of here. Any idea where we are, or which way I should go?"

He held the shell to his ear again. If Charlotte was speaking to him, he couldn't make out her words.

Luke guessed that he was on his own.

He turned to close the door to Gein's lair, and at that moment a dove appeared from inside the room and flapped away down the hall. It must have gotten pulled into the tunnel before the door on the roof slammed shut. Maybe it knew the way out of here.

Luke dashed down the passageway after it. The corridors weren't wide enough for him to fly–he figured his wingspan was over fifteen feet–but he was able to get a little lift if he held the wings in certain positions. And they were perfect for taking corners at top speed, so he was able to keep the bird in sight most of the time.

The dove seemed to know what it was doing, but even if it was just as lost as he was, he didn't have any better ideas, so he kept following it. After what seemed like endless miles of tunnels with turns, flights of stairs, ramps and even a spiral staircase, the bird emerged onto a long platform that filled the length of an underground chamber of vast size, lined with pillars hewn from living rock. Here the dove stopped and began to peck around underneath a stone bench. Luke sat down on the bench, staring up at the single yellow lightbulb-in-a-cage that lit the cavernous space, and wondering what to do next.

The dove pecked ravenously at a piece of bagel which skittered across the platform. The dove fluttered after it and pecked again. Luke watched idly.

Famebeau. This place was so strange. Sometimes he appeared to have power over the very forces of nature and physics. The next time he turned around, he discovered he was subject to rules he couldn't understand. And to the wills of terrifying spirits.

He wondered about the lady in the tunnel. It seemed to him that the diagram had been pointing to her, somehow. A thought struck Luke for the first time. Had the intubated girl somehow been a conductor for all the power of the vortex, and the prism that it fed into? And if she were, what did it mean that he had released her? Would the pyramid even be able to transform material forms, now?

Would Buzz ever come back to life, or return to her rightful self?

He ached for the nameless goddess. He had held her so briefly in his arms, only to lose her again. He had been searching for her, and she had been there with him all along. Now the condor was a lifeless slab of meat.

And what of the urgent mission that had led him here? He had been trying to figure out a way to help Charity and the kids, but so far he could barely manage to make it from one hour to the next without being destroyed in some bizarre incident.

It was no picnic, that was for sure, being dead.

A sound like an enormous quantity of sand sliding down a mountainside distracted Luke from his thoughts. He looked up to see a cyclopean cylinder sliding along in front of him. It was a worm the size of a whale, glowing brightly with a greenish tinge, gliding alongside the platform like a train pulling into a subway station.

The worm stopped moving, and an opening appeared in one of its segments. The dove flew toward it and landed inside. Luke quickly followed, stepping in just before the door slid shut.

He was in a hollow tube with pink cubes lined up on either side, one for each segment. The dove was strutting about on the leathery curved floor. The worm started to slide forward again, which it did in sections, so that the cubes stretched apart as the segments extended, and then came back together again, having moved forward by some distance in the process. As the floor contracted, Luke was thrown about and grabbed for one of the cubes, thinking he would be better off sitting down. However when he placed his hand on top of the fleshy cube, it was wet. He tried to pull his hand away, but it was stuck–*really* stuck. His whole hand had sunk into the soft, moist surface. He realized his arm was being sucked down into the cube. Were what he had taken for seats actually mouth-like organs that trapped and devoured riders?

Was he was riding a man-eating subway worm?!

Luke was only able to extract his arm from the sucking pink box with some difficulty. Now it was wet to the elbow with sticky mucus.

He decided to stretch out on the floor of the worm's interior, so as to avoid getting tossed onto one of the voracious cubes. When the worm pulled up at another platform, and an opening appeared, he exited in haste.

The dove flew out with him as he skidded over the rubbish-covered platform. The bird fluttered up and up, and Luke took wing, and followed. They were flying up toward a light high above that speared down through the vast stone chamber. The light picked out the side of a pillar and an expanse of the littered floor, leaving everything else bathed in deep gloom.

The dove flew on, higher and higher. The light was much further away than Luke had supposed. It was tiring to fly up and up, carrying the heavy backpack with its gruesome load. Luke was a beginner at flying, and he probably wasn't getting the most efficiency out of his strokes. As he panted and labored through the air, Luke felt anxious about getting a cramp in his wing, and even more, about running into some large object that he couldn't see in the dark. As he approached the square of sunlight he worried about what was up above him in the light of day. What new horrors might he find when he emerged?

At last the dove reached a structure set into the ceiling of the stone chamber. It was a rectangle two meters deep and one by two meters wide, with two hinged steel trapdoors, and one of these was open. The dove flew out, and Luke grabbed onto the edges of the opening with both hands, folded his wings, and pulled himself through.

He found himself staring into the surprised face of River Phoenix. Luke had just emerged from the dumpster by the satellite station.

"Luke!" River gasped. "What happened? Where have you been?"

"It's a long story," Luke said. He opened up the backpack, and dumped Ed Gein's head out onto the pavement.

He told the whole story then: about getting sucked down the tunnel, finding Charlotte and freeing her from the tubes, the fight with Gein, and the strange journey that brought him back to the dumpster.

The only thing Luke didn't mention to the others, was the moment when Charlotte had become a tiny firefly of light, and entered the cowrie shell that he still carried on a chain around his neck.

"So the question is, was she the power source?" Luke concluded. Everyone decided to troop into the quonset hut to see what had become of the vortex.

Luke opened up the backpack, thinking to shove Gein's head back into it. When he did, the collar that was still chained to his wrist slipped down from its place. Luke had been wearing it wrapped around his arm, to keep it out of the way. The circlet had now fallen down into the interior of the bag. When Luke dug down into the bag in order to extricate the collar, he saw that it had slipped around the severed neck of the vulture. As Luke watched Buzz's head, tucked in beside the body, moved slightly like a magnet attracted to another larger magnet. Then it suddenly snapped back into place.

"Skrawk!" Buzz struggled frantically. "Get me outta this freakin' bag!"

"Buzz!" Luke cried, "You're back!"

Once the condor was freed from the backpack, up into the air she rose, beating her wings.

"Yay!" River cheered, "Buzz is alive again!"

"Goddammit!" Luke said as he watched her settle onto his leathery green forearm. He was back, too–back to being a zombie. "Why the fuck does this keep happening?"

"Sorry, kid," Buzz croaked. "I don't make the rules."

"That's a bunch of bull," Luke whispered. "If you don't make the rules, who does?" The raptor just stared at him with her horrible pink head to one side, silent, then nibbled at her tail feathers.

Luke stood in the quonset hut with Oscar, Charlie, River and a crowd of others. They all gazed down into the whirlpool of bright specks.

"It's so much dimmer, now," Luke remarked.

"If this change is the result of disconnecting Charlotte from Gein's diabolical device, that could indicate that she was indeed the power source, a sort of human transformer-battery," said Marie Curie.

"Where's the Countess?" asked Oscar.

"Ada returned to the control room some time ago," Curie responded.

"We must mount an expedition immediately to find Charlotte," Boadicea insisted.

"Is that wise?" wondered Chaplin. "Judging by Luke's adventure, there will be many perils in the labyrinth."

"But we must rescue the poor girl!" insisted Jeanne d'Arc.

"We can just use the cable to lower ourselves down," said Janis Joplin, who had already climbed up a ladder to investigate the transfer station roof and satellite array.

"We mustn't do this blindly. We must learn more about the forces at work here," Madame Curie replied.

"Yeah," said River. "Who is this Charlotte, and could she be dangerous?"

"Luke, what do you think?" asked O'Neill.

"Yes, Luke, we must rely on you for information," said Boadicea.

"Luke?" cried River, detaching from the group and looking all around the quonset hut.

But Luke was no longer among them. He had slipped away unnoticed.

Just then Clark Gable arrived with Errol Flynn, Josephine Baker and Billie Holliday. They came in chatting and joking, apparently having a wonderful time.

"The golems have all awakened!" cried Josephine.

"At first it was only the mind-controlled slaves like us who came to their senses," said Billie.

"But once the system powered down, even we grinder golems began to revert to our former personalities," marveled Gable. "I was hiding out in a photo of myself that was part of the display in the palace entrance hall. Once the system powered down, natural forces pulled me back into my body. Other doppelgangers simply vanished."

"What about mine?" Wilde wondered.

"We didn't see him," said Josephine.

"Too bad, I always wanted to meet Oscar Wilde," said Oscar.

"The crocodiles in the swan lagoon are gone, and the swans too," Billie remarked.

"I remember how much Bette enjoyed watching the crocs eat those swans," Chaplin remarked with a shudder.

"Many of the missing celebrities remain un-accounted-for," Gable pointed out.

"Some of these are likely to be found in Gein's lair," Chaplin suggested. "So long as we're searching for Charlotte, we'd better organize a task force to retrieve the remains, and attempt to reanimate the victims."

*  *  *

Luke jogged around to the back of the building with Buzz in tow, and opened up the hatch.

Buzz tried flapping away, but Luke was insistent.

"We've gotta go down to the pyramid chamber," he said.

"Why do you wanna go there?" Buzz squawked.

"As if you don't know," Luke retorted. "Now stop making trouble and come on." Buzz reluctantly allowed herself to be caught.

He tucked the condor under one arm and began his descent down the long steel ladder. Emerging in a short while into the control

room, he saw that Ada had returned, and was working on adjustments to the machinery.

"I need to go in there," he said. "Is it working?"

"The system is crippled," Lovelace said, "and the power is on
standby level. The imagimatrix is no longer functional. But the reset
field is still working inside the pyramid. All the manual adjustments
are offline, though."

"Reset is all I need," he replied. "I may be a while. Don't let anyone disturb me, okay?"

"As you wish," Ada said.

"And . . . can you please switch off the monitor? I want some
privacy."

The Countess looked at him suspiciously. "Yes, sir!" she responded with more than a hint of sarcasm.

Luke ignored this. "Thanks!" he called as he ducked through
the door and entered the chamber, releasing the vulture, who flapped
down to the floor mat.

The transformation took a few seconds. The condor's image
stuttered and hummed and finally winked out, and the goddess stood
before him, in an attitude of melancholy. She was robed in a smoky
fluff of drapery that wisped around her like the spray from a sneeze.
Heavy braided ropes of pearls were wound round her neck, wrists
and ankles like fetters. Luke seized her by the shoulders, and looked
searchingly into her eyes.

"Who *are* you?" he asked.

Tears poured down her cheeks as she gazed at him.

"My Lord," she said with a sob, and wiped her eyes with the
back of her hand. "Forgive me, I beg you. I cannot bear this!"

He'd been trying not to be angry with her ever since she died,
awash in feelings of betrayal and mistrust, which was, he had to
admit, in large part a projection of the guilt and anger he felt toward
himself for allowing her to be decapitated. However, there was one

thing that justifiably pissed him off. She'd been lying to him the whole time, pretending to be a vulture, and her deceit had only been revealed to him by accident.

But now . . . she was so lovely, so helpless, and there was a sweetness, a humility to her manner that wrung his heart. Instantly, he forgave her for everything.

"Oh Jesus," Luke said. He took her face between his hands. Her gaze was as loving as it was inconsolably sad. He kissed her, slowly, then again more deeply. She was so soft, she seemed to melt in his arms. "Oh god." He held her to him fiercely, like he wanted to merge with her, right then and there. After a few minutes of urgent fondling she fluttered against him, and he reluctantly released her.

"Can't you please tell me what's going on?" Luke begged. "Can't you at least tell me your name?"

"I have many names, darling Luke," she responded. "But you can call me Kore."

"Okay, Kore, thank you. And why the vulture act, may I ask?"

Kore hung her head. "That . . . that's a punishment."

"A punishment?" Luke was taken aback. "For what?"

"What we did . . . in the Hall of Ten Thousand Pillars . . . was unlawful."

"What are you saying? Are you telling me that I got turned into a zombie, and you got turned into a vulture, as a punishment for *fucking*?" Luke was outraged.

"Your current form is not a punishment, Luke. It's a manifestation on the path of your destiny."

Luke considered this oft-repeated assertion. Was she telling the truth? He figured he had to assume so, until he learned otherwise. "So only you are being punished? By who?"

Kore looked so small and frightened now. Tears started in her eyes again. Luke put his arms around the trembling creature, kissed the dark curls on the top of her head, and spoke more softly. "Please,

Kore, tell me. Who's punishing you?"

She put her lips to his ear and whispered, "My husband."

The words struck Luke like a blow. He shut his eyes and breathed deeply. Her husband. Okay, that was unexpected. That was not good news. But he couldn't be angry any longer with this exquisite creature who had, it seemed, suffered so much on his account.

It wasn't the first time Luke had accidentally slept with someone who was married, but it was an arrangement that did not tempt him, one that he avoided if forewarned. Charity had never been the jealous type, and had reeled out a good long leash for him when he was on tour, so there had been opportunities a-plenty. But he'd been bullied and threatened enough over the years to understand that his fame would pose no obstacle to a jealous husband, or wife for that matter, hell-bent on beating the crap out of him. Besides, he'd concluded that he was simply too possessive to share.

But as he had gotten himself particularly worked up over the goddess, and her intoxicating proximity made him feel like a god, and as he was in fact already dead, he decided to abandon all caution. Kore was his now, he told himself, the chain that still bound them together was proof of that. He opened his eyes and looked into hers.

"Fuck him," he said emphatically. He took the houri in his arms, kissed her again, running his hands over her body.

Kore pulled away slightly. "My husband is very powerful!" she cried.

"Is he here right now?" Luke wondered contemptuously, and continued to address himself to the maiden's delicious body.

"He is everywhere, Luke, he sees all. But here inside the pyramid, I think, is the one place where he cannot see us."

"Good," said Luke. "Then I think we should stay in here for a long, long time." He enfolded his wings around her, lifted her. Her legs wrapped sinuously around his waist, and with a sobbing cry, Kore gave herself to him. This was what he's been longing for. This.

And this. And this!

When Luke had been making love to Kore for what seemed like hours, he became aware of irritating voices on the intercom. They buzzed like sugar-hungry wasps hovering near the window screen, trying to get into his pirated hideaway. Luke ignored them.

His thirst for Kore was still far from slaked when she seized his ear between her fingers, and murmured, "I think we are about to have company."

"We're coming in, Luke. Ready or not!"

Luke rolled up onto one elbow and attempted to conceal Kore's tender parts under one of his wings, as Janis, Josephine, Jeanne, Jack Kerouac and Oscar entered together.

Josephine spoke. "We, the Goddess Alliance Forever Force, claim this apparatus for her majesty, Persephone, the Queen of the Dead."

Kore blinked, peeking out at the GAFF members from behind Luke's feathers, her cheeks reddening. While they stood staring, looking exactly like statues of surprised and acutely embarrassed people, at her resplendent loveliness, Luke could hear Ada's voice over the intercom.

"Sorry, Luke!"

"Your . . . Majesty?" Oscar faltered.

The members of GAFF now gazed at Luke. Luke in turn stared at Kore with a mixture of reproach and adoration. She shot a look at the committee, pursed her lips, and her eyelashes batted shyly. Luke encircled her with his arm protectively.

"For-forgive our intrusion," Wilde floundered on. "It was not known to us that–that you had already, ah, taken possession of the prism."

"You may go," whispered Persephone, Queen of the Dead. The delegation quit the chamber with hasty apologies, and Luke was alone with Kore once more.

He lay flat on his back, arms stretched out wide, looked up at his Queen, and rolling his angelic head back and forth, began to sing.

*"I-I-I'm just a gigolo-o-o, everywhere I go-o-o-o-o . . . people know the paaart I'm playin' . . ."*

He stopped singing, sat up quickly. "Kore?"

She had her back turned to him. She was shaking.

"Are you crying? Tell me you're not crying."

She sniffed.

"Darling Queen, don't let this embarrass you!" Luke begged. "It's nothing!" He put a hand on her shoulder, but she shook him off. Finally he lay back on the floor with a sigh.

"I love my husband," Kore said softly, looking away from him. "I've always loved Hades. But he truly is the cruelest of the gods . . ."

Luke sat up again. He had found his destiny. This was the task he was born to. His adoration would bear all before it. He had chosen to ignore the existence of this so-called husband, but she wasn't making it easy.

She peeped at him guilelessly. ". . . Except of course, for you-know-who."

"No, I don't know," Luke said huskily. Her words had for some reason brought a stab of panic, and he now fastened upon Kore with vivid attention. "Who is the cruelest of the gods, O Persephone, Queen of the Dead?"

She seized his hands and held them in hers, kissing the palms.

"Why Eros, of course," she murmured. "The god of love."

"Well then, Eros can go to hell too," Luke said. "I say we stay right here, you and me, fucking, for all time! And to hell with all of them." He made to kiss her again.

That was when she burst into tears. Again.

Luke rallied. He reminded himself of all she'd been through, most recently being killed, carried around in a bag of body parts, and finally brought back to life as a chained vulture. She had every right to be fussy.

"My Queen, my darling, what's wrong?" he said.

"Oh Luke!" she wept. "Don't you see–this–this situation!?" And she seized the chain fiercely in her delicate hands.

"Don't worry darling. Bondage doesn't make you look fat."

"Ohh!" she howled, tears cascading from her eyes. She apparently did not find his joke funny at all. "How could he–how could you!" she wept. "Treat me like a . . . slave!"

"What? What did I do?" Luke protested. "I'm not the one who put you in chains!"

"Aren't you?" she blubbered.

"I'd gladly take them off in an instant if I could," he insisted.

"When did you ever think about how I felt?" She wiped her eyes on a curl drawn from the curtain of her hair. "When did you ever show me kindness, or respect? When did it ever occur to you, that maybe it would be wrong to take advantage of this woman, goddess though she be, who had been placed in your power?"

Luke was utterly taken aback. "Power? Me?" he said in disbelief. But he remembered now, all the times he'd been cruel to Buzz, or domineering. All the times he'd cursed the goddess in front of the vulture. For the first time, it dawned on him that he might be in trouble with the Queen of the Dead.

He might actually be in very big trouble indeed.

Worse still, she had been talking while he was thinking these things, and he'd missed what she was saying. Shit!

". . . I'm not allowed to speak of, that if a word passed my lips, untold miseries would commence. But shouldn't it have been obvious–?"

"Okay, I didn't know it was you, did I?" Luke broke in. Kore just looked at him with a sad knowing smile.

"I–I thought . . ." Luke said slowly.

What could he possibly say in his own defense? He had known

she was the goddess from the Hall of Ten Thousand Pillars, since their first visit to the prism. And yet he had let her get killed by the Minotaur. And then . . . had he really *forced* her to come in here? She had a beak like a pair of meat cleavers. He had figured she could defend herself, if she'd wanted to.

He opened his mouth, and sounds came out:

"What I really thought was, I'm the luckiest guy in the universe right now. I thought, wow, she loves me. I hope–I wasn't wrong. Was I?"

"I do love you. Of course I do. Everyone loves you, Luke."

"I don't want everyone. I want you."

"And I also love Hades, cruel Hades. I may be the only one who really does. He needs me, Luke. You don't need me, but he does."

"Kore. How can you say that I don't need you?" Luke was becoming agitated. "What do I have to do to show you how much I adore you? God, I–I worship you! What do you want me to do? Just tell me. I'm the one who's *your* slave. Don't you get it?"

"That's not the way it seems to me," she said. Her voice cracked. She was going to start crying again.

"Well forget about the past, Kore. That was then, I was blind. Everything's changed." Luke stroked her arm gently. The waterworks had already resumed, however. Kore was a salty fountain. "What do you want me to do?"

"I just don't want to be–*waaah!*–punished anymore," she wept.

"Okay, look. I will chop off my hand right now, if that's what you want. Voilà. You'll be free of me. All right?" Luke looked up at the closed-circuit camera. They were probably out there watching them right now, trying to figure out what they could do to separate him from Kore, dreaming up new ways of making his death difficult for him. Goddammit.

"Sword, please!" he called out to the silent watchers.

"Luke, that won't work, and you know it," Persephone said reproachfully.

"It could work. Just grab the hand real quick, pop it into an iron box, lock it up and throw away the key. I'll never play guitar again, but who cares? If that doesn't work, you could cut off my head too, grind it to a powder. That should help. Grind up my whole body, if all else fails. That oughta do the trick."

She only cried harder with every word, *boo hoo hoo.* Luke was feeling decidedly uneasy about the way things were going. He shouldn't have been so sarcastic just now. He went into emergency contrition mode.

"I'm sorry, Kore," he said soothingly. "Please forgive me. It's just my bitter sense of humor, that's all. I adore you! I'll make it all up to you, I swear. I will, I will. Don't cry. Talk to me. Talk to me, and we can figure this out. You and me. Right?"

She hiccuped, and sniffed. "Will you really listen to me? Will you really listen, and not interrupt me?"

"I swear I will. Scouts honor," Luke said, smiling and holding up three fingers.

Persephone took a deep breath, dried her eyes, and began to speak in a low, emotional voice.

"I am the daughter of Zeus, who is my mother Demeter's brother. That's all you need to know about me, to understand how messed up my childhood was.

"Daddy was never around, but Mother talked about him constantly, complained bitterly about him. Our extended family was so dysfunctional, that the most appalling and cruel behavior was treated as a matter of course by everyone.

"But Mother was having none of it. She would talk about how hard she worked, tending the whole planet and caring for humanity and all the plants and gardens, keeping track of the seasons. Meanwhile everyone else on Olympus ran around screwing like rabbits, getting into fights, creating endless problems that she had to solve.

Nobody seemed to care whether the whole planet went to hell. But she cared. It was so much responsibility, and Artemis and Athena, Hecate and Hebe were the only ones she could depend on to help.

"I wanted to help too. I begged and begged, and at last she gave me a job to do. I was the artist of the flowers, a really lovely occupation, and I still do a bit of floral design work even now."

"Nice! I've always loved flowers," Luke said.

"I was still barely more than a child, and had been visited by the moon time once only, when Uncle Hades came to our airy complex of rock-cut caverns at Eleusis.

"It was the first time I'd ever met him. Mom was very protective of me, smothering really. She mostly kept me away from the family– especially Daddy, of course.

"Hades was a dark, poetic god with a gloomy expression. He'd come to consult with Demeter about burial rites, she being an earth goddess, and they talked for hours about matters that bored me. But from the moment I clapped my eyes on Pluto's handsome face, I knew he was dangerous, and that he would be a bad man for me to know. His eyes struck through me to the core, he solemnly winked at me, and I was in love.

"I was in my workshop perfecting a tiger lily when he came in unannounced. He has a cap of invisibility, you see, and you never know where he's going to turn up. He startled me."

Luke looked around him uneasily, wondering if Hades might even now slip up on them unawares.

"But he was gentle and courteous, and he told me stories while I worked. He who ruled a subterranean land of great wealth, told me of the wonders beneath the ground, the glittering gems, the fairyland caves, the perfectly still pools. He told me of the halls of Elysium, where all great men and women, all heroes and poets, go to converse with the Lord of Death under the earth, to feast and make merry for all eternity. He told me too of the terrible justice inflicted on the perfidious, the murderers and criminals who all came down into his realm in the end.

" 'And over all these things, you will one day rule as queen,' he said, kissing my hand.

" 'And what does my mother say of this?' I asked pertly. But secretly I feared him, for I was but a young girl, and he was tall and strong, and I saw that he was fair, but cruel, and that he was a god who was accustomed to having his way in all things.

"Now, I knew that my mother had it in her mind that I would never marry, for she called me Kore, which means the Maiden, and many times she had told me that she wished for me to remain always with her, chaste like the other maiden goddesses who watched over women and men. But I chafed against this fate. I had never been loved by my father, and the love of women was all I had ever known. I wanted to know what it was like, to be the queen of a man's heart, and of my own realm. And so when Pluto drew his seductive picture in my heart, I welcomed the temptation.

" 'Come with me,' Hades whispered, 'And see all these wonders, and if you wish it after visiting my kingdom, then we will go to Demeter and tell her that we are already married. But if you do not wish it, then you shall come home to your mother, and I will not trouble you any more.'

"Now in my secret heart I knew that Hades was not to be trusted. I knew that he would use upon me persuasions of every kind to keep me in his underground domain. But I did not want to listen to my secret heart just then. In that moment, I was flushed with pleasure at the thought of escaping from the burden of Demeter's fussy, demanding and over-wrought care. I even anticipated her discomfiture with relish. And so willingly I went with Hades to the Land of the Dead.

"But I was unprepared for the depth of his subtlety. He never compelled me, but spoke to me sweetly, asked me what I wished for, tempted me with pretty toys and flattery. In this way I began to see the gloomy realm below the earth, the land of dead things, as more special and more magical than life itself, which is the greatest of all magic. I thought I loved death because Hades had given it to me as a plaything, and had told me that I was beautiful and powerful.

"I can only imagine how distraught my poor mother was when she learned that I had descended to the underworld with Hades. Of course, she immediately tried to manipulate and exert control over me. She sent me a long letter describing in detail how the fields and gardens were all dying, because I had taken away her happiness. Come on, Mom. We all know what that really means: *Right, so you're gonna leave me? Fine, the whole world can starve until you come back.'*

"I ignored her.

"I was deeply enchanted with the way Uncle Hades gazed mournfully, longingly into my eyes. I was enamored of the way he dressed me, like a prized doll, in lace and gems and silken gowns, and of the way he held me on his knee as if I were still a little child, and fed me from his own plate. Never did he insult me, but he caressed me constantly, tracing his hand on my arm or shoulder, stroking my waist, touching my neck so gently and sweetly that my body tingled. Then he would send me away with a kiss on the forehead. I had never felt such things before, and as the days went by I began to crave his touch within parts of me that had never before been awakened. I began to desire that he would make of me a plaything for his own pleasure.

"I am sure that my mother was frantic. She spread it around that her darling girl had been abducted by Hades. This was false, of course. I was seduced, I was manipulated, but I was never abducted by force, not by my uncle Pluton.

"Mother hates the underworld, but bringing along her basket of honey cakes, she made the trek past the Styx and Cerberus, and marched right up to the thrones where Hades and I sat, ruling together.

"  'My darling daughter,' Demeter said. 'How pale you look!' Then she addressed my uncle. 'She is but a child, too young to be taken from her home.'

"Hades didn't answer, but looked to me. 'Before you say anything more, Mother, I'm not going back,' I said. Mother was furious.

"  'You selfish girl!' she cried. 'What of me? How am I to go on alone, giving everything to all the world, and receiving nothing in return? If you don't come home, I'll take to my bed, I'll let all the flowers die, I swear it!'

"  'You aren't going to make me want to come home with your hysteria and complaints about the chores left undone.' I replied coldly. 'Don't you see? I am the Queen here, and my darling Hades has seen to my every wish.'

"  'Oh, I'm sure he has,' Mother said sarcastically. Then she burst into tears, and called me cruel.

"  'Perhaps if you weren't so bossy you'd have someone to take care of you too,' I retorted, not kindly. I knew how hurt she was that Daddy never helped her. 'But it's not my job.' I said. 'I have my own life to live.'

"She drew herself up then, and pulled her starry blue cloak close around her lovely neck. 'Well then, we'll see what your Father has to say about this,' she uttered, and stormed off.

"My Mother Demeter has told me the story of what happened next, so many times. She went straight to Olympus, where she found Zeus in his chariot-house. She begged him to interfere.

"  'Persephone won't listen to sense,' she complained.

"  'Well, is she happy with him?' Daddy asked.

"  'What does that matter?' Demeter demanded to know. 'Persephone's gone to the land of the dead with her gloomy, mad uncle, the Lord of the Damned! What else is there to discuss? My Kore, my lovely flower doesn't belong in that awful place!'

" 'He's rich enough to take good care of her,' Daddy pointed out.

" 'He's the oldest of us, an ancient god, and she's a mere child. He stole her from me, and now he's convinced her that I'm the enemy. I cannot permit this! I want your support.'

"Zeus spoke. 'I will offer you my support on one condition. If Persephone wants to leave Hades, of course she can and should, and if Hades is keeping her there against her will, then I will personally come and see that he releases her. There, are you satisfied?'

"Demeter was sorely disappointed that Zeus didn't realize the extent to which I was, according to her, being deluded by Hades.

" 'Of course she doesn't want to come home, she's in love! But you know what a lunatic our brother is. How can you bear the thought that he has her in his claws? By the time she comes to her senses, it may be too late!'

"I can hear her now: 'You're insensible to the harm Hades is doing to the child, just as you've always been insensible to the harm you've done to myself and to our daughter. You are her father!'

"Of course Daddy hadn't been to visit us in ages, and maybe he wanted to get a look at me and find out what his brother had seen in me. Whatever the reason, Mother prevailed upon him to help.

" 'All right,' he said, 'I'll go there myself and get her.'

" 'No, I will go,' said Demeter. She didn't trust him one bit. 'Just give me the two dragons that guard your store of thunderbolts, and your chariot. I will take her to a secret location where she'll be safe.' And so Zeus ordered the dragons to be hitched to the chariot and brought to Demeter.

'Now these dragons have the ability to fly through any material, be it stone or wood or steel, and Demeter lashed her whip and the dragons spread their wings, and a moment later she arrived in the underworld. There I was with Pluto, listening to a concert being played by Orpheus, when Mother showed up and the dragons breathed fire all over everything. One of the dragons leaped forward and landed on Hades, pinning him. Demeter seized me by the hand, dragged me into the chariot, and cracked her whip again. The dragons leaped into the air and disappeared.

" 'Well, did you do it?' she asked me. 'Did you sleep with him?'

" 'Of course not, Mother. He's my dear sweet Uncle, not a pervert.'

"But the truth was, I was on fire for him. Just the previous evening as I sat on his lap, he had kissed my lips, not chastely but deeply, for the first time. In his mouth were the seeds of a pomegranate, and he held them gently without breaking the skin of a single ruby fruit. As he pressed his lips to mine, he crushed the pomegranate gems one by one onto the roof of my mouth with the tip of his tongue, so that the sweet juice ran down my throat. When he did this, I trembled and flushed, and felt a sensation in my sex that made me swoon.

"Hades carried me then to a bower lit by the stars of the everlasting night and laid me down. He gently and slowly unlaced my bodice, and bit by bit he worked the laces of my gown open, until my bosom was bare. But he did not touch my body, he only kissed my eyes, letting his breath caress my bare nipples so that they contracted into knots. He left me there in that state to toss sleeplessly all night long.

"My desire for him had become almost unbearable. Why had Mother interfered?

"Mother guided the flying chariot to Sicily and landed it on a sandy spot at the mouth of a grotto, where a sweet little waterfall tinkled in a lovely pool. Demeter thrust me into the cave and set the dragons to guard me.

" 'I see you will marry, even if it is against my wishes. Fear not, darling child, for I will find you a proper husband, somebody who will not take you away into the dark forever,' Demeter said. Off she flew to find Hermes and enlist his help.

"Meanwhile I wept in the cave, longing for my love, until my eyes were sore. I tried to escape but the dragons were so fierce and powerful, they frightened me. At last I cried myself to sleep.

"One of the dragons was much larger than the other and I had watched it wrestle its companion to the ground. The magnificent creature then stared into the other dragon's eyes until it was hypnotized, and the smaller dragon fell asleep. Late in the night the enormous golden dragon slithered into the grotto. It flicked its tongue in and out, touching my body as I slept, and my robes parted as if by magic. Its tongue flickered over my bosom and I moaned. The dragon's tail wrapped around me, holding me tightly in its coils. Now its tongue flickered over the slit between my legs, decorated with curling down, and that is when I began to stir and realize that it was no dream. I was in the grip of a serpent, and its huge powerful head was nosing between my thighs. I struggled to escape, but the dragon gripped me inexorably, like a snake that has its victim in its coils. Resist as I might, my legs were forced apart by the serpent's heavy coils, while its tongue played about the entrance to my cavern like flame.

"The dragon tasted the nectar between my thighs, and I sobbed in terror, but its tongue did not cease lapping. I whimpered and sighed but, trapped in the grip of the powerful creature, I could not stir. The dragon's tongue then entered me and writhed inside me as I trembled and cried out.

"The dragon knew now that I was still a virgin, for his sensitive tongue could detect the hymen. In this moment of triumph he took his true form, and ravished me.

"For it was my father Zeus who held me in his powerful arms. He had determined what he wanted to know, that Pluto had not as yet deflowered me. It was he who raped me, he who took my virginity, both through deception and by force.

"Meanwhile Demeter had found Hermes, for the god had just returned with a message from Hades. Pluto insisted that I be restored to him. I was his by right, for I had eaten the seeds of a pomegranate and according to the Fates, now I must stay in Hades forever.

"In fact I had eaten many feasts in Hades, but the pomegranate seeds counted more. Now you know the reason why.

"Mother was incensed and decided to appeal again to Zeus, but first she returned to the cave to check on me. Of course she found Zeus there with me, raping me every which way he could think of, her barely pubescent child. Daddy was clearly besotted with me, but in his moment of surprise I tore myself away from him and ran to Mother, weeping. They had the most terrible fight. Daddy wanted to take me away with him, Mother wanted to take me away with her, and all I wanted was to go back to Hades.

"Sometimes I wonder if Daddy might not have prevailed and kept me for himself, if it were not for those pomegranate seeds. But due to the decree of the fates, he was forced to permit me to return to my love for one month out of the year, for every seed I swallowed from the tongue of my gentle lover.

"I soon learned that I was pregnant by Zeus, and in time I gave birth to Zagreus. Hades of course would have nothing to do with the child, but my father was so pleased with the boy that he took him back to Olympus, where the tot crawled up onto the throne and declared himself the new King. Whereupon poor little Zagreus was torn to pieces by the Titans.

"Hades never let me forget my shame, and has always guarded me closely. To this day when I depart from Hades I return directly to my Mother. I certainly don't have anything more to do with Daddy than necessary.

"Every Fall I would bid my mother goodbye, and make my way to the deep places of the earth, where I'd find my black-eyed lover waiting for me, filled with longing and adoration. Hades and I have two daughters.

"For a while my life was delightful. But Hades always became depressed when I left him alone, and in recent centuries he has become increasingly withdrawn. All he does is party, and gamble, he never takes care of the judgments or rewards anymore. He pays no attention to me at all. For a thousand years, I've had nobody to keep me company but the endless stream of the dead."

Luke digested all of this before answering. He knew a good deal depended on what he said now.

"I . . . can't believe your Dad did that to you. That's despicable!"

Kore sniffed, and slid her hand into his.

"But now . . . now you don't have to be so lonely, right?" said Luke. "Now that you have me."

A sob escaped her lips. "I never meant to do it. I don't know what came over me. I never meant to get involved with you."

"Well I'm glad you did," he said, stroking her shoulder.

"Don't you see? As soon as it happened, my husband found out. Maybe he was watching me, maybe he just knew, but he seized me by the hair and threw me to the ground. He threatened to kill me!"

"Oh! God–I'm so sorry," Luke said.

"Then–" Persephone sobbed, "then he accused me–of having seduced Zeus. He said that all I'd ever wanted was my Daddy, that he had been nothing but a substitute, and that after Zeus tossed me to one side, I came crawling back to him, and that he had taken pity on me. And . . . it's not true!" She dissolved into weeping.

"Then–then he snapped the collar around my neck, dragged me to his throne, and flogged me with the chain until I was black and blue. 'You'll never rule beside me again!' he cried terribly, and then when he saw how he had bruised me in his rage, he wept. 'Kore, Kore,' he cried over and over, and I knew then that I had broken his heart."

"I would never whip you with a chain," Luke pointed out. "Not a chance."

"It's because of you that I was whipped!" Proserpina said sharply. "It's because of you that I am in disgrace, punished. And I know,

I know that Hades will never relent, not in ten thousand years. His judgments are eternal. He has sentenced me to be a vulture, chained to your wrist, forever. And either he doesn't know that you have found a way to suspend the spell, and to ravish me–"

"Come on! You wanted me to!"

"I am in chains, Luke!" she retorted. "What am I to do? Can I run from you? And either my husband knows nothing of my plight, but will take vengeance soon enough, or he knows, and does not care." And at this Persephone sobbed bitterly and long, and would not be comforted.

Maybe Luke had lost her now, or maybe he had never had a chance with her. At last he wearily spoke.

"What do you want to do, Kore? Do you want me to go to him, and tell him that it was all my fault? That I seduced you, raped you? Do you want me to beg him to punish me, but set you free? I would do that for you, if it would stop your tears. Would it make you happy? Would it help you to win back his love?"

Kore stopped crying, turned her head and looked at Luke for a long while.

"You would do that for me?"

"Darn tootin'!" Luke replied with a sad smile. "But I'd rather find some other way to make you happy. One that didn't involve being forever an enemy of the Lord of the Dead."

"It's too late for that," said Persephone, "for both of us."

They lay there side by side on the floor of the pyramid chamber, silent, for some minutes. Luke waited for a sign, and bided his time.

At long last she breathed in a deep, quivering breath, and let it out gustily. She sat up and began arranging her hair. Luke dropped a kiss onto her shoulder, and then another. Kore did not repulse him. He stroked her back with his hand.

"Well, the way I see it, it's exactly like we're married," Luke pointed out. "The old ball and chain, huh? And if we're going to spend the rest of eternity together just because we were lovers once, we might as well do it again, whenever we get the chance.

"Don't you agree?" he asked, pulling Kore to him. "I mean, we've got nothing if not time," he wheedled.

Kore buried her face in Luke's neck. She did not say, *What about your quest to help your family back on Earth? What about the accusations against your wife?*

Luke thought about it, though, as he kissed Kore's shoulder. His hopes had been pinned on finding the goddess and begging her help. It looked now as though Kore was as much a prisoner here, as he was.

*Eternity,* **Hades**

Hades had been depressed for days. He was listless, he'd been sleeping a lot. In fact aside from getting fitted for a new suit, which usually cheered him up but had failed to this time, he'd done practically nothing for three days.

Three days had gone by since he had turned Persephone into a vulture for cheating on him.

He'd been angry at her infidelity, of course, but what really depressed him was how unexpected it had been. That, and knowing who she'd done it with. After all these centuries as a faithful little wife, devoted and sweet, she'd suddenly had a rutting spree with some dead junkie singer with a bad voice. It made no sense.

Hades was disturbed by what that said about himself. He realized, suddenly and devastatingly, that it would come as no surprise to anyone but Hades, that his relationship with Kore had gotten to such a state. He hadn't had a conversation with her in years. He'd been neglecting her. If she had lost interest in him, he was to blame.

The truth was, Hades was out of touch, and he knew it. He was old hat. And knowing that made him defensive. There were places, most places in fact, where his worship was a travesty. Who gave him his due any more? The so-called goths? Goth fashions and horror films were laughable trinkets to a god who'd ruled a hundred thousand terrifying priests and been fed with rivers of actual blood.

But he was still among the mightiest of the gods. All men were his fodder. So for his goddess wife to randomly couple with a short, greasy trailer-trash kid was utterly incomprehensible. What had she seen in the fellow?

Well, she would have to get used to the rascal now, because she was going to remain chained to him like Prometheus's eagle for all eternity. And even that wouldn't be long enough to heal Hades's wounded pride.

Hades bent down, sniffed up another long line of coke. He needed to wake himself up a bit. He'd been bingeing on downers till yesterday. Once he started to slide down into depression, he had to go all the way down before he could come back up. The black beauties sped up the process.

But he would perk up soon, he hoped, and then he would stroll down to the counting-houses and take stock of his hoard. He always enjoyed seeing what new gems had been added to his collection. He could gloat over a priceless necklace, of rubies and sapphires perhaps, and muse on how Proserpina might have received it as a present.

If she hadn't decided to go and have sex with that kid.

Gloating was one of Hades's favorite emotions. Gloating summed up his personality, at least when he was cheerful. Voracious was another word that suited him. No matter how much he had, he wanted more. He would devour everything in time. It was his function.

Oddly enough, the one thing Pluto seldom hungered for was sex. He was very good at it of course, as he had pointed out to Persephone many times, but he was not addicted to the carnal act the way Zeus was. Death had access to far better drugs, or at least, drugs that were more effective in his case. Also he didn't have his brother's easy, charming manner and seductive prowess. There was a coldness to him, an automaton grace and perfection, that women found curiously loathsome. He disliked looking at himself in mirrors for the same reason, and had banned them from his kingdom.

And yet Hades was beautiful, a tall imposing figure of a man built like a gladiator, with large liquid eyes brown as loam, a roman nose, baby-sweet coral lips, and a crest of white hair that flowed back from the widow's peak on his high pale forehead. Moreover there was a commanding magnetism to him that was irresistible. With these qualities, he ruled over his vast kingdom with ease.

Power was second nature to Hades, but love remained a mystery to him. What was love, if not possession? He must love his daughters, he supposed, for he guarded them fiercely and took an interest in every aspect of their lives. Certainly he had loved Persephone. From the first moment he saw her, it had become necessary to possess her, and to protect her from the rapacious appetites of her father Zeus.

And up until now, this was the one vital thing that he had failed to do. A distressing thought. Hades put it out of his mind, the way he always did, when he could.

He reassured himself with the recollection of his own nobility, in taking Proserpina back after the rape. And that he had been faithful to his wife, for the most part, for millenia–what is that, he protested to himself, if not love?

And still she had betrayed him with that punk, that weakling. She had destroyed their perfect union to take into her bed no immortal, no great man of the times, but a mere flash in the pan, a low-level seedling in the euhemerism beds of Famebeau.

He had wept when he discovered her perfidy, wept for the first time he could remember. What did it matter that untold billions of the dead were under his heel? He could not control his own wife. He was shamed and brought down by it. Zeus would find out sooner or later, and then his brother, his vain, sexed-up, overweening baby brother, would never let him forget it.

She had to be punished, naturally, but how to achieve this had puzzled him. Appealing to Zeus was out of the question, and according to Olympian Law, he could not act as both judge and plaintiff. Hades had elected to employ Themis and Hecate to settle the matter. Accordingly he had sent his servant, the winged monkey god Hanuman, with gifts for the divine judges: for Hecate, a black cat with one green eye, and one blue; for Themis, a magnificent mantle embroidered in gold. Pluto's presents were accompanied by a request for "counsel on a matter of importance."

*I am composing a policy manual for my staff,* the Dark Lord had written, *and I have need of thy wisdom on a matter related to the divine rights of the Olympian goddesses.*

To Hecate he wrote:

*What is to be the fate of a mortal man who assails the virtue of a great goddess?*

To Themis he wrote:

*How must the law treat a great goddess who has betrayed her lord in matters of love?*

Hanuman had returned the following answers.

Hecate: *A mortal man who assails the virtue of a great goddess must suffer the most terrible of fates. To be torn to pieces by dogs would be a mercy unto him. Far better that he be chained to a hyena, a vulture or some such scavenger, to be tormented for all eternity by having his living organs devoured.*

Themis: *Should a great goddess betray her lord in matters of love, let the law mete out to her the same justice as is accorded to the gods. Let her lord relinquish his control over her, and permit her to join with her lover, for he himself may do as he chooses.*

Upon reading these answers, Pluton had taken from them the meanings that he desired. Kore would join with her lover, but as a vulture, to feed upon him for all eternity. He had the letters of the Judges to prove that he had sought their counsel: a flimsy defense, he knew, but better than none.

Hades adjusted his tie, downed a shot of espresso. Before he walked out, he wanted to check up on Persephone and her endless torment, as well as that of her lover. He needed a little gloating time.

He pressed the flashing button on the answering machine on his desk.

*"You have . . . three hundred and twenty three . . . new messages,"* said the mechanical voice. Hades sighed. He used to enjoy the obituary updates his secretaries prepared for him, but he'd gotten behind

on them lately. Maybe there were reports from Hanuman somewhere on the tape, though.

He'd lost touch with his agent in the flash flood. It had been counter-productive to wash them all away in a raging torrent, and Death knew it. But sometimes he just needed to express himself.

Now, he wondered where his wife had ended up. Was she still in one piece? He should really check the messages first, bring himself up to date. He began to scroll through them, listening to those that caught his interest.

If Pluto had been looking forward to some schadenfreude this morning, he was disappointed. As he listened to a series of recordings from the monkey god, the news increasingly disturbed his peace of mind.

*"Alpha Om, this is Country Cousin. The queen has entered the cosmic vortex. Repeat, the queen and the zombie have entered the vortex."*

*"Alpha Om, this is Country Cousin. The queen has emerged from the cosmic vortex. Repeat . . ."*

*"Alpha Om, this is Country Cousin. The queen has entered an ectoplasmic regenerator field . . ."*

Hades had drowsed through more of a catastrophe than he had foreseen. Had he been aware that there was an ectoplasmic regenerator field in Famebeau, he would have been more careful. He shuddered to think what might have already occurred inside the field. The command that held her in bondage eternally would remain in force, but if the queen and her lover could both resume their original forms . . . That meant that Hades had in essence punished his wife and her lover, by presenting her to him in chains, as a delicious slave.

This was far from ideal, but he could only guess at the outcome. He scrolled on through the messages.

*". . . The queen and the zombie have exited from the ectoplasmic regenerator field."*

"*. . . Repeat, the queen has been decapitated and the collar removed . . .*"

"*. . . This is Country Cousin. The queen has been reanimated and the collar is back in place . . .*"

Hades felt his heart thudding as the implications of these revelations unfolded in his mind. He skipped ahead to the last message.

"*Alpha Om, this is Country Cousin. The queen has entered the ectoplasmic regenerator field, and has been recognized by your subjects. Repeat, the queen and the zombie have been recognized . . .*"

Pluton needed to talk to the operative immediately. He jabbed at a button on the machine with his finger. "Country Cousin, this is Alpha Om," he said. "Come in, Country Cousin." His voice was instantly transmitted to a tiny device behind River's ear.

"This is Country Cousin," whispered a voice a few moments later. River Phoenix was holding to his lips the beaded disk on his hippie necklace.

"What's going on?"

"The Queen and the zombie are under the prism now, sir."

"What does that mean? Are they inside the regenerator field?"

"Yes, Lord Hades."

"What are they doing?"

"I do not know sir. They have been in the chamber some hours. The others, sir, have recognized the Queen. She sent them away."

"Well turn on the camera, and get in there."

"Sir!" whispered River, "That would blow my cover!"

"I don't care if it blows your head off. Get in there now. That's an order!"

"Without delay, Lord." River switched on the camera hidden in the necklace, allowing Hades to see that he was in some sort of research lab or control room, half-filled with gift baskets of fruit and other tribute that had arrived from various quarters for the Queen. Phoenix picked up one of the baskets, and entered the pyramid.

"This came for your Majesty, and I thought you might–" River began.

Hades could see his Queen within the chamber, and she was indeed restored to her divinely beautiful form. She lay on her back, naked but for her jewels, her feet wriggling in the air, while between her thighs a head bobbed and nuzzled. Proserpina's voice tinkled, a sound somewhere between crying and laughing, and evocative of ecstasy. Accompanying the melodic song of her bliss were a series of loud blowing, smacking and farting noises.

The view was quickly obstructed by the face and curly white mane of Hanuman, wearing a beaded hippie necklace.

"They haven't seen me yet," he whispered.

The pale brow of Hades became moist. As his anger mounted, his dark eyes flashed with red sparks. He vowed to find a punishment for these two, one from which they could not escape.

"I'm coming," he said tersely, and switched off the receiver.

Hades, though he had adopted the power suit and tie of a modern business executive or mobster, though he possessed wealth ten thousand times a king's ransom, had never bothered to bring all his equipment up to date. The new telecommunications system he'd installed in the early 20th century was already becoming antiquated, and as for transport, he had no desire to replace his serviceable mounts. He opened the door to his chamber and called out to one of his retainers, "Gryphon!"

Within moments a winged, eagle-headed, lion-bodied steed was saddled and ready. Hades mounted and disappeared in a swirl of wings. Three minutes later, he had landed on the roof of the quonset hut in Famebeau. One minute after that, he had slipped down through the vortex, and was inside the pyramid chamber.

He materialized beneath the prism with an angry thunderclap, a gesture that failed even to register with his errant wife. She was perched on the boy, who hovered fluttering in the air on angelic wings. Her dazzling haunches flashed up and down with rapidity, while the two vocalized in unison, as lovers do at the climax of their sport.

Not a hair of Hanuman's blue-and-white hide was to be seen.

Hades folded his arms over his deep chest and glared at the heedless couple. He raised two fists, brought them down sharply as though conducting an orchestra, and an earthquake shook the pyramid violently. Still the goddess of Spring and her seducer yelped and shuddered in orgasmic oblivion, as though the earthquake had proceeded from the violence of their own passions. When their spasms had calmed and they were spent, Hades cleared his throat and spoke in his deep and resonant voice.

"Is this how you demonstrate your remorse, my wife?"

Persephone now floated with her head on her lover's bosom, her hair covering him like a mourning shawl of lace. She raised her eyes and saw her husband standing there in a red-hot penumbra of fury.

"Hades!" she cried, and shrank back in fear.

At this Luke alighted on the floor and put Kore quickly behind him.

"You must be Death," Luke said pleasantly, and reached out a hand in friendship toward his foe. *Insufferable puppy.*

"Down, cur!" shouted Pluto, striking out with a jet of red flame that emitted from his palm.

Persephone screamed, "Luke! Get out of the way!" but the boy ignored her, stepping forward to intercept the blow.

The fireball ought to have been powerful enough to incinerate the boy's astral body to ash, indeed it might easily have fried the disgraced woman behind him to a crisp as well, though being immortal, she would have surely survived to endure a lengthy and wretched torment. But apparently the Queen was quicker than he, for the firebolt was met midair by a blue shield in the form of a translucent trefoil.

*What's this?* Hades fell into a defensive crouch, as his bolt redounded with force, striking him like a heated whirlwind.

*She's not that powerful,* he told himself in disbelief. He trained a beam of fire on his rival and watched the infernal blast curve harmlessly around the force field that protected both him and Proserpina. The boy merely blinked, appearing bemused that the universe had protected him from annihilation. Pluton began to suspect that there was something exceptional going on.

"It's not fair to blame your wife, Hades," the youth said.

"Luke, please," cried Kore, tears starting in her eyes. "You mustn't do this!" She had drawn a heavy purple peplos over her lustrous skin and pinned it at the shoulders so that its folds engulfed her, clinging to her body's curves.

There was something familiar about Luke, that Hades couldn't place. Had he known the father? He wasn't sure. He had already read the boy's file. Nothing unusual there, just a small town kid with no education and a loud guitar. Still, maybe it would be better not to try again to destroy him, until he found out more.

But it was difficult to restrain himself, when the gormless lad continued to interpose himself between the Queen and the righteous anger of her lord.

"She made every effort to resist me, but I was relentless," he drawled. Who was this wight? Curse him, he looked like an archangel, with all the vitality and passion of a daemon.

*I won't rest until the viper is eliminated,* Hades told himself, grinding his teeth. But whoever this stripling was, he had come here with some high level protection. Persephone could never have saved him alone. Though Hades loathed the human insect and wanted nothing more than to crush him, it seemed just possible that he could not do so on his own.

Yet Hades had no desire to appeal to a higher court for justice, as that meant going to Zeus.

"Look, if you want my advice, let her go," Luke went on confidentially. "She loves you, dude, she told me so herself. But you aren't going to get on her good side with this cave man act. Girls don't go in for that sort of thing, not for long, in my experience."

Death stared at Luke in disbelief. Was this presumptuous maggot giving him relationship advice? It was really too much.

He had at his disposal a simple way of ridding himself of his rival instantly. He could send him back to Earth.

Hades stepped between Luke and Kore, took the slender but unbreakable silver chain in his hand, considered it, then glanced at Luke coldly. "Tell me, my boy," he said softly, "how did you die?"

"The way I always wanted to," Luke replied, then his face clouded. "The way I always knew I would," he murmured with a slow blink. "Heroin."

"Strange, isn't it?" Hades knitted his noble brow. "That you would find yourself in this predicament? Here in the prism of course you are whole, but the moment you step outside, you will once again be, ah, sadly exposed."

"Yeah, I get the joke," the angelic boy replied scornfully. What impudence. "The zombie thing. Very funny."

"The zombie thing?" The Lord of the Underworld murmured faintly. He appeared to be infinitely bored, he knew, but he was in fact dangerously alert, and accessing all his faculties.

"Zombies eat brains, not the other way around, by the way," the idiot was babbling. "And everyone knows heroin turns you into a zombie. Great sense of humor, there, Lord Death."

"Yes, thank you." Hades stared at Luke balefully for a few moments. "But what if you aren't really dead, Luke?"

"Stop!" the goddess Proserpina cried.

Pluton ignored her. "What if you've been lying in a coma, and all you ever had to do is . . . wake up?" he went on.

Kore aimed a kick at the leg of her stately mountain of a husband. "Pluton, stop it!!"

Luke lunged at Persephone, seizing her arm. "Kore? Is all of this just a dream?" he demanded.

His hands were on her! This impertinence could not be permitted. Hades reached out and lifted Luke in the air with one mighty arm, and shook him till his teeth rattled. Kore beat at Hades with her fists, and her angry tears poured down, but for the Lord of the Dead this only enhanced the savor of his vengeance.

Hades finally put Luke down and patted, or to be precise batted his head a few times, just as he might chastise an annoying dog. Luke didn't try to fight back, just glared at Hades with such disgust that the vengeful god felt a surge of delight. At last, here was someone he could really enjoy punishing. As pleasure surged into Pluto's eyes, Luke's defiant stare became ever more panicked.

The Lord of Death laughed, *"Ah HA HA haha haha ha!"*
Luke looked at Kore in fright.

"I'm merely saying, what if you could go back," Hades smiled cruelly, "could always have gone back, if you truly wanted to?" He drew Luke to him and stared deep into the boy's frightened eyes. "And what if by dallying here with *my wife*, you wasted too much time?" Death smiled a little wider, and Luke shivered, said nothing.

"Pluton, please!" Kore begged.

"But just look, my darling, he's not dead," Hades said sweetly. He raised his left hand and a green light emitted from the palm, filled the prism.

Persephone gasped. In the ectoplasmic glow could faintly be seen, emanating from Luke's belly, a phantom umbilical cord. The strand of luminescence wound off, and disappeared through the wall of the prism.

"How tenuous it is, Luke. I do believe you are running out of time. But right now, it's still so very easy to go back." *And if you do, will you ever really . . . wake up?*

"Don't listen to him, Luke. It's a trick!" cried the Queen of the

Dead.

Luke stared at the thin line holding him to life, and the Lord of Death effortlessly read his thoughts. The lad was thinking about what he naturally would at such a moment.

*That shining trail leads home . . . home to Charity's sweet pussy!*

"No hard feelings," Luke babbled. He spoke in a nasal voice, as though unconsciously pretending to be a nerd. "I understand how it is. There's something mystical about the vagina of a woman who's given you children . . ." Bands of translucence appeared across his form, flickered, multiplied. He was fading.

"I'm entitled to an appeal! I call upon Isis!" Proserpina announced hastily, holding her head high as she glared accusingly at her enormous spouse. "If Luke was never among the dead, I broke no Law!"

"You broke my Law, Kore," Death said sadly, "and I rule here. Let the sentence stand: eternal slavery, the eating of carrion, and with the destruction of the bond to the host upon which you feed . . . annihilation!"

At that very moment Luke winked out, and Persephone went limp. Hades watched numbly as she collapsed to the floor. He stood there motionless for quite some time, looking at her.

Suddenly he felt terribly tired and depressed.

*April 4, 1994* –Brooklyn, NY

Rosetta awoke from a peaceful sleep. There were no dreams of tragic mistakes, dead bodies or police investigations to record in her journal. No Luke Mandrake crawling out of the crypt.

Rosetta did not remark upon the absence of her haunting spirit. She simply made coffee, got out her sketchbook, and spent some time in the art studio adding color glazes to the oil painting of the balloon fairies. Later on, she strolled up the street to the market where she exercised her god-given right, as an artist, to charge the week's groceries and beer on her credit card.

However, when she passed the newspaper rack and saw the headlines, Rosetta's fingers went numb. A large jar of pickles slid out of her hands and down into the basket of her shopping cart, injuring a potted hyacinth.

LUKE MANDRAKE'S BODY FOUND, the headlines trumpeted.

*CORONER: SHAMBALA FRONT MAN DEAD THREE AND A HALF DAYS.*

www.ingramcontent.com/pod-product-compliance
Lightning Source LLC
Chambersburg PA
CBHW070440120726
47910CB00003B/868